"Steeped in dark dangers and ...., Annwyn is a world not to be missed! Renwick rocks!"

—National bestselling author Sylvia Day

"Sophie Renwick has created a sexy cast of heroes and loads of intriguing story twists."

—Joey W. Hill

"FASCINATING. [*Velvet Haven*] scores a trifecta as fantasy, romance, and erotica. Four and a half stars. A top pick!"

—*Romantic Times*

"Sophie Renwick dreams up an enthralling new world with this deliciously sexy paranormal . . . an unforgettable tale."

—Fresh Fiction

"For those who love paranormal romance, who love suspense and good mystery, who love the world of the Fae, and who long to find a way into the world of dreams and visions, this multilayered story is for you. . . . The twists and turns were completely unexpected. FOUR AND A HALF STARS!"

—Book Binge

Books by Sophie Renwick

Mists of Velvet

Velvet Haven

Hot in Here

MISTS OF VELVET

Sophie Renwick

HEAT

HEAT
Published by New American Library, a division of
Penguin Group (USA) Inc., 375 Hudson Street,
New York, New York 10014, USA
Penguin Group (Canada), 90 Eglinton Avenue East, Suite 700, Toronto,
Ontario M4P 2Y3, Canada (a division of Pearson Penguin Canada Inc.)
Penguin Books Ltd., 80 Strand, London WC2R 0RL, England
Penguin Ireland, 25 St. Stephen's Green, Dublin 2,
Ireland (a division of Penguin Books Ltd.)
Penguin Group (Australia), 250 Camberwell Road, Camberwell, Victoria 3124,
Australia (a division of Pearson Australia Group Pty. Ltd.)
Penguin Books India Pvt. Ltd., 11 Community Centre, Panchsheel Park,
New Delhi - 110 017, India
Penguin Group (NZ), 67 Apollo Drive, Rosedale, North Shore 0632,
New Zealand (a division of Pearson New Zealand Ltd.)
Penguin Books (South Africa) (Pty.) Ltd., 24 Sturdee Avenue,
Rosebank, Johannesburg 2196, South Africa

Penguin Books Ltd., Registered Offices:
80 Strand, London WC2R 0RL, England

First published by Heat, an imprint of New American Library,
a division of Penguin Group (USA) Inc.

First Printing, February 2011
10 9 8 7 6 5 4 3 2 1

HEAT is a trademark of Penguin Group (USA) Inc.

LIBRARY OF CONGRESS CATALOGING-IN-PUBLICATION DATA:

Renwick, Sophie.
  Mists of velvet/Sophie Renwick.
      p. cm.—(The Annwyn Chronicles; bk. 2)
  ISBN 978-0-451-23260-1
  I. Title.
  PS3618.E64M57   2011
  813'.6—dc22   2010039715

Set in Adobe Caslon
Designed by Alissa Amell

Printed in the United States of America

PUBLISHER'S NOTE
This is a work of fiction. Names, characters, places, and incidents either are the product of the
author's imagination or are used fictitiously, and any resemblance to actual persons, living or dead,
business establishments, events, or locales is entirely coincidental.
  The publisher does not have any control over and does not assume any responsibility for author
or third-party Web sites or their content.

To all the fans who have embraced this magical world—
thank you.
And to my daughter, Olivia, who first gave me the idea of an
angel falling from the sky . . .

ACKNOWLEDGMENTS

A book is never simply written—it's rewritten until it comes together as it should. While an author writes the story, so many other people are part of the process that turns a story into a book.

I have to thank my wonderfully patient editor, Tracy Bernstein, for always making my writing stronger—and for keeping me on track when Suriel wants to take over! As well, I have to thank the art department for the gorgeous covers they've given to my Annwyn world. Finally, kudos to the copy editors who make me look like I know what I'm doing and to the marketing department for getting the word out about this series.

Thank you for all your hard work. I really, really appreciate it.

PROLOGUE

Once there was peace. Now there is war. In the past, Annwyn was filled with light, but now only shadows reign.

The Dark Times have come.

As foretold, Annwyn is at the mercy of a Dark Mage who seeks a flame and an amulet that have been hidden away for centuries. Into whose hands these fall will dictate what will come—peace once more, or annihilation.

This master magician has a prophesized apprentice called the Destroyer whose identity remains carefully hidden. It is known only that he is an immortal who will possess the ability either to save or to destroy both Annwyn and the mortal realm.

These Dark Times that surround us will bring betrayals, deaths, and utter blackness before the dawn of light may once again creep between the trees of the forest.

I have seen Annwyn's greatest weapon—the sacred nine, bringing the beginning and ending of all things. But their future is not fully told. That, I cannot see, for one among them is the Destroyer.

The time has come. The nine shall gather. When they find the amulet and bring it back, our roles in this prophecy may be set forth.

To aid the nine immortals, the Sacred Trine will be revealed— women whose virtues are Healer, Oracle, and Nephillim. Their powers complete the prophecy. Yet it is not only the warriors who wish to find the trine, but the master magician whose powers continue to grow stronger with each ritual of dark magick. The warriors must find and protect this Sacred Trine if they are to have any advantage over the mage. For if the mage finds these women, all will be lost.

Thus far, the mage is winning, but in times of darkness, there is light, and with that light there is still hope.

The Scribe of the Annwyn Chronicles

CHAPTER ONE

The king was coming.

Bronwnn sensed it. The trees whispered of his presence. The winds sang of his strength, and the evening air tasted of his power. Annwyn was alive, humming with the magical aura of the great Sidhe king.

His approach was slow, deliberate, like a wolf stalking a stag. Without haste he came, seeking any and all advantage as he traversed the hallowed groves to the temple—a place he well knew would not fully welcome him; a place that would try to bend the king to the will of the leader of their ancient order. All this Bronwnn knew, for she was one of them—a member of the order of the goddesses.

Long had the goddesses ruled Annwyn. For thousands of years, Annwyn's many races had been united in their awe, enthralled by their beauty and mystery as well as their powers. But Bronwnn knew something her sisters did not. The order was changing. The Dark Times would see to that. Soon the old ways would change—out of necessity—to make way for a new order.

Closing her eyes, Bronwnn focused on the elements that surrounded her. They spoke of this change, too. They showed her the shadowy image of a new and powerful being who far surpassed the magic of Cailleach, the Supreme Goddess. Did Cailleach know? Bronwnn wondered. Or was it yet another mystery she must keep hidden?

A strange vibration hummed along her skin, and she opened her eyes to see the mist shrouding the sacred temple shimmer, then part, allowing the king's progress toward the inner sanctum where the Supreme Goddess held court.

Bronwnn did not need to hear the warning of the Sidhe king's arrival murmured throughout the forest, for she had felt him long before the leaves shimmered above her, telling of his nearness to the temple.

His was a power divined from the earth and the elements. His strength and magic preceded him, making him the most powerful force in Annwyn. Once, it had not been so. Once, the Supreme Goddess had been the most powerful, but Bronwnn had seen the subtle shift of power. Cailleach, of course, did not recognize it yet. But Annwyn did. All living creatures revered the king, bowed to his magic, and stood in wonder of the human queen whose powers made her husband so potent.

Their union was a force no magic could have forged. They were destined to find each other, fated to love each other. For that was the way of mating in Annwyn. It was fated in the moon and stars, a destiny forged in the cosmos. No one could outrun his fate—nor want to. The desire to find and claim one's mate was an irresistible force, and the Sidhe king was as helpless before his own destiny as any other creature in Annwyn.

It was said there was one special soul to match every living thing in the world. One could live lifetimes before crossing paths with one's soul mate, but in the end, the two destined spirits would finally make their way to each other, just as the king's and queen's spirits had merged despite one being human and one Sidhe. The new queen had made her king powerful.

Even now the earth seemed to pulsate with the king's authority, and soon all in Annwyn would pledge their fealty to the Sidhe king, and to his eight warriors.

She had seen it. She did not doubt this vision. It was only a matter of when, for it would happen. Her gift did not lie.

Sitting on the window ledge, Bronwnn gazed out from her spot high in a temple chamber, watching the clear waters of the meandering river snake toward the horizon, where they would eventually tumble over a waterfall. The climb up to the temple was steep, and the terrain treacherous, designed as it was to protect the ancient order housed within these thick stone walls. A castle supposed to be a sanctuary for her kind, it had never felt like a safe haven for her. For Bronwnn, it had been nothing but a prison.

The wind picked up, blowing long strands of white blond hair from her braid. The hair tickled her eyes and obstructed her view of the mighty Sidhe king. Brushing the wayward strands from her eyes, she tucked them behind her ear, pressing forward in order to watch the king step out of the forest. Behind him was the queen—Mairi was her name—and when he embraced his wife tightly to his body, Bronwnn closed her eyes and absorbed the current of desire that emanated from them.

She had once seen the king taking his wife. She had watched as the queen rode on top of her husband. She had studied them, enraptured, as the king made love to his wife on the sacred altar of the Sidhe.

Bronwnn had been walking through the grove in an attempt to shake off the feeling of restlessness that had troubled her for weeks. The sound of their passion had drawn her to the king's Nemed—sacred place.

From between the trees, she had been at first startled, then intrigued to see the king and queen in the act of loving. Decency decreed she leave, but that restless feeling inside her forbade it. Instead, she watched them, wishing she might one day find the same passion with her own mate.

Later that night, she had dreamed of a lover taking her body. His hands, large and warm, had touched her in places that seemed to bloom beneath his fingertips. It had been her first dream of *him*—not of the king, but of another: a lover she had dreamed of every night since, only to awaken in the morning in a state of unspent agony.

Her time was coming, she realized, as she saw fleeting mental images of a dark-haired man with large, powerful arms and beautiful hands. She was reaching sexual maturity, a time in the life of a goddess that was spiritual and pure.

Except the feelings and needs that assaulted her were not spiritual. They were carnal, lustful. She craved sex; she hungered for it—burned with the need for it. Did other goddesses feel the same, or was the need naturally stronger for her? As the goddess of sexuality and fertility, was she *meant* to have more powerful needs, or was this yet another abomination she was to live with?

Now she watched the king and queen kiss and felt her own body come alive, just as it had that night when she watched them make love.

Would she ever have this? A mate to touch her this way?

Or would she forever be Cailleach's servant, with only her fevered dreams to bring her pleasure?

While the other young goddesses were schooled in the arts of sexuality, Bronwnn had been sheltered, forbidden to prepare for the sacred act of Shrouding. Left on her own most of the time, Bronwnn used the ancient texts in the library, learning what she could while trying to find a way to relieve the ache of what was coming—being left behind while the others were courted by Annwyn's warriors, who would fight over them in a show of male strength. Only the strongest would lie with a goddess, for it was the greatest honor to share a bed with one of her kind. Every man dreamed of it. Every goddess rejoiced in it, for it was their duty, not only to sustain the order but to cement the bonds with the inhabitants of Annwyn.

The others would experience it, and Bronwnn would be left alone in her chamber to wonder what it was like. Perhaps she might be able to hide in the shadows to watch and see what would be forever denied her.

Bronwnn had never been told why she was kept separate from the others, but she believed it was because of the unusual powers she had, powers that Cailleach feared. So the Supreme Goddess segregated her, keeping her alone, to attend only her. This ensured that Bronwnn was always within sight, and within reach, as though whatever she saw in Bronwnn's eyes worried the Supreme Goddess.

Why? Was what she saw inside Bronwnn so horrifying that she must be kept from all the others? The thought made her lie awake at night.

Their hands still entwined, the two lovers parted, slowly releasing, unwilling to let go; the image replaced the worrisome thoughts of Cailleach. The king was devoted to his queen, and to Annwyn. That was the reason he was here today. He would honor Cailleach's summons.

Reaching up on tiptoe, the queen kissed him, and Bronwnn saw the love shining in her eyes as they parted. It was wise for the queen to leave the king to his business, for she would not have a warm welcome here at the temple. The Supreme Goddess did not like her or fully accept her, for the queen was mortal, and Cailleach viewed mortals as inferior and useless. Rodents, she called them.

But Bronwnn knew Cailleach would have to change her view of mortals if she wished any sort of assistance from the king. Times were changing, and Annwyn was now thrust into darkness. Even the temple was cast in a pall. Its mists, which had once shone like a rainbow, were now a gloomy shade of gray. The sun no longer rose over the temple but left it cast in a cloud of melancholy.

Evil was present. Bronwnn felt it, that persuasive darkness that spread throughout Annwyn like a cloying vine, wrapping its tendrils around anything that got in its path. Annwyn, she was afraid, was succumbing to the dark magick.

The Sidhe king watched his wife disappear into the forest before he shape-shifted into an elegant raven. He soared, high and graceful, catching the current of wind so that he dipped and banked. Fascinated, Bronwnn studied him, watching how he became one with the animal inside him. The king seemed to embrace both man and beast.

Slipping away from the window seat, Bronwnn made her way down the curved staircase to Cailleach's private solarium. She was not expected to wait on the Supreme Goddess while she spoke with the king, but she was far too curious to let such an opportunity pass her by. She hid behind a curtained screen, watching through a tiny crack as the king landed in the middle of the solarium, his bird form gone, replaced by a tall, imposing Sidhe.

"I received your summons."

Cailleach's pet owl flew from the back of her throne to his velvet perch by the window. The bird's shrewd eyes watched the king, and Bronwnn pressed farther back to the wall, hoping to avoid the owl's gaze. Cailleach, she noticed, did not rise to greet the king. They were not equals in her mind. She and the Sidhe king ruled Annwyn together, but the Supreme Goddess had always held ultimate power. Cailleach still clung to the old ways, despite the old ways having allowed the Dark Arts to be reborn.

"Sit, Raven. Do you care for some wine?"

"I care to get this over with."

Bronwnn watched as Cailleach's cheeks reddened with anger. "I see marriage has done little to soften you, or improve your manners."

"You've taken me away from my investigations. I demand to know what is so important that you've interrupted my search for the Dark Mage."

"That Soul Stealer is what has me summoning you."

Sitting in the chair opposite Cailleach, the king watched her warily. "Have you information for me?"

"One of my handmaidens has the sight." It was Bronwnn she was speaking of. Now her ear was pressed tightly against the gossamer fabric of the screen. She hoped her shadow was not evident. She should not be eavesdropping, but she couldn't leave now, knowing the Supreme Goddess was speaking to the king about her.

"Do you recall the book I had you find? It belongs to her, and to her mother before her."

"And what care have I for this handmaiden?"

Cailleach sent him an annoyed glance. "Because you understand the significance of this book, that is why."

"Do I?"

Cailleach's expression turned murderous. "Play your games with your courtiers, Raven, if games amuse you. However, they only provoke and irritate me. Surely you can see that this farce of cat and mouse we play together has made our alliance and our rule ineffective."

The king cleared his throat and shifted his large body in the chair. Curtly, he nodded. "Continue."

Cailleach took a sip from the gold chalice, then carefully set it aside. "You will care about this handmaiden, because she can successfully prophesize the future. She records her visions in the book, then reports them to me."

Not all of her visions, Bronwnn thought. She had kept many things from the goddess—things she could not understand or explain; things that might prove dangerous if they fell into Cailleach's hands.

"And what has she told you, Cailleach?"

"How do you think I came by the knowledge that there would be nine warriors to find my amulet and the missing flame?"

Intrigued, the king sat forward in his chair. "So that is what this summons is about. Now who is playing games, Cailleach? Why not come out and admit it. You want the names of my warriors."

"It's been weeks since you wed. I've allowed you enough time to woo your queen. Now it is time to see to your duties."

He smiled, then sat back in his chair. "I can see you've never been wed, or wooed," he said with a chuckle, "for you would know that weeks are not nearly long enough when spent with a lover."

The queen stiffened and glanced away. "My handmaiden has told me it is time for the nine to arise and begin the hunt. Dark magick is sweeping across Annwyn. We cannot delay."

"Let me speak with her," the king demanded.

"Impossible," Cailleach scoffed. "She has taken a vow of silence. She has not spoken a word since she was a child."

That vow had been for her own protection. Visions constantly flooded her, and Bronwnn could never be certain her secrets would not come spilling out along with her visions. There were things about her that the goddess didn't know. Things that could get her banished from the order. She shuddered to think of what could happen—something much worse than being segregated from the others; that was for certain.

"Well, isn't that convenient?" Suddenly the king's gaze darted to the screen, and she froze. He saw her. He had pinned her with his mismatched eyes, and she was caught.

Preparing herself for Cailleach's wrath, Bronwnn held her breath. The tirade never came. Cailleach was still sitting on her throne, and the king's attention was still focused on where Bronwnn was hiding. There was a warning in his gaze and a message in his eyes. She knew then she must stay, and he would speak with her after his meeting with Cailleach had ended.

Suddenly, his gaze left her, only to be pinned on Cailleach. "I sense that this handmaiden is not entirely what she appears to be."

"Bronwnn would never dare cross me. She knows the price of betrayal."

"Fear does not instill loyalty, Cailleach. Trust is earned and freely given."

Cailleach's expression turned mutinous. "You dare presume you know of our ways? You are a Sidhe. Sidhe know only how to fight and mate."

The king glared at Cailleach. "Speak carefully, Cailleach, for it is very early in our truce. I am not above severing it."

Cailleach's pale green eyes turned a frosty shade. "Our truce is for the benefit of Annwyn, not each other. I will speak as I find fit. Now, then, the symbol you showed me, the one painted on the wall in the mortal realm—when I showed it to Bronwnn, she was able to see that only one magician is performing these rituals. He invokes Gwyn, our god of death and ruler of the Shadowlands, as well as the Dark Angel of the mortals' religion. Two separate deities, but one man."

"So Suriel was correct. He told me the mark referred to an angel named Uriel."

The Supreme Goddess actually shivered at the name, but she recovered almost immediately. "Now we know we hunt one man—for now. He is either an angel or a mortal with extensive knowledge of both angelic and Druidic lore. An occultist, a practitioner of the most dangerous of the Dark Arts."

"And did she tell you what this man looked like?"

"She writes the word 'chameleon,' over and over again. Do you know what it means?"

"It is an animal that exists in the mortal realm. It resembles a small dragon, except this animal is able to change its appearance to blend in with its surroundings. It's a protective ability."

"So it seems our enemy is able to change his appearance. That will make it very difficult to discover his identity."

Bronwnn had not known what it meant. She had only heard the word, time and again. It had been said with such pride and gloating. And now she knew that the evil she saw in her visions was always changing; it was always one step ahead of them.

"It is time, Raven. Name your nine, if you please."

The king's gaze volleyed back to Bronwnn's hiding spot, assuring her he was not done with the topic. "Very well. I've given the matter great thought. I know the nine."

"And?" Cailleach asked impatiently.

"Mairi."

"She's a mortal!" the queen spat.

"You will recall she has an incredible power—the one to heal me and those I care about," he growled. "I will not undertake anything if Mairi is not at my side. Even you in your blind hatred of mortals can see how beneficial Mairi's power is to our cause."

Grudgingly, Cailleach acknowledged the fact. Waving her hand impatiently, she muttered, "Go on."

"Carden, of course."

"An excellent choice, if you could find him."

"I *will* find him." The king narrowed his gaze. "Can your seer not aid us?"

"I haven't yet asked her to envision your half brother." Cailleach shrugged elegantly. "Perhaps if I were assured of your full cooperation . . ."

"I gave you my bloody word," he snarled. "Don't fuck with me, Cailleach."

Her gaze turned murderous. "Do not speak in that common way to me, Raven. This is a holy temple, not that filthy mortal club, Velvet Haven. If in no other place, you *will* respect my position here."

"I do not give my word lightly. Do not question it again."

They stared at each other for long moments—adversaries more than corulers. The feelings of mistrust and anger simmered, making Bronwnn's breath catch.

"As to Carden, I will set my handmaiden to the task. Her visions are reliable, so if she sees something, you can be assured it is the right path to follow."

"Thank you."

Nodding, Cailleach rose elegantly from her throne and walked around the long table to stand before the hearth. It was cold in the chamber, and the goddess rubbed her hands together, her rings glimmering in the flickering firelight as she used her magick to make the fire grow warmer.

She was stunningly beautiful, standing in the warm glow. A vision of such majestic, ethereal beauty. But beneath the stunning veneer lay a cold and powerful woman bent on revenge.

"Perhaps you might consider an alternate, in case Carden is not found?"

"He'll be found."

With a sigh, Cailleach turned and met the king's gaze. "With you, that is only three. What of the other six?"

"Suriel, of course."

The queen's expression blackened. "I forbid it. A fallen angel? No, absolutely not. I will not have him *or* his kind in Annwyn."

"I need him as a bridge between Annwyn and the mortal realm. His knowledge of the mortals is invaluable."

"It is very dangerous to involve him in our matters. His allegiance is to himself."

"I concur, but there is nothing else that can be done. I need Suriel, whether we trust the bastard or not."

"I don't."

The king nodded once. "Nor do I, but the truth is, this is a matter that threatens not only our world. The mortal realm is also at stake."

"Can he be relied upon? I doubt it. Do you even know where he is?" Cailleach demanded. "Hiding, no doubt, like the snake he is."

"Mairi knows."

"Tread carefully, Raven, for I sense deception on Suriel's part. His motivation is not clear. His role in your mate's life is most perplexing, and I am not afraid to say it worries me."

Cocking his brow, the king drawled, "Why do you suppose I want him nearby? I believe in the adage, 'Keep your friends close and your enemies closer.'"

"The last time an angel was in Annwyn," Cailleach said with a shudder, "it was catastrophic."

"You have my word that I will keep Suriel in check."

"And the others, will you be able to keep them in check?"

"I'm certain. I've picked those I feel I can trust, and who can add the most to our search."

"And who would they be?"

"Sayer, for his ability to use Enchantment magick. Keir, who is well versed in divination. As a Shadow Wraith, he also has invaluable reconnaissance abilities. I've also enlisted Drostan, the griffin with the power of summoning, and Melor, the phoenix. He has great fighting skills, and he is also familiar with necromancy."

Cailleach whirled on him. "Allow me to get this straight. Your sacred nine consist of a mortal female, a stone gargoyle, an unscrupulous Selkie who practices his magick to seduce the opposite sex, a fallen angel with dubious loyalties, a firebird with a link to the very evil we are trying to defeat, and a griffin who is nothing but a mercenary for hire?"

"Exactly. Drostan's summoning magick is so valuable that, if pressed, I will pay him in whatever currency he desires. We need him."

"I forbid this—this motley assortment of so-called warriors. There is not one elf or sprite or nymph among them. You've overlooked very powerful allies."

"Nay, I haven't. I've banded together warriors whose magick controls all the elements, air, fire, water, and earth, as well as all facets of magick. And as for Melor and his ties to necromancy, we need him to help us fully understand the Dark Arts. To know your enemy, Cailleach, is sometimes to become like him."

"This is madness."

"This is strategy." Crossing his leg over his knee, the king contemplated the goddess. "What do you fear, Cailleach?"

"Nothing."

"I think you do. I think you object to my warriors because you have no dominion over them. They don't fear you and your wrath as the elves and the nymphs do. However, I did note that you left one warrior out of your condemnation—the Shadow Wraith."

"He is the only sensible ally," Cailleach retorted. "As mysterious a race as they are, their powers are immense. It is almost impossible to defeat an opponent who can become invisible. And," she said more slowly, "it is a gesture that will not be ignored."

The king's gaze grew alert. "You desire an alliance with them. You know that from the Wastelands, the wraiths have no fealty to you, or to the Sidhe."

"Yes," Cailleach whispered. "Theirs is the only race that does not flow with the power and blood of my order. Think of it, Raven—the power of the wraiths bred with the power of the goddess."

"What are you suggesting, Cailleach?"

"That we draw the wraiths into the war to save Annwyn by wedding one of their kind to one of my goddesses. Uniting the two races would secure our control."

"You mean *your* control," the king corrected.

Cailleach ignored him. "I have the right woman. She is coming into her maturity. And as she is the goddess of sexuality and fertility, she is ready to procreate and cement the bond between the Shadow Wraiths and the goddesses, between the Wastelands and Annwyn. With her powers, she can propagate a small army—for my purposes."

Gasping, Bronwnn pressed her hand against the stone wall for support. *She* was the goddess Cailleach spoke of. She was the one to be sacrificed to a Shadow Wraith. Cailleach was making her a pawn. Yet, to be mated with a wraith would enable her to leave the castle, and to be free of Cailleach . . .

"You leave my warriors be, Cailleach, and I will not interfere with your plans for the Shadow Wraiths."

"Agreed. Now, Keir, the wraith, is he here in Annwyn, or does he still lurk within that vile mortal club?"

"He has been in Annwyn more of late."

"Yes," Cailleach said softly. "The mortal woman, I presume. How does she fare?"

"Not well. Her death is near, I think."

"I am sorry Annwyn was not able to slow her fate."

The king's expression fell as he lowered his gaze. "Mairi is beside herself with worry. Her only hope is that she will be able to heal Rowan when the time comes—just as she heals me."

"And so the wraith visits the mortal, then?" Cailleach asked.

"Along with Sayer," the king answered. "The three of them are trying to assist me in finding Carden. I believe Rowan is an oracle of sorts; when Sayer enchants her, she is able to shed her conscious thoughts and help us to decipher the riddle to Carden's whereabouts."

"I have no wish to interfere in your search for Carden. If he is to be one of your nine, he needs to be found. However, as soon as he is able, the wraith must come to me. He will be shrouded with the goddess Bronwnn, uniting our two races, and our power."

The king stood, caught Bronwnn's gaze, then very slightly tilted his head, indicating the hall where he would meet her.

"Raven," Cailleach called. "The mortal, Rowan. She may be buried here in Annwyn if she and your wife wish it."

The king stopped and stared at the goddess before bowing to her. "Thank you, Cailleach. You are most generous. Mairi will be pleased to have it this way."

She waved away his praise. "She reminds me of someone," Cailleach murmured. "Someone I should have taken better care of. Perhaps I may atone for the sins of my past with this gesture."

The door to the solarium opened, and Cailleach's voice rose once again. "Do not think you fooled me, Raven. You named only eight warriors. Who is to be the ninth?"

The king pinned Bronwnn with his gaze. "I am not yet certain, but I believe I know someone who will be able to provide me with an answer."

"Think on the elves, Raven. They are cunning, and at times, quite merciless."

The chamber door closed. Bronwnn watched as Cailleach sank into her chair and closed her eyes. The owl flew from his swing to land on the velvet sleeve of Cailleach's robe. Shaking his head, he hooted softly until Cailleach raised her hand and brushed his snow-white wing. The goddess looked tired. Her light was fading. Reposed like this, she looked like a vulnerable woman, not the powerful Supreme Goddess she was.

"You haunt me," Cailleach whispered as she gazed up at the jeweled ceiling. "Day and night, you haunt me."

Not knowing of whom Cailleach spoke, Bronwnn decided to take advantage of the Supreme Goddess' distraction to slip away from the screen. Bronwnn did not dally, climbing the stairs to the hall where the king was waiting for her. He would ask her questions and probe her thoughts. She must keep her secrets. And she must, she thought, find the man who was to be her mate, for he was not safe from Cailleach. She did not need a vision to know that. She felt it deep within her. Cailleach was hiding something, and Bronwnn felt the overriding animal instinct to protect her mate.

CHAPTER TWO

Sometimes being mortal was a real bitch. Like tonight, when he was trying to open the wooden door to Annwyn—a door that mortals should know nothing about. Except he wasn't just an average anthropomorphic.

Frustrated, Rhys slammed his shoulder into the thick oak, hoping the antique door would give under his strength. The damned thing didn't so much as budge. He gave it another shot, this time pushing with his body.

Damn his great-uncle Bran for placing the protection spell on the portal. The Sidhe king had enchanted the door so that mortals like him would stay the hell away from the realm where the immortals dwelt. The inhabitants of the Otherworld guarded their home and their secrets well, and their greatest fear was that humans would discover their world and destroy it.

"*Cocksucker*," he swore as he pounded his fist into the door. "God damn it." He took the brass handle in his palms and jarred it up and down. Christ, he must look like a five-year-old. But the fact was, he didn't want to admit defeat. He didn't want to come close to admitting what he truly was—your average, garden-variety human.

"Hey, buddy, back away from the door."

Rhys sent a lethal glare over his shoulder. The bouncer, who was really an immortal, a troll in a human's guise to be precise, paled when he saw his face. "Apologies, Mr. MacDonald. I didn't realize it was you."

"It's me, and I suppose that apology doesn't extend to opening the door for me?"

Farley rubbed his big palm over his shining bald head. "Sorry, man, but I have strict orders from my king."

"What about the orders of your boss?"

"In my world, no one outranks the Sidhe king, except perhaps the Supreme Goddess."

"Well, we're not in your world, Farley. We're in the mortal realm."

"Still—it's just that—well, from what I understand, you've been banned by the king."

"Tell me something I don't know," Rhys snarled as he shoved past the bouncer and headed back to his office. *Fucking Bran.* Who the hell did he think he was? This mansion, this club, and that damned passageway to Annwyn were Rhys' birthright. He'd inherited everything from his great-great-grandfather Daegan, who had abdicated his throne and Sidhe powers for life as a mortal. In Rhys, there had to be some Sidhe blood, no matter how minuscule an amount. But try as he might, he hadn't been able to summon any magical powers, and as a consequence, that damned door remained permanently off-limits to him.

Normally, he didn't give a damn about Annwyn, but this

was the third time in a week that he had seen Keir disperse the Enchantment spell and slip past the door into Annwyn. Not that Rhys cared what Keir did in his downtime, but it was really strange for Keir not to tell him what he was doing or where he was going. His recent behavior—agitated, almost strung-out—perplexed and worried Rhys.

Jesus. It sounded like a damned love affair—which it wasn't. This was Keir he was talking about; Keir he was worried about.

Keir—his Shadow Wraith; his protector since birth.

"Some fucking protector," he snarled as he slammed the door to his office. Not that he needed a babysitter. He was quite capable of handling himself, not to mention taking care of mortal or *immortal* troublemakers who liked to stir up shit in his club.

No, it wasn't fear for his own life that had him all juiced up; it *was* worry. Something wasn't right with Keir. Always intense, lately the Shadow Wraith had gone from quiet intensity to downright lethal menace. Keir wasn't himself, and no one knew that better than Rhys.

In some grand cosmic fuckup, he'd been given a male Shadow Wraith to protect him from the family curse. The previous firstborn males of his line had always been given females, which was nice, considering the intimate nature of the bond between them.

But Rhys' wraith was a male. The universe, he was sure, enjoyed shitting on him.

Be that as it may, Rhys relied on Keir's almost constant presence to keep him safe from a curse that had spanned two centuries, and Keir's survival depended on Rhys' feeding him.

At first, Keir had survived on Rhys' emotions—good or bad. But with the onset of puberty, the wraith had come to crave emotions less and less, and sexual energy more and more. And, strangely enough, it didn't bother Rhys. Their relationship was more than that of a protector and a protected. They had a deep bond, and if Keir needed to survive by sharing some hot sex with him and a woman, then so be it.

A fucked-up relationship for certain, but it was what it was. Besides, within the walls of Velvet Haven there was no end to female companions who dug the whole threesome thing.

Things had been going well, as they had from day one when Keir had parked his ass by Rhys' cradle. Business as usual—well, as usual as it could be for a Shadow Wraith and a mortal descended from faeries. But two weeks ago, the usual had been butchered by a sadistic ritual killer who had the fucking nerve to carve up his last victim outside Rhys' club. Throw in some dark magick, a pissed-off Sidhe king, and a dangerous fallen angel—that was the new normal.

Shaking his head, Rhys sank into his chair and scanned the papers that littered his desk. He was as much in the dark as he had been two weeks ago, when the murder happened. All he knew was there was a killer using death and sex magick, both in Annwyn and here in the mortal realm. The rest of the information was kindly spared him because he was "just" a mortal.

Not just, Rhys thought as he wiped his hands over his face. Because no other mortal he knew had a Shadow Wraith protector, or lived under a curse. Nor could any mortals he knew of boast that his great-uncle was the Sidhe king and coruler of Annwyn.

Of course, in the king's eyes he was just a pain-in-the-ass

relative with no powers to exploit and no brains to solve any-thing magical.

He'd expected that out of Bran, but he hadn't expected it out of Keir. In all the thirty years Keir had been keeping Rhys alive, they'd never had secrets between them. This odd behavior wasn't like Keir.

Fighting his second headache of the day, Rhys reached for that morning's copy of the *Examiner*. He had a few hours yet before the club opened. Once it did, he would be busy monitor-ing the goings-on between the immortals and mortals in Vel-vet Haven. But for now, he had some time to kill. Maybe the solitude would settle his nerves and allay the gut feeling he had about Keir.

Flicking open the paper, he scanned the headlines, then flipped to the sports page where he searched for the results of his favorite teams. At the back of the sports section came the classifieds and the obits. Normally, he didn't read them, but this morning there was a picture of a woman that sent chills down his spine.

Trinity Fergus—she had been the girl murdered outside his club two weeks ago. It was an "in memorium" write-up, and Rhys grimaced when he read that she had been only twenty-one when the psycho butchered her.

There was a mention of an ongoing murder investigation, but Rhys knew the cops would not be able to solve this case. While he didn't know who the culprit was, he knew *what* he was. He also knew the devil didn't leave prints. This case would go cold. There would be no satisfaction for Trinity's family.

Skipping over the other obituaries, he came across some photos of happy couples in wedding announcements and silver-anniversary notices—not something he'd ever be putting in the paper. What woman would marry a guy who lived with another guy? A guy who was attached to him like Velcro? Yeah, not happening. Rhys knew his fate—a series of kinky chicks who liked getting it on with two guys; a life of one-night stands and no-strings-attached sex.

He'd long given up the hope that maybe he could live like a normal man with marriage, kids, pot roast on Sundays. He had only to look at his own parents to know the unlikelihood of happily ever after. His mother couldn't hack it—the secrets, the feeling that his father was cheating on her with his "best friend," his Shadow Wraith. Maybe if his dad had come clean, she could have stuck it out, but coming clean about Annwyn and a centuries-old curse didn't come easily, or believably. Finally, his mother had bailed on him and his dad. Rhys didn't know her—couldn't even remember her. But more disturbing? He didn't feel the loss of her.

His father had suffered, though. Regretted not telling Rhys' mother the truth. Which only cemented the thought that Rhys would never live a normal life. He was sure no woman would believe the fantastical story, or trust him and accept him as he was.

Yeah. It sucked. But this was his life, and he couldn't deny that he appreciated what Keir did for him. Hell, he wouldn't be alive without him, but he did regret that his life could never be normal. And he felt bad that Keir had also been denied a life. As Rhys' eternal shadow, Keir was chained to him until Rhys drew his last breath. After that, he had no idea what Keir's life would entail. Maybe he would be cast back to the Wastelands where others of his kind lived. Maybe he would cease to exist like Rhys. In any event, Keir had no life of his own, because he'd been sentenced to babysitting duty.

Both of them were fucked. Even if Rhys wished to get rid of the wraith, he couldn't. Keir was his. A wraith only ever belonged to one person. And Rhys himself? He wanted to mean something to someone—someone who needed him; someone he could protect, and make love to. Not just screw, but make love to. That sappy, bone-melting passion they showed in the movies—that's what he wanted.

But women were constantly out of his reach—well, the kind of woman he wanted. The easy kind—he always had those. They were fine for a night, but long term? No, he didn't want the type of woman he screwed in the back of Velvet Haven. He wanted wholesome. Lovable. Sexy—and a good cook. Hell, he was mortal. He liked to eat.

A cursed mortal, he reminded himself, which of course made him question for the millionth time that day where the hell Keir was. He hadn't seen him since daybreak, when he opened his eyes to find Keir slinking out of bed and out the door.

Just what the hell was going on in Annwyn, and why the fuck was he being kept in the dark? Sure, he was mortal and would die. But he wasn't a pansy ass. He could hold his own.

Rhys' teeth ground together, making his head pulse harder. Reaching into his desk drawer, he popped open a bottle of Tylenol and took two tablets, along with a swig of cold coffee. Propping his Doc Martens on his desk, he leaned back in his chair and put his arms behind his head. Focusing on the copper tin ceiling above, Rhys allowed his mind to go blank.

It was time to locate the wraith.

Closing his eyes, he stilled his breathing, trying to sift

through his anger and frustration to locate Keir's thoughts. Their bond was strong, stronger even than his father's bond with his wraith, who just happened to be Keir's mother.

Immediately Rhys felt Keir, but he couldn't hear him or see him in his mind. Was it possible he had cloaked his thoughts? Wraiths had the power to do that, but Keir had never done so with Rhys. Their thoughts and emotions were an open book. It was what made their bond so strong.

Rhys lingered in Keir's mind, nudging a bit harder while he waited patiently for the wraith to talk. But Keir's voice never came, and a black curtain suddenly drew down over Rhys. He'd never seen such a thing before. He had no idea what was happening—why he couldn't hear Keir, despite sensing him— and couldn't seem to shake off the sudden exhaustion that claimed him. Struggling against the blindness, he gave in and let the beckoning black velvet suck him in. Sleep overcame him, and he felt his arms drop to his sides and his head fall back.

The minute Rhys felt the woman, he knew he was dreaming. This was no astral projection. The thought was confirmed when he discovered he was in bed with only her. No way was that happening in real life. Keir was always present. Together they pleasured the women Rhys wanted. But this woman? She wasn't even his type. She was too angelic, too pretty, and untouchable.

The women he bedded had a bit of an edge to them. They knew what they wanted, and he gave it to them. But this one looked shy and virginal as she kneeled on the bed before him, her pale eyes watching him with excitement but also wariness.

Her long hair was a silvery blond. Her skin was pale, except for the faint glow on her cheeks, which were stained with her blush.

She didn't look of this world, he thought absently. She was too perfect; too ethereal. But that body was anything but ethereal and innocent. Hers was a body straight out of *Playboy*, and suddenly he wanted to tear away the strange-looking gown she wore and reveal her naked form.

The image hovered in his mind, lingering before his eyes and taunting his mind and body with the temptation to reach out and touch her, to cup one breast in his palm and clasp a hand behind her neck, bringing her forward so he could take her mouth. He had a primal, almost animalistic urge to claim her.

He realized it was not the first time he had seen her in his dreams. Once before, he'd had a fleeting image of a pale-haired woman riding him. He'd awakened sweaty and hard, shaking with pent-up desire. He'd figured his dirty mind had created both her and the sex dream. But this dream felt different— more intimate and passionate. There was an emotional as well as a visceral sensation running through his body as he watched the dream play out before him.

Who was this woman? He'd never seen her at the club, and he'd certainly remember her if she'd been one of his one-night stands.

Maybe Keir was getting lucky in Annwyn and Rhys was witnessing what was going on between them . . . Most likely that was it.

Rhys could sense and feel his wraith, as Keir could also sense him. Maybe Rhys had stepped into Keir's thoughts while he was in bed with this woman, or maybe it was just an erotic dream Keir was having.

But that was the weird thing. He'd felt Keir's presence before he fell asleep. But now he didn't. He felt only *her*—this incredibly hot woman who appeared to be totally into him.

Pale hands went to the hem of her gown, and slowly she pulled it up, revealing a set of long legs and nicely shaped thighs. He swallowed, waiting for a glimpse of that tantalizing triangle between her thighs. Suddenly he was parched, and as eager as a twelve-year-old at a peep show. She shifted, and the hem skimmed over her backside that was nice and round. He saw his hand reaching out, ready to run his fingers between her thighs and feel her pussy on his fingers—when he was abruptly wakened.

Instantly alert, Rhys bounded out of his chair, crouched and ready to fight the culprit who had kicked his feet off the desk and so rudely interrupted his X-rated dream. And there he was, standing with arms crossed at the side of his desk. It was Suriel—all six and a half feet of him, wearing his trademark leather, army boots, and a shit-eating grin.

"Must have been some kind of dream."

The bastard knew. Of course he did, Rhys reminded himself. Suriel was a fallen angel. Angels always knew what mortals were thinking and dreaming.

"Not really," Suriel responded as he strolled, uninvited, to a chair across from the desk. "It was more what was standing at attention that gave it away."

Rhys colored then. Shit. He was still hard and aroused, and angry as hell that Suriel knew of it. The bastard laughed as he sank into a plush velvet wingback. It was an antique, but with typical Suriel indifference, he sprawled out his large frame and swung one leg over the chair's arm.

"All alone? Where is your little friend?"

Keir was hardly little, but Suriel liked to amuse himself by insulting the immortals who staffed the club, as well as Bran and Rhys.

Rhys sank into his own chair and carefully adjusted his denim-covered cock beneath the privacy of his desk. Man, he was still hard. Forget the dream, he thought, and deal with Suriel. That would call for his undivided attention.

"You're like the Grim Reaper, Suriel, popping up at the most inopportune times. I thought you were in hiding, or was that just another one of your lies?"

Suriel flashed him a false grin. "Hiding with my tail between my legs isn't my thing. I prefer to fight with guns blazing and balls out."

Rhys snorted. Guns? Not Suriel's choice of weapon, not when he possessed untold powers in his elegant fingertips. Now, balls out, he could buy. Suriel didn't give a shit about anything, or anyone—most especially the mortals he was supposed to love and guide. In fact, Rhys would bet, Suriel didn't really care if he himself existed or died. There was something tortured in his black eyes; something that told of unspeakable pain. But Suriel would never admit that.

"So, where have you been hiding?" Rhys inquired. "Bran has been looking for you."

Suriel picked a speck of dirt off his coat and flung it onto the carpet. "Oh, here and there. Nothing permanent. I prefer to be nomadic. And if I wanted the crow to find me, I would have left a trail of bread crumbs."

Rhys could just imagine what his arrogant great-uncle

would think if he heard himself being referred to as a crow. Still, Bran wasn't here, and Rhys could use Suriel's unexpected appearance to learn more. Not that Bran would thank him for the assistance.

"So, while you have been . . . nomadic, what have you been doing?"

"Facilitating a few mortal souls to their maker. Nothing too exciting. You?"

Rhys did not feel a moment of ease at Suriel's flippant attitude. "Just trying to keep my club going. That business with Trinity caused a huge problem with the cops."

"They're not going to solve the case, MacDonald. It's beyond them. It's up to Bran and his merry men to do that. Speaking of merry men, where *is* the Shadow Wraith?"

What the hell did Suriel want with Keir?

"I thought you were all-knowing, Suriel," he muttered while he cleared the papers from his desk and placed them in a drawer. "Why don't you tell me where he is?"

Suriel's amused gaze flickered to his face. "You flatter me, MacDonald. But the truth is, upon occasion some facts elude me. I'm afraid this time is one of them."

"Bullshit."

Suriel shrugged. "Believe what you like."

"I will. And I believe that you're here to stir up shit—again."

Suriel's smile was a blend of cynical amusement and deviousness. "And why do you think that? I am fallen, not evil."

"Doesn't that mean the same thing? You sinned and lost your wings, didn't you?"

"No, I still have those. They're just black now."

Rhys leaned back in his chair and regarded the angel sitting before him. Tall. Well built. Hair that was thick and shoulder length, the color a dark brown—almost black. His eyes were dark, too, fathomless. Rhys didn't like to look too long into Suriel's eyes. It was the one thing in the world he feared—what he would find in Suriel's black eyes. No doubt there was nothing but death and terror to be found inside this particular fallen angel.

What had been his sin? Rhys wondered, not for the first time. What powers had God gifted Suriel? And what made him take them away?

Suriel pressed forward, his eyes growing darker with hatred. "You want to know what I did? I got laid." Suriel waited for a reaction, and the bastard smiled when he perceived the tremor of trepidation that flickered down Rhys' spine. "You flesh bags get your dicks wet whenever you feel like it and are spared his wrath. The one time I do it, I'm banished for eternity. Hardly fair." Suriel sat back and propped his booted feet on top of Rhys' desk. "So now you know. I had sex. Tasted the flesh of a woman. And now I'm here, walking this hellhole till He decides that I've properly learned my lesson. But do you know what? I've already learned everything there is to know about your kind. And that ain't saying much."

"What do you want, Suriel?"

"Believe it or not, I've come to warn you."

Rhys snorted. "About what?"

"Your stupid curiosity and macho hero tendencies. That's right," Suriel said with a chuckle, "I saw you trying to open the portal."

"Big deal," Rhys muttered, trying to act nonchalant. In truth, he was utterly unnerved. Where had Suriel been lurking?

"Eyes and ears, my friend," Suriel reminded him as he rose from his chair and allowed his black wings to unfurl from beneath the long leather trench he always wore. "It's the mark of a good guardian angel."

"You're not *my* guardian."

Suriel shrugged. "Who the hell else would put up with you?"

"I don't need a babysitter."

"You're not getting my subtlety, MacDonald."

"And you're not getting mine. So let me be clear. I don't want anything from you. Stay the hell away from me."

Two large hands slammed down on the desk. "Shut the fuck up and listen to me. I'm trying to help you, even though it goes against everything I feel. Now," Suriel said quietly, "do not make another attempt to go beyond that door. What it leads to is a world you cannot be part of. There are dangers there you cannot begin to fathom."

"I already know about Annwyn and Cailleach and all the other fairy tales that have been passed down."

"But you don't know this one." Suriel turned his hands over. Angelic script appeared tattooed on his palms. The ink was blue and vibrant, and Rhys felt his gaze latch on to the strange symbols. "Life, with the left hand," Suriel murmured. "Death with the right. If you go beyond that door, this"—Suriel held up his left hand—"cannot save you."

"What makes you think I'll need saving?"

Suriel reached out, and it took everything in Rhys not to

flinch as the angel touched him. Suriel's fingers were hot as they swept beneath the neck of his shirt. "Do you believe in this symbol, MacDonald?"

Rhys looked down to see his necklace lying in Suriel's hand. The ornate Celtic cross glistened against the script tattoos.

The cross had been a baptismal gift, bequeathed to each firstborn male of the MacDonald line. Daegan had brought the cross with him from Scotland. The story went that Daegan had the cross blessed with the waters from a sacred pool in Annwyn.

It was a protection talisman; one Rhys had never taken off.

"Do you believe in it?" Suriel snarled. The look in his eyes was rabid.

"I believe."

Although he wasn't a churchgoing type of guy, he believed, and what was more, he had immense faith in the power of the cross he wore around his neck.

Seemingly satisfied with his answer, Suriel lifted away from him and stepped back. Rhys heard the silky sound of Suriel's wings scraping against the hardwood floor. "Good. Use that faith. Never let it waver. You'll need it."

"What is your purpose here, Suriel? The truth."

"Use your head, MacDonald," Suriel snapped. "What do I care if you go into that forsaken tunnel and get yourself butchered in Annwyn? I don't give a shit. But He does, apparently."

"How did you know I planned to go into the tunnel? Maybe I just wanted to open the door and have a look."

Suriel snorted. "You don't lie well. Besides, how do you think I know? He told me."

Rhys' gaze dropped to Suriel's palms. The markings were gone; erased.

"Erased, just as you will be if you venture beyond the door. Remember that. I've done my duty," Suriel growled. "Now it's up to you, stupid human, to do what you want with the knowledge I've given you."

And then the angel was gone, disappearing before Rhys' eyes. As he shook off the unease he felt, Rhys' gaze was drawn to the wooden box that sat on the corner of his desk. Engraved on the lid was a Celtic cross. He'd been raised Presbyterian— the Church of Scotland—and he believed. As strange as that sounded, as fucked-up as his life was, he still believed in God and the angels, in heaven and hell. A little piece of him even believed that Suriel was telling him the truth. Annwyn didn't want him, and if he ventured into the Cave of Cruachan, God couldn't—or wouldn't—help him.

The warning was clear. But then, he'd have Keir . . .

"You needed me?"

Rhys looked up from the wooden box to see the wraith standing in his office.

"How long have you been here?"

"Long enough to hear Suriel warn you away from the cave."

Rhys shrugged and glanced away. "Suriel's a fallen angel. Why would you or I believe anything he had to say?"

"Because your God speaks through him."

Rhys snorted. "Yeah, right. If God spoke to Suriel, he wouldn't be fallen, would he?"

"The Dark Times have come to Annwyn. They've also come to the mortal realm. Perhaps your God is in need of Suriel's knowledge of the seedier side of the human race. Maybe Suriel is God's hope for humanity."

Rhys met Keir's electric gaze. He had looked into his eyes a million times; yet somehow tonight they looked different. Gone were the silver eyes rimmed with violet. Now they were white like ice, edged in a darker purple that looked almost black in this light. Keir was different. He was worried about something—or someone.

"Don't go near the door again," Keir commanded him. "It's off-limits."

The wraith's tone made him bristle. Both of them were angry and tense, and they needed an outlet for the rage. They didn't typically use each other this way, but it was different now. They both needed to let off steam, and they were each other's convenient whipping post. "I'm not five anymore!"

Keir crossed his thick forearms over his chest. The divination symbols that ran up his hands and arms began to glow softly.

"Do not think of putting any sort of magical spell on me," Rhys snarled. "I mean it, Keir. You think I'm pissed now . . ."

The symbols faded to a blue-black color. They now resembled ordinary tribal tats. But they were far from ordinary, or innocuous.

"It's my duty to protect you, Rhys."

"I know that."

"There is no place in Annwyn for you."

"I know that, too. But this mortal gig is pretty damned boring. Especially when I know for a fact you're involved in something and are deliberately leaving me out."

"For your own safety."

"You make me sound like a weakling."

"No. Just a mortal."

Rhys bit back his thoughts. He really hated to be reminded of his mortality. When you spent your life with magical and powerful creatures, being human was a disappointing
vocation.

He knew he wouldn't win this argument with Keir, so he
tried another tack. "So what's going on in Annwyn that has you
going there every day?"

"I want to see Rowan."

That was the truth. Rhys felt Keir's honesty, and his despair. But there was another reason for going. Rhys sensed it.
And he didn't like that Keir was able to keep something from
him—not when Rhys' life was an open book to the wraith.

But pummeling Keir wouldn't work. And neither would
pestering him into spilling what the hell was going on in
Annwyn.

"Suriel does not lie about what will happen to you, Rhys."

"How do you know?"

Keir winced, glanced away, and dragged his hands through
his black hair. "I have seen it."

Tarot cards. Keir's special kind of magic was divination.
He used scrying and detection spells, and sometimes fire. But
mostly he used the tarot. And some of the shit Keir saw was
downright terrifying.

"You believe me. I sense that." Keir stepped into the office,
closing the door behind him. "You know I would never lie to
you about these things."

Rhys watched as the wraith paced the width of the room.
The heavy soles of his Doc Martens pounded the floor. It was

the only sound in the room, and Rhys suddenly felt unnerved—oppressed—by the quiet.

"The woman in the alley," Keir began. "I have seen more like her. The killings will not stop. They will continue on both mortals and immortals. The torture worse than before. The rituals will become more complicated, and through these sacrifices, the mage and his apprentice, the Destroyer, will become stronger in their power."

Keir stopped before his desk, his eyes now a muted silver, a sign he was in an altered divination state. "The greater the sacrifice, the stronger the powers. Do you understand?"

"I understand the bastard needs to be caught before he kills again."

"No. You're not listening. The greater the sacrifice—"

"Why don't you explain it—plainly?" Rhys demanded, exasperated. "I'm just a mortal, remember? I don't get all this magical stuff."

"If you forfeit your safety to look for me in Annwyn, you'll have more than Cailleach to worry about. The mage will see you as a wondrous offering. Your struggles to save yourself will empower him. And what if," Keir said quietly, "I cannot get to you in time? Do you really want your soul stolen and given up to the Dark Arts?"

Keir watched Rhys carefully as he continued. "Your courage is admirable. Your worry for me appreciated but not warranted. Your mortality makes you—"

"Weak?" Rhys snarled. "Inconvenient? A general pain in the ass?"

"Vulnerable," Keir finished for him.

It always came down to this—how ineffectual he was, trapped between two worlds and belonging to neither.

"I gotta go," Rhys snapped. "It's opening time, and I have a full night to put in."

"Do not worry, Rhys. Soon the mage will be caught, and this chapter will be over. We'll be able to return to normal."

Rhys stopped and glared at his friend. "What the fuck makes you think anything about you and me is normal?"

CHAPTER THREE

"You could have been a tad more forceful."

Keir watched as Suriel emerged from the shadows. "I've already aroused his suspicions. He's like a damned pit bull with a bone. His jaws are locked, and he's not going to let go. He won't give up until he wins."

"An admirable quality," the angel mocked, "if one desires to be bound to an altar and mutilated."

The fierce protectiveness that came naturally to him all but swallowed up Keir's rational thought. "He's a mortal. He has free will. He will do as he chooses, regardless of warnings."

Suriel shrugged. "I think you could have stopped him from a fate we both know is awaiting him."

"Rhys isn't suicidal. And he isn't magical. He won't be able to open the door to the cave, and he won't intentionally get himself killed."

"Fate is a funny thing," Suriel said. "You cannot outrun it, or alter it, no matter how hard you try. It is the same even in your world, is it not?"

Fisting his hands at his sides, Keir strived to keep his emotions under control. But the truth was, he was unraveling. Something was happening to him, and he couldn't explain it. A piece of him was dying inside, and it had nothing to do with what was happening in Annwyn, or Rhys.

"What are your motives?" Keir suddenly snarled. He didn't trust Suriel, and he didn't believe for one minute the angel was all he appeared to be. This concern for Rhys was some kind of ruse to deflect Keir from Suriel's true purpose.

"My motives are my own. What about yours?"

"Mine?" he choked. "What the hell are you insinuating, Suriel?"

"Just that we all have parts to play in this prophecy. And those parts are preordained. Like fate, we cannot alter what we are."

"What are you, Suriel?"

"A fallen angel. And what about you, wraith? What are you, really?"

"You know what I am."

Suriel's slow smile raised the hair on Keir's nape. "Yes. I do. I do know."

"Just stay the hell away from me, and Rhys, too!" Keir thundered. "Stick to your mortals here on Earth, and I'll worry about Annwyn."

"Very well." Suriel moved to leave, then stopped. "There will come a time—very soon, in fact—when you will humble yourself before me. You will request a favor of me, and I will not be able to grant it."

"What a surprise," Keir mocked.

"Fate, wraith. Remember, it cannot be altered."

"So why bother to tell me?"

"Because when that time comes, I don't want you to believe that my refusal to give you what you desire most has anything to do with this petty disagreement today."

"I want nothing from you, Suriel."

"You will. Now, I have one more visit to make; then I'll be gone again. Give my regrets to the crow for missing him, and tell him not to bother trying to find me again."

Keir watched as Suriel disappeared in a shaft of glimmering crystals. Bastard. He didn't like him, but more importantly, he didn't trust him—never had. There was a darkness to Suriel. He had seen it in a divination, as well as with his waking eyes. Suriel was hiding something, and that made him more dangerous than ever.

Perhaps if he weren't so damned tired and weak, he might be able to reason it out, to discover what it was that set his nerves on edge whenever Suriel was around. But the truth was, his brain was fried, and his concentration was shit.

Flopping down into Rhys' chair, Keir placed his head on the desk and pressed his eyes shut. He felt out of control, angry, insolent. He was worried about Rhys, and he felt guilty as hell for the way he had been leaving him alone the past few weeks, not to mention the way they seemed to be bickering like an old married couple.

He'd tried to tell himself that Rhys was safe enough within the walls of Velvet Haven, but he knew better than that. The human woman had been taken from the club and sacrificed out in the open. No place—and no one—was safe from the Dark Mage.

Especially not a mortal like Rhys. He had plenty of Sidhe pride, and fiery Fey blood, but none of the magick.

Damn it, Keir knew better than to leave. He was Rhys' Shadow Wraith, created to follow him through life, guarding and guiding. But he'd been doing a shitty job of it.

But it wouldn't be forever, he reminded himself. Soon, the reason for his distraction would be gone.

The pain of that admission cost him. If he had a heart, it would be twisted and squeezed, making him breathless. It was unbelievable to him that he had done the unthinkable. He had fallen in love with a mortal woman. And not just any mortal, he thought with hatred, but one who was dying.

Rowan. Even the image of her flashing in his mind caused him pain. He couldn't lose her, but he knew he was going to. There was nothing he could do; it was fate, just as Suriel said. As much as Keir despised the truth, he knew it was so. There was nothing in the mortal realm or in Annwyn that could save her.

If only his love could.

Jesus, he was fucked up. He was a Shadow Wraith, his existence tied to Rhys. But his soul was overtaken by a dying mortal, who didn't even realize he loved her—wanted her and fantasized about being deep inside her.

If he could only have her—just once, to feel her and keep her memory alive. Just once, and she would live forever in his memory.

A gentle tapping at his hand made him open his eyes. Cliodna, his little wren, pecked gingerly at his thumb. All seers—or shamans, as they were known in Annwyn—had animal allies who bonded with them; he had been chosen by this wren. It had always made sense to Keir that this little bird had chosen him. In the Otherworld, the wren, or *dreathan-donn*, was a sacred bird, considered to be a messenger from the deities. Cliodna's magical musical voice and complex song were a source of divination for him.

Picking her up in his palm, he met her black gaze. "What is it you wish me to know?" he murmured while brushing his thumb along her back.

Cliodna began to sing, and while she did, he focused on her gaze, the feel of her soft plumage beneath his thumb. He quieted his thoughts, so her magical song could bring him into a trancelike state. He was weak, having not fed from Rhys' energy in days, which made it much more difficult to alter his state of consciousness.

Patiently, his wren sang, until he could at last enter his meditative trance. Instantly, his spirit was transported to Annwyn, while his physical form remained rooted in the mortal plane. He saw himself in a dark chamber, a woman's form on a bed, draped in white.

Keir felt his mind begin to race, despite his deeply entranced state. It was Rowan. He felt her and the instant desire to take her and claim her. But she was still, her face covered with the white cloth.

Cliodna sang louder, and he glanced away from the body on the bed to the wren. That was the trouble with divination. One could not pick and choose when it came to visions, or bring one to an end when it became too disturbing.

He didn't want to continue, but the wren sang on, forcing him to interpret her musical notes as verbal directions.

Pulling the sheet off, Keir was not shocked to discover that it was Rowan lying beneath the sheet. He knew her shape, her scent, as intimately as if he had lain with her. But he hadn't, and he likely never would. Perhaps that was the reason he stood now, studying her, absorbing every nuance of her beauty and innocence.

She was naked, her body full and voluptuous, despite her illness. Her pale skin was smoothed and unmarked. The turquoise eyes he found so enticing were closed, giving her the appearance that she slept. But her chest was still, her breathing silent. It was not the repose of slumber; it was the repose of death. A feather quill, an inkwell, a candle, and a piece of folded paper were placed above her head. An athame, its blade tip stained with something rust-colored, was placed to her left. Beneath the blade, three perfect drops of blood glistened upon the white sheet. And in her hand, peeking out from between her fingers, was a feather. *Cliodna's feather*.

The wren's song pierced his thoughts, and he heard words rise up between her musical notes. *"So must it be done."*

"No!" he roared, severing the astral link. He awoke as his mind and soul slammed back into his physical body. Sweating and breathing hard, Keir opened his eyes, his mind whirling with what he had seen, his body exhausted from the journey. Cliodna was still perched on his hand, her head cocked to the side as she studied him with eyes that suddenly looked sorrowful.

"Was it a vision of what is to come, or a possibility that may be altered?" he asked.

And for the first time since his little wren had chosen him, Cliodna's song was that of silence.

In the darkened hall of the temple, Bronwnn stood in awe of the great king. His magical powers were palpable, and the fear he lit within her was very real.

"You are the seer Cailleach speaks of?" he asked.

She nodded, and started at the sound of a bird approaching. Cailleach's *oidhche*, no doubt. The owl was not just Cailleach's pet, but a spy she enjoyed sending out into Annwyn.

"There is nothing to fear," the king murmured as he cupped her chin, forcing her to meet his mysterious, mismatched eyes. "'Tis only a wren."

The little bird flew out of an alcove and then out through the arched window that led to the inner courtyard. She had seen that particular *dreathan-donn* on her travels through the woods. The bird's hauntingly lovely song was embedded in her mind, because seeing the wren always preceded a vision of her lover—a dream lover she now realized was going to be her mate.

"You have taken a vow of silence, I am told."

Refusing the urge to look away from the king, she nodded. He looked down upon her, watching and studying her as if she were some strange new creature he had never before seen.

"You have a look about you, little one. Something familiar," he murmured. "The memory is so close; yet whenever I try to reach out and claim it, it floats away like mist."

Bronwnn allowed him to tilt her chin as he looked at her from all angles. "Have you ever been to Velvet Haven?"

She shook her head. She had heard of it, of course, but had never gone farther from the temple than her walks in the woods and the little cottage that was her secret from Cailleach.

Releasing her chin, he allowed her to take a step away from

him. Her hands no longer shook, she realized, as she smoothed them along the front of her white gown.

"Cailleach informs me you are the order's scribe. Your visions are prophecies."

She inclined her head, hoping he would not ask how she came by her visions. That secret she could not give up.

"I sense something in you. A great power. I wonder if Cailleach senses it. Is that why she wishes to gift you to the wraith?"

He was thinking out loud. He did not need an answer from her. And thank the goddess, for she would not know how to reply.

"You heard me name my warriors. What do you think of my choices?"

A shrug was her answer. She knew little outside her world. She knew only what her visions had foretold—that there would be nine warriors, and one of them would be a Destroyer; a powerful, powerful apprentice to the Dark Mage, who would either destroy Annwyn and the mortal realm, or the very master he served.

The king seemed to understand her, despite her silence. "Tell me, do you know which of the nine will betray Annwyn?"

She shook her head vigorously, hoping he could see her seriousness.

He sighed, but he looked kindly at her. "We are allies, are we not?" he asked as he held out his palm to her. "I will protect you. Even from Cailleach. All I ask is that you come to me with any new visions that may aid us. You can trust me, Bronwnn. My word is my bond—and my honor. I do not give it lightly. But you can believe me in this. I will not let you suffer, not under the wraith, nor under Cailleach."

She smiled, feeling light with joy. She had an ally in the king. As he started to move away, she reached for his hand and clutched it in her own. Turning his palm up, she traced the lines with her fingertips and closed her eyes.

He was searching for his brother, and Bronwnn vowed to gift him with anything she might see. If the king had vowed to protect her from Cailleach, it was the very least she could do.

Images of water came to her—a long snaking river that traveled through darkness. A tunnel? A cavern? A pathway? It was a cavern of sorts, with strange symbols not of her world; yet the river was in Annwyn.

Opening her eyes, she met his gaze, then reached into the little satchel she wore at her side and pulled out the notebook she carried in order to communicate with Cailleach. *Begin at the reflection pool*, she wrote quickly, *and follow the river, until it leads to a cavern, where you will see mortal cipher. Your brother waits at the end.*

Tearing the page free, she pressed it into his palm, then slipped away, knowing she had stayed too long in the hall. Cailleach would have need of her soon, and Bronwnn did not wish to arouse her suspicions. But before she could leave, the king clasped his fingers around her wrist and stopped her. The wren was back, she noticed, perched on the thick stone sill.

"I am in your debt. You have only to ask, and whatever you desire is yours."

She turned and looked at him. *I want what you have*, she thought silently. *A love so powerful and beautiful. I want to belong to someone, and have him belong to me.*

Despite the darkness, he saw his reflection. His were eyes designed to see through anything—light or dark; good and evil. He loathed what he saw—a human known as Aaron.

It was not his real name or appearance, of course. He reviled fleshlings for their frailty, their mortality, their place in heaven. It went against his nature to hide his splendor beneath such a disguise. But the time was not yet right to reveal himself, or his intentions. "Soon," he whispered to himself. Soon, he would shed his chameleon ways. Then he would possess the powers of heaven and hell in the mortal realm, as well as those of the Summerlands and the Shadowlands in Annwyn.

The Dark Arts, he thought with amusement, were not so difficult to master. Not for one such as he. The witch Morgan had been a most agreeable tutor. But he was done with her. Her death had been necessary and enjoyable. She had taught him all she knew. Once he had exhausted the witch's talents, he had turned elsewhere, to another who had been exceedingly adept at sex and death magick. But like Morgan, she, too, had worn out her usefulness. What he needed now were more victims—sacrifices; offerings to the Dark Arts so that his magick could grow. There was so much that could be learned in Annwyn—much more than in the mortal realm.

And he was learning, growing, and becoming the most powerful creature to walk in either world.

Chains clanked together, and a groan rumbled above the metallic scrape of metal against stone. His captive was rousing yet again, despite the fevered beating he had dealt.

Strolling over to the naked, dirty form, the mage bent and reached for a handful of black hair and used it to pull his captive's head back.

"Why won't you die?" he snarled.

"Because I have something to do first," came the weak reply.

"After a thousand years?" he asked in disgust. "There is nothing left of the world you once knew, *Brother*."

His prisoner, weak of body and spirit, still had enough strength to mock him. "I have something you don't, and that is my faith."

"Faith is for mortals," he spat. "Not your kind."

"Are you not one of my kind?"

"Shut up!" he snapped, shoving his captive's head against the cave wall. "You know nothing of me."

"You have blinded me, Brother, but I still know your voice. Even after all this time, I know."

"You were always such a stupid, blind fool, Camael. Blind to everything but your desires."

"My desires are not so different from yours. I hungered for the flesh of a goddess. You hunger for power. You seek a kingdom to rule, Uriel, because you've been banished from God's."

He had not heard his name in so long, he had nearly forgotten it. He had become someone other than what he had been. The Dark Mage he was now, but hearing his rightful name once more forced him to recall what he was.

"And the angels who did not keep their own position," Camael whispered, his voice broken and hoarse, "but left their proper dwelling, He has kept in eternal chains in deepest darkness for the judgment of the great day."

Uriel did not need any biblical quotes or reminders. Camael was a fool. It was so much more than hatred for the humans. It went even beyond Uriel's desire to triumph in his banishment.

"Your chains are metaphorical, Uriel. You did not keep your position, so He banished you. You have imprisoned yourself with darkness, and chained yourself to its seductive call."

"And why shouldn't I?" he snarled. "When He banished me, He left me to rot among His filthy creations. Keep my place? No," he growled. "My place is not with the fleshings. My position is my own. My kingdom is to come. And then we will see what He has to say on His great day of judgment."

"Angel of prophecy," Camael said mockingly, "what will you do when you discover you have fallen victim to your divination?"

"I will cause pain and destruction. I will turn the righteous into sinners. I will turn the Destroyer into a creature of darkness and despair. I will take, and take, without thought or reason. I will take to hurt, to fulfill my greed, just as I did when I took your goddess lover."

Camael gifted him with his struggle against the chains, the pain etched on his face. He could almost see the hatred that would have been in his old adversary's eyes, but the orbs had long been plucked out.

"Your precious Covetina." The whimper of pain that whispered past Camael's lips was like the stroke of a lover to Uriel. His cock was hard. He was aroused by the pain he felt shuddering through his brother. "What was she ... Oh yes, the goddess of the well and the womb. A healer, a protector of childbirth ... and as lusty as any common whore. But as pleasurable as it was to bed her, it was far more delightful to watch her blood spill onto my hand."

"No," Camael cried, struggling to be free of the chains.

"Did you think her still alive? Oh no, Brother. It was from

her grimoire that I first learned of death and sex magick. Its power to control others—to aid me in my cause. Her body was my first sacrifice. I drank her blood and infused all her powers. And do you know what?" he whispered menacingly. "I can still taste her."

Camael went limp, and Uriel watched as the angel before him crumpled. Pulling the hood over his head, Uriel walked around the still form of his brother. "There will be an offering tonight. You will listen to it. Just as you have all the others. But this time, in your mind you will hear your beloved's scream."

Uriel's boots scraped against the stone. He reached for the heavy door, but Camael's voice made him pause.

"Do you know why I won't die, Uriel? Because I'm not the one without a flame."

"Fuck you, Camael."

The door slammed tightly, and Uriel bolted it. It unnerved him to know that Camael had discovered his secret. An angel without a flame was vulnerable to death. Anyone could kill him, even a lowly mortal. How had the blind and imprisoned Camael discovered his innermost secret?

"Well?" spoke a deep voice. "Do you have what I asked for?"

Uriel turned to see Gabriel move out of the shadows.

"You promised me Suriel!" Gabriel snapped. "I want him now. And I want him with his powers intact. Do you understand?"

"You will have Suriel." *And I will have the Sacred Trine, the flame* and *the amulet*, he silently added—*and all the power to rule the mortal realm and Annwyn.*

Gabriel's eyes blackened, but Uriel felt no fear. His brother might be one of God's favorites, but he was as corrupt as Uriel. Both were ruled by greed and lust for power. "Patience, Brother. My apprentice is not yet ready to embrace his preordained fate. There is still considerable resistance to the dark path."

"Then find a way to illuminate the path."

"It isn't that easy."

"Do you even know who this Destroyer is?" Gabriel sneered. "I'm beginning to think you're full of lies. And this Sacred Trine you speak of. Have you found it?"

The Oracle, the Healer, and the Nephillim. The trine was the most important part of the prophecy. He needed all three to control both realms. But something told him that Gabriel wanted the trine for his own purposes. For what, he would have to discover. Until then, he must distract Gabriel by giving him Suriel. That was Gabriel's most pressing concern.

"My investigations have led me closer to them," he lied.

Gabriel towered above him, glaring down into his face. He was searching for the lie in his eyes, but Uriel had been blanketed in sin for so long that his conscience no longer shone in his eyes. There was only blackness there—a deep well of unrelenting hatred against everyone in the mortal realm, and the goddesses in Annwyn. He was so close. He could smell it; taste it. Soon he would have the trine, and his apprentice.

Gabe was a tricky bastard, but Uriel was smarter, more devious. He would have what he wanted, despite what Gabriel decreed. Suriel would not be handed over to Gabriel. No, he had something else in mind for Suriel and his *gifts*.

CHAPTER FOUR

Scanning the crowd, Rhys let his gaze slip to a silver-haired woman. The color wasn't real—most likely it was a wig—but it would make the fantasy that much better. He hadn't been able to stop thinking of the woman in his dream, and suddenly he was consumed with the thought of taking a woman who looked just like her to bed, to finish what the dream had so teasingly started.

Normally, he didn't treat the women he took to bed like sex objects. He pleasured them and enjoyed them while they were together. The women he knew sexually were after the same thing he was—sex with no strings, one night of pleasure. There was no drama, no desire to keep seeing each other.

Tonight, though, he felt like a user, because of that damned dream that wouldn't leave him alone and because he was still taut with sexual need. He needed to get off, and why bother with his hand when the woman was staring at him that way?

"She'll do."

Rhys glanced over his shoulder to where Keir was standing behind him. He was used to the way Keir could appear and disappear in a shadow or a shaft of moonlight. He wasn't surprised to see him come out of the darkness of the corner. "You need to feed?"

"Yes."

Rhys sensed the desperation within the wraith. He needed energy, not only to survive, but to perform magick. But something was holding him back. Keir was normally eager to climb into bed with any woman. He enjoyed sex, but tonight it looked like a necessary evil—a sacrifice, if Rhys was interpreting Keir's clenched jaw correctly.

"I was wondering about her friend. The blonde. She's pretty."

"No blondes," Keir snapped, "and no one too . . . full."

Now Rhys understood. Keir didn't want any reminders of Rowan—a full-figured, stunning blonde he couldn't have.

"It's too much," Keir murmured. Even though the techno goth music was pulsing loudly through the club, Rhys heard Keir's anguished voice in his thoughts. "I can't be with someone who looks like her. It's wrong. I . . ."

"It's okay. I understand." Rhys felt the wraith's instant relief. "Let's get back to the one in the silvery blond wig," he suggested.

"Nice," Keir replied, trying to sound as if he were into this whole threesome thing tonight, although Rhys knew he wasn't. "You think she'll take us both?"

"Well, her eyes seemed to light up even more when you appeared. One can hope."

"If not, there's always Abby."

Rhys searched through the flashing strobe lights and colored laser beams for the red-haired waitress. She'd been trying to get into bed with them ever since she'd started at the club a year ago. Trouble was, doing this kind of thing with the staff was risky. He didn't like it. It made the night after sex awkward, and she was a good waitress. His customers liked her, and he'd hate to lose her if she wanted more than just a night of hot and sweaty sex. He'd have to let her go if she got all clingy—especially if she got suspicious about Keir. Normally, the whole magical, immortal thing wasn't a problem. Humans saw what they saw, and to them, most of the patrons were just like them—human. But if Abby took it into her head to get close with them, things might change.

On the other hand, Abby was the farthest thing from Rowan. And she was the complete opposite of his dream lady. Maybe that was what they both needed—to lose themselves in a woman who reminded them of no one.

"Hey," Abby said as she sashayed past them. She was wearing her customary black leather dress that looked to be at least one size too small, and black fishnets with thigh-high black boots. Her hair was dyed a burgundy red and worn in a bob. Her look was dominatrix, and Rhys wasn't sure if what he wanted tonight was something rough or . . . simpler. Straight pleasure.

"If you're wondering about Silver Bunny," she said, pressing forward so they could get a view of her cleavage, "she's good to go. She was asking me about you." Then she smiled and pressed closer. "But if you want someone who can handle both of you, there's me."

With a smile and a laugh, she sauntered away.

"Silver Bunny," Keir said as he nodded in her direction. "Pick her. You want her more than Abby. I'll meet you upstairs."

Then he was gone, evaporating into fog, which mixed in with the vapor of the dry ice. Rhys followed the writhing form as it made its way to the stairs to their rooms in the part of the club that remained the mansion.

Picking his way through the crowd, he pressed against the woman, preparing to ask her to dance, when she pressed back against him and kissed him.

Obviously, small talk wasn't required. From the feel of her breasts pressing against his T-shirt, her nipples were already hard, and her tongue . . . It was definitely searching for more.

"You sure?" he whispered in her ear as he kissed his way down her jaw. She moaned and pressed against him, her hand sliding down his abs to his crotch. She cupped him and said breathlessly, "I'm sure."

"What about my friend?" he asked as he pulled them deeper into the shadows and toward the stairs. Her body vibrated against him with the suggestion of the threesome. He could smell her excitement, could feel it as she wrapped herself around him.

"What about him? Is he willing?"

"More than willing."

She practically purred as he took her hand in his to lead her to the staircase. "I've never done this before."

"I know." They always said that, pretending innocence, then clawing at him and Keir as soon as they were alone.

She looked up at him, her eyes outlined with black eyeliner. She was pretty, and he was turned on. And Keir needed to feed. With a smile, she reached for him and pressed another kiss against his mouth.

"I'm ready," she murmured against his lips, "for the ride of a lifetime."

Keir paced the room where Rhys was going to bring the girl. His mind was consumed with Rhys' feelings, the lust coursing through his blood. The woman was reaching for his cock, stroking and cupping him. He could hear Rhys' growl; he could feel his need to press the woman against the wall and lift her skirt, sinking his cock deep inside her. The excitement built within Rhys, and Keir felt his body absorb the sensations.

As Rhys got excited, Keir fed.

Keir felt them outside the room. Already the woman had Rhys' shirt off, and her hands were working on the fastening of his jeans. He heard Rhys' heart speed up and the blood rush in his veins—and to his cock.

The energy built, and he allowed it. This was what he needed to survive.

The door opened, banged against the wall, and Rhys and the woman fell into the room. She was wild and experienced, and Keir gave thanks that she would not take long to fuck them.

He had no desire to seduce tonight. He wanted to take; not teach; not reassure. He wanted someone who knew what she was getting into.

Rhys moved to the bed, and the woman, now half dressed, fell back onto it. Rhys stood at the side of the mattress, his fingers unbuttoning his jeans.

Moving to stand behind him, Keir pulled his shirt over his head and allowed it to drop to the floor. The woman's eyes widened as she took in his markings; then her gaze slipped to Rhys' cock, and she took in the size of that.

Keir could smell her excitement. She was wet; already her core was opening, waiting for them. He heard her thoughts, a breathy voice in his head.

"Oh my God, they're beautiful. I can't wait to feel them . . . and to see them together. I wonder if they do each other."

Keir mentally reached out to Rhys. *"You know what she wants."*

With a nod, Rhys reached for her and brought her to her knees. Then he pulled her top off, baring her breasts.

"Both, right?" she asked as she watched Keir climb onto the bed behind her.

"If you can handle us both," Rhys said with a grin. He reached for his cock, stroking it in his hand, as Keir cupped her breasts from behind, shoved them together, and offered them up to him.

Rhys licked the mounds, wetting them for his cock, which he wanted to slide between them. He normally kissed and touched, preparing the woman and easing their way into the threesome, but this one was ready for it. Her gaze was hungry. He could feel the stinging of his back from where her nails had dug into his skin.

Keir tugged at her nipples as Rhys licked. Then Keir pinched them, and Rhys sucked on them. She moaned, then slid her hand down the front of her skirt, playing with herself as Keir parted her breasts and Rhys slid his cock between them.

She watched, Keir's hands on her breasts, Rhys' cock pumping between them. Keir circled his finger around the wet slit of Rhys' cock, then brought it to her mouth. She sucked his finger in deep, then licked the drop of pre-cum from his finger.

There was no way in hell that she'd never done this before. Keir looked at him with amusement, then took his cock in hand and rubbed her hip with it.

She moaned and bent sideways, trying to see Keir masturbating. Her mouth bumped Rhys' cock, and she bent forward, taking him in her mouth and sliding deep.

With a groan, he closed his eyes, allowing himself to feel and allowing Keir to feed.

"Fuck," Keir moaned as he pumped harder. One hand gripped her breast, then squeezed, conveying the thought that he liked what he saw, but Rhys knew it was him, *his* feelings that made Keir groan in satisfaction.

Holding her over his cock, Rhys slowed her down and met Keir's gaze over her back. She was moaning and writhing as Keir lifted her skirt and brushed his cock along her ass. She was still fingering her pussy. Then he ripped the skirt from her and tossed it aside. No panties; no bra—she was just a woman eager for two men. Her mouth was sucking him, and her hand was stroking Keir as he fondled her breasts.

Closing his eyes, Rhys tried to think of her. She was beautiful and experienced. She knew how to suck him; how to stroke Keir's cock as she worked his with her mouth. It was every guy's dream, but he wanted more. That empty place in his chest yawned deeper, and he tried to forget about it, to think of something else, but then the image of his dream woman came to him, and the hole in his chest got bigger and darker.

⚘

Keir sensed Rhys pulling away. He knew why. He was think-ing of his dream woman. His emotions got murky, his excite-ment waned, and Keir felt frantic. He wasn't done feeding. He needed more.

"*Don't think of her,*" he mentally murmured to the mortal. *"Just as I won't think of Rowan."*

The woman fell back onto the bed, her thighs spread, wait-ing for them to come to her. They both crawled to her, and Keir bent to suckle her breasts while parting her sex with his fingers, inviting Rhys to pet her.

Their fingers touched. The electric charge slammed through him. Only when he fed did they feel it. It was arousing, binding, and Rhys brushed against him again, just to feel the connection once more.

Keir's cock was hard and aching, and the woman was reaching down for Rhys' hand. Then, she was placing Rhys' fin-gers around Keir's cock.

The woman's excitement vibrated around the room as Rhys stroked him. When Keir reached for him, then wrapped his hand around Rhys' neck, bringing him closer to him, she purred and rubbed her thighs together. When he grabbed Rhys' cock and began stroking him, she cried out and touched herself.

She watched, her eyes wide, her fingers stroking her cunt as Keir and Rhys touched each other. The arousal ramped up, and Keir felt his hunger abate—he also felt the empty spot in-side him begin to fill the tiniest bit. There was a special connec-tion between them, especially during this—sex.

He heard Rhys' thoughts: he wanted—needed—to come. He wanted inside the woman, to fuck her hard; he wanted to watch Keir take her as well.

Keir wanted all that, too.

They left each other. Rhys then lifted the woman so that she was on her knees, her back to his chest. Keir kneeled in front of her and placed her legs over Rhys' thighs, exposing her core. Gripping her hips, Rhys lifted her up, sat her on his cock as Keir worked one breast, and slid the other hand to her pussy.

The woman cried out in pleasure as she slid down on Rhys' cock, and he thrust upward. Keir watched as Rhys took her, his cock sliding in and out. Her bottom slapped at Rhys' thighs, and her tits bounced enticingly, making him reach for one.

Her sex was stretched wide with Rhys' cock; she was moaning. He played with her and watched her breasts bounce; he pinched her nipple and felt her cunt grow wetter on his hand. Her core clutched at Rhys, and he groaned, gripping her hips harder. As Keir took in the picture before him, he wondered if Rowan would ever be this way with them—with him.

Could he share her like this? Could he stand to see Rhys thrusting into her? Could he part her thighs, lower his mouth to her core, and have Rhys there, watching? Touching?

No. He couldn't. Whatever he did with Rowan would be beautiful; too sacred; too important to him to share—even with Rhys.

"Oh my God," she kept chanting as Rhys took her. Keir was sweating, his teeth grinding together. He was close, and he fed off the inner struggle Rhys was waging.

He didn't want to come—yet.

Circling her, Keir stroked her core, then Rhys' cock.

"You bastard." Rhys' panting breaths entered his thoughts. *"You know you'll make me come."*

The woman liked it. She changed from "Oh my God," to "Yes, yes." She wanted to be fucked by them and then to watch them take each other.

Keir met Rhys' gaze before he lowered his head to her breasts. Rhys lifted her breasts to Keir's mouth, brushing her nipples against his face, and Keir caught them in his mouth, biting down softly.

Her arm flew behind her, and her fingers clutched Rhys' hair. Her breasts bounced, Rhys lifted them higher, and Keir took them hard, suckling her, kneading her in time to the stroke of Rhys' hands and his cock. Their fingers brushed again, and the electric shock was shared once more.

Then Keir moved down, lower, lower, until his mouth was at her sex and he could see Rhys' cock filling her. He watched for a second, turned on by watching. Rhys' cock was thick, glistening, and the woman was taking him, swallowing him whole. And it looked so fucking good . . .

Rhys heard the woman scream as Keir sucked her clit. The bastard's fingers were sliding around the base of his cock, spreading the wetness down to his balls. Then Rhys felt Keir's tongue circle the part of his cock that he could reach. As he withdrew, Keir's tongue swiped hot and wet—in, then out again, only to have Keir's tongue wrap around him.

Biting his lip, he fought for control. His emotions were unraveling, and Keir was taking them deep, feeding off his lust.

He was lost now, no longer thinking about anything, just the mindless need to come. How good it felt to be inside someone; to have Keir here, a presence in his mind, and his body. He was connected now with Keir, so Rhys could hear the woman's thoughts drumming through his mind.

"Oh my God, he's licking his cock!"

Even though Keir was licking her cunt and playing with her nipples, she wanted to see Rhys' dick in Keir's mouth.

Keir decided to give her what she wanted.

Lifting her away from Rhys, he left the woman on her knees, his hand buried in her pussy as he bent over and took Rhys' cock deeply in his mouth.

Both he and the woman moaned at the same time, and Keir's body tensed, infused with power.

"Finish me," Rhys commanded the wraith as he sucked deep, pulling him. The wraith laughed, his voice ringing in his mind. *"Not yet, mortal."*

Keir was having way too much fun.

Pulling away, Keir bent to the woman and kissed her, his tongue tangling with hers. "I like the way you taste on him."

She moaned, pulled Keir down on her, and spread her legs. "He tastes good on you, too."

Keir gripped her hair and licked her neck. "Did you like it, watching me suck his cock?"

She moaned, liking the conversation. Keir used his thigh and brushed the contoured edge between her sex. She came down on him, rubbing him hard. Keir's thigh was glistening wet.

"Take me," she begged, arching her hips.

Rhys watched as Keir slammed into her. He was rougher, more aggressive, but the woman liked it—took it. It was always this way. Rhys was the seducer; Keir the dominant. Once Keir was fed, he was strong, his natural dominance coming to the forefront.

Rhys tore his gaze from the two bodies as the woman slid her hand along the bed, reaching for him. He moved closer, watching the way Keir worked her. His cock was thick, pounding in and out of her, and Rhys watched, mentally commanding the wraith to go harder, faster.

He obeyed and lifted the woman's legs over his shoulders, exposing her, deepening the angle for his penetration. The side view turned Rhys on. He saw Keir's cock filling her, thrusting deep, and saw her cunt open to him. The woman moaned, and Rhys glanced down. She was sliding her fingers around his cock, pulling him closer, to her mouth. She liked what was happening between the three of them, and she was hungering for more than one of them.

As she sucked him, Rhys allowed himself to touch Keir. There was a jolt between them, which Rhys felt infuse his body. The woman was working him faster and harder as her climax came upon her. He was close to coming, and so was the wraith. The woman's mouth worked his cock, as her pussy worked Keir's. Rhys and Keir had a rule—the woman's pleasure before theirs. So Rhys leaned forward and flicked her clit, and he felt her explode, the cry wrapping his cock.

Then the wraith stiffened, and Rhys felt his orgasm, along with his own, rear up.

Keir held his gaze as he pulled out of the woman, emptying on her belly. She held Rhys close, inviting him to come in her mouth, but he pulled out and instead pressed the head of his cock against Keir's, coming in pulsing white streams that coated the head of Keir's cock.

The three of them were panting, and Rhys was left with the sensation that both he and Keir had needed something different tonight. It was more than their bond. They had needed to fill that empty space inside them that neither of them understood.

"Holy shit," the woman breathed. "That was fucking hot."

Keir pushed away and reached for his shirt. He wiped the woman's belly clean and tossed the shirt onto the floor.

Then he leaned over and caged the woman with his arms. "Look into my eyes."

She did, and Rhys knew the drill. Keir was going to wipe her memories clean. She wouldn't remember much more than taking Rhys upstairs. Neither of them wanted the women to remember what they did to each other. It was personal; a private expression of their bond.

"You will remember one of us. Not both. And not us together."

She nodded, her eyes glazed. "Yes."

Keir's silver eyes flashed, and he moved away. "Thank you," he said to her, helping her sit up. "You were perfect."

Keir sent Rhys a smile, then turned to dress. Rhys watched the tableau and felt a chill race down his spine. When he was younger, he couldn't have imagined it any better—hot, anonymous, kinky-assed sex. He'd loved it. Now he was left feeling empty. That woman hadn't wanted either of them—not really. She'd wanted the sex; the excitement of a threesome; the novelty of seeing two guys together. But it hadn't been anything more than base, sexual desire. She didn't want to know them or to connect on anything other than a physical plane.

Keir glanced at him over his shoulder, his look conveying that he felt the same thing.

"You're alive, and I'm alive. It's as good as it's going to get."

Keir left the room, and the woman, who was just finishing

pulling on her skirt, gazed up at him. "Ah, I think you ripped this."

Rhys went to the wardrobe and pulled out a pair of jeans. "It's all I've got."

She grabbed them and tossed her hair over her shoulder. "So, uh, I have some friends to meet downstairs."

"Sure."

"I'll see you around?"

"Yeah."

He watched her pull on his jeans, which were, of course, too big, and followed her out the door. When she was walking down the stairs, Keir came out of the shadows.

"I'll lock up tonight."

Rhys glanced at the wraith. "Is it enough for you?"

"It has to be. She enjoyed it. She's downstairs now telling her friends what a stud you are."

Rhys reached for Keir. "You thought of Rowan. When you came."

The wraith nodded, then looked away. "I couldn't help it. You saw what she looked like in my thoughts."

"I tried not to, but it was damned hard. You have a vivid imagination."

Keir winced. "I know. It drives me fucking mad at night."

"You should go to her."

"No." Keir brushed his hands through his hair. "She's too good for me. You saw me in there. I'm a beast, and Rowan needs someone gentle. No reminders of her past. I would . . . want to claim her when I was with her. Hard, fast. I'd be possessive and dominant, and I'd only terrify her."

Rhys knew it was a losing battle. Keir wouldn't go to

her, especially not now, when the memories of them with the woman were so fresh in his mind. If Keir hadn't needed to feed, Rhys knew he would not have come to him and the woman tonight. Tonight had been purely about survival for Keir. And maybe it had been that for him, too.

CHAPTER FIVE

Sunlight filtered in through the stained glass window of the breakfast room. It was nine, and Rhys was alone—again. The wraith had left before dawn, but Rhys had seen him change form, creep across the floor as a shadow, and filter beneath the door. He still hadn't returned. Rhys wasn't going to worry about him. The wraith had been well fed, his magical abilities replenished. He could take care of himself, just as Rhys could.

Frowning, Rhys picked up the box of cereal. It had been two days since the confrontation in Rhys' office with Suriel and Keir, and still, the memory stung. Rhys hated being kept at arm's length, but what he despised more was the ignored request he had sent via Keir for Bran, the Sidhe king, to come to Velvet Haven and talk with him. Rhys wanted answers about what was being done to discover this murderer and the kind of protection he was going to have for the club's guests. As the owner of the club where inhabitants from Annwyn mixed with mortals, Rhys felt he was entitled to a little information. The psycho killer was sacrificing both mortals and immortals, so no one was safe.

Of course, Bran had ignored the request, which pissed Rhys off. Bran thought him either incompetent or insignificant. Either way, the Sidhe was wrong, because Rhys had no intention of being kept in the dark or brushed aside.

Maybe Bran had reasoned out that Rhys was going to ask to be allowed to join the group of nine who were hunting for the Dark Mage. After all, he was involved, and he owed it to his own kind—mortals—and to the patrons of his club to make it as safe as possible. But instead of telling Rhys to his face that he wasn't wanted, his uncle chose to ignore him like a child, really ramping up his pissed-off state.

Sitting around during the day while his club was closed allowed Rhys too much damned time to stew and brood over the injustice of it all. He was an action kind of guy, and inaction made him irritable and snappy. His nerves were stretched thin, and the whole situation was beginning to wear on him. So, too, were the dreams he kept having of the sexy blonde. He couldn't close his eyes without seeing her image. Hell, he didn't even have to close his eyes. Sometimes he caught himself daydreaming about her, and those daydreams naturally evolved into steamy vignettes of sex.

Sure, he had a healthy sex drive, but lately he was acting like a hormonal teenager. He had a perpetual hard-on, and it was making him bad-tempered. Maybe he could find a woman who looked like his dream woman. He could pretend she was that dream woman, and he could act out all the things he thought of doing. Then, he could purge her from his dreams, and his mind, and carry on with his life, living as he had before the murders started. But last night, he'd had a woman, and it hadn't made it easier to forget his dream goddess. It had only made him want her more.

"Hey, what's for breakfast?"

Rhys watched as a shadow crept across the carpet, only to solidify and become Keir. "I gave Maggie the morning off. It's cereal or toast." Rhys narrowed his gaze. "Where have you been?"

"Annwyn."

So why did he have to change his shape and slink out of the room at the crack of dawn? Rhys wondered. No, Keir was lying. But why?

Keir poured himself a cup of coffee and took a sip. "Sleep well?"

"No," he grumbled. "I didn't." His dream lady kept visiting him, and his conscience was eating away at him. He hadn't really wanted that woman last night. But he'd taken her anyway. It didn't sit well with him.

"You?"

Keir shrugged and sat back in his chair. "Not really. I haven't slept in weeks."

"Rowan?"

"That's not up for discussion."

They sat in silence for a minute. Then Keir suddenly snapped, "Do you have to do that?"

"Do what?" he growled. Apparently, both of them were in a bitch of a mood.

"Slurp your milk. It's damned annoying."

Rhys scooped up a hefty spoonful of Froot Loops. "What's your problem this morning?"

"Nothing."

Rhys grunted as he wolfed down his breakfast. Keir and his mood swings were getting out of control. For weeks, Rhys had tried to give the wraith the space he needed to tend to Rowan and accept her fate. But it wasn't working. Keir was becoming only more sullen and withdrawn.

"I'm fine," Keir grumbled, obviously hearing his thoughts. "You gave me enough energy for a month."

The mention of the woman and the night of hot sex should have brought back some satisfying memories. Instead, it reminded him of *her*—his dream goddess. Rhys felt his cock harden, and he groaned. He emptied the box of Froot Loops into his bowl and ate, trying to think of anything other than the woman—or sex.

"So, you want to tell me what's going on?" he asked Keir, who was busy gazing into a cup of black coffee. "You left early this morning, and in shadow. Which tells me you didn't want me to know you were leaving."

"You know what it is."

"I know it has something to do with Rowan, and there's also something else you're trying to hide."

Keir shrugged. "Bran has named me one of his nine warriors."

Rhys waved his spoon. "Too late. I already figured that out. I'm mortal, not stupid. So, tell me what you're really trying to hide. And don't bullshit me. Remember, we're connected."

"It would be better if you didn't know anything—"

"If you're going to insinuate that it would be better for me because of my mortal status, you can prepare for a pounding. I'm getting sick and tired of being treated like a goddamned kid."

"I've never seen you this way," Keir accused, "so angry to be what you are."

"Well, I've never had to feel ashamed that I was a human. You know, in my world, I'm considered a hard-ass. In yours . . . you treat me like a wilting flower, and it bugs the shit out of me."

"I'll talk to Bran. But I think you already know his answer."

"Just tell me this—is it revenge? You know, finally getting back at Daegan through me?"

Keir shook his head. "Bran has accepted his fate. When Daegan abdicated and left the Sidhe throne to Bran, he was enraged. But he's had centuries to reconcile himself to being king."

"So, what is it, then? Is it because I have no powers? Because he thinks I'm some sort of fuckup who would ruin his plans?"

"I can't speak for the king, but I believe it's because of the curse Cailleach has placed upon the males of Daegan's line. Bran doesn't want the extra worry of having to protect you from the goddess."

"That's what I thought. He thinks he needs to babysit me. Well, I can handle myself."

"The Dark Times have already consumed Annwyn. There's danger everywhere, even for those who have lived there always. Safe harbors are no longer safe. If the immortals do not know where to hide from this mage, then how can you be expected to survive while hiding from him *and* Cailleach? It's just not safe, Rhys."

Rhys felt his temples begin to pound. He didn't know what it was, but he felt the overwhelming desire to prove himself, not only to Keir and Bran, but to Annwyn; to show the Otherworld that he belonged.

"No one is questioning your ability to fight, Rhys. Bran knows you can handle yourself. That's not the issue."

Rhys wasn't normally the macho, dickhead type, but lately,

his actions had been leaning in that direction. He really didn't have anything to prove to anyone, but maybe this feeling he had was the need to prove something to himself.

"So, what else are you hiding?" Rhys grumbled, preferring to talk about something—or someone—other than himself. "I know you are, so you might as well come clean."

Sighing, Keir sat back in his chair and raked his long fingers through his hair. "I have been using the cards to try to investigate Rowan's past."

"What'd the tarot tell you?"

"Nothing. I mean, it's so bizarre. I know she's not fully human. I can feel it. And so can Bran. But what the other part of her is . . . I can't determine."

"And this other part? Do you think you can use it to save her?"

Keir looked at him sharply. "What do you mean?"

"If she's immortal, can you use whatever immortality she has to save her?"

"That's not the way it works. You're either immortal or you're not."

"I already know that." Rhys had tried to perform magick, and fuck-all had happened. He was a mortal, with violet-colored Sidhe eyes—the only sign of his immortal blood. Nope, not one magical cell in his body. Just about his only special talent was with a bow and arrow. As a kid, once he'd accepted that magick wasn't in his blood, he'd picked up a different hobby—archery. He was good—*really good*—at it; a natural, his instructor had said. He'd always believed that one day, his talent might come in handy. But when compared to magick, playing with arrows was . . . well . . . so nursery school.

"I figured if I went to the cards, they might help me to learn more about her, but it was just cloudy images, until . . ."

Keir swallowed hard and closed his eyes. Rhys felt Keir's agony. The way it ate at him. Rhys had never been in love, and he was suddenly glad for that, because he didn't want to experience one ounce of what the wraith was going through.

"This morning, I left the club and went there," Keir whispered quietly, his voice cracking. Rhys knew exactly where Keir meant—Rowan's old store, which housed her inventory of new age stuff. Keir was a devout practitioner of the tarot.

Keir glanced at him, and Rhys knew the wraith could hear his thoughts. "I needed to be close to her, and I needed to know her. I went to see if I could discover her past." Keir shot him a hooded look. "Instead, I saw her death."

Rhys shoved the bowl away and pressed forward, trying to catch Keir's gaze. But he was a million miles away, lost in the memory. "I saw it in the cards—it is heat and flame and ash. And when the embers die away, and the wind whispers over her grave, the ashes fly up and around, and there is nothing left but a bit of silver that is melted and distorted."

"Jesus, Keir," Rhys murmured as he reached out and clutched the wraith's shoulder. "You should have told me sooner."

"Why?" Keir looked up at him with desperate eyes. "Can you change it?"

"You know I would if I could."

His friend nodded and pushed his coffee cup away. "It's all just bullshit, you know." Keir stood and moved away from the kitchen table, prowling like a caged lion. "I shouldn't even care what happens to her. I've known her for what? A month? Hell, I haven't even slept with her. And yet, the second she looked into my eyes I felt something . . . like destiny, or my fate unfolding. I can't explain it. I just feel it so deeply, that she is meant for me."

"I know what you mean." And he did. He felt the very same thing whenever he dreamed of the woman. Yes, he wanted her sexually, but there was something more than lust connecting him to her.

Keir shook himself. "I apologize for leaving you high and dry here. I've just—just been consumed with Rowan. And if I'm being honest, it's hard to see her spending so much time with Sayer. That damned Selkie is using his Enchantment magick on her to help with the search for the king's brother, but my gut tells me he has his own motives, and they aren't pure and innocent."

"There's no need to apologize. You're not my babysitter, and I'm not your wife."

That earned a half smile from the wraith. "Shit no. I wouldn't marry you. You talk in your sleep."

Suddenly, Rhys was on the alert. "Oh yeah, what do I say?"

"Very naughty things. You've been dreaming of a woman for a week."

Amusement melded into jealousy. He didn't like that Keir might be able to see his dream woman. Hell, he didn't even like the idea of the wraith's knowing about her.

"Easy," Keir grumbled. "I got my own female problems."

Only slightly relieved, Rhys pushed his chair back. He didn't want to think about Keir's knowing about the woman. For some asinine reason, he was starting to become highly jealous and possessive. "I have some business to do in my study. I'll catch up with you later."

"Just stay away from the portal, right?" Keir reminded him.

Rhys flipped him off, making Keir laugh for the first time in weeks.

Keir watched Rhys walk out of the kitchen. The mortal was tightly wound this morning. It had been stupid to admit he knew of Rhys' dreams and the woman. He was overstepping bounds. He knew it. But somehow he had to find a way to make Rhys realize that things weren't always as they seemed.

That woman Rhys was dreaming of? She was going to make things very difficult, and very complicated.

With a groan, Keir sat back at the table, allowing his head to fall into his hands. Things were going to get down-right ugly—and soon. Closing his eyes, he recalled how he'd been awakened in the night with the near-deafening screams of Rhys' thoughts in his head. He could still feel the mortal's desire swimming in him. And the things he had wanted to do with the woman . . . *Christ*. He glanced down at the button fly of his 501s. *Ah, shit.* Not again. Wasn't it bad enough that he'd suffered through a hard-on all night while listening to Rhys get it on in his dreams? But now, too?

Damn it. He couldn't help it. Everything Rhys wanted to do with his woman was what Keir wanted to do with Rowan.

Okay, he had to check it. To get the memories of Rhys' thoughts and yearnings out of his head. But Christ, he couldn't stop hearing him. Even now, Rhys was thinking of her. Keir heard his thoughts and his sexed-up voice. It was a terrible in-vasion of his privacy. He should have shut off the sounds—he

had the power to—but he was so strung out, so fucking desperate that he didn't have the strength. He was desperately in love
with Rowan, just as Rhys was falling in love with a woman he
could never have, for Keir was powerless to deny the destiny
that was unfolding. The woman Rhys dreamed of would not
belong to him. She would not be his mate.

Instead, she would be Keir's.

In time, Rhys would have to know the truth, but not now.
Let him have his dreams. As long as Rowan was alive, Keir
would do everything in his power to change their fate—a fate
that would destroy Rhys.

"You will open your eyes and awaken when you feel my touch."

Rowan felt the gentle caress along her cheek. Lashes fluttering, she slowly lifted her lids to see Sayer sitting before her.

"Well?" she asked.

He shook his head. "Nothing new. The riddle is the same.
No more or less was revealed."

"I'm sorry, Sayer," she whispered. And she was. She had
so hoped that by allowing Sayer to enchant her, she would be
able to help uncover the location of Carden, the Sidhe king's
brother.

"We'll try tomorrow. I have other techniques I can use."

Rowan knew her mental resistance was the roadblock.
Sayer, despite his powerful Enchantments, could not break past
that one last barrier in her mind. This was the barrier that protected her innermost thoughts and feelings and the dwelling
place of her horrible memories of being raped.

Cupping her cheeks, Sayer looked deeply into her eyes. His pupils were long, elliptical—beautiful, and the mystery she saw in his eyes drew her in. "You know you can trust me, Rowan. I need that trust to be able to get inside your mind completely."

"I know I can trust you . . . but . . . I can't let you in there. I . . . can't."

Kissing her forehead, he soothed her fears. "It's okay. It's too soon yet. That's all. Don't worry, we'll find a way around this."

Pressing her face into his neck, Rowan allowed herself to absorb Sayer's heat and the safety he provided. He was a good friend, but obviously not good enough for Rowan to shed the memories of her body being abused by the caretaker of the orphanage where she had lived since the age of five.

On the outside, she appeared to be a together type of woman; someone who had survived being raped as a teen, and was still able to heal and grow. And she had, in some respects. But in her mind, she hadn't. She hid those memories, and the fears, from herself and others.

Trembling as the memories came back, she held on tighter to Sayer. A month ago, if someone had told her she would find comfort and friendship in an immortal Selkie who practiced Enchantment magick, she would have laughed, then promptly called the psych ward for the poor, deluded individual. But now, it seemed almost normal.

He held her for a while, allowing her to breathe in his calming scent. He smelled of the ocean—clean, salty; the aroma always brought her a measure of peace and calm.

"You need to rest."

She wasn't tired, but the opportunity to be alone was too

much to resist, so she nodded and allowed Sayer to press her back onto the bed. She shuddered as his chest came down to hers. Suddenly she felt smothered, just as when she was sixteen and the caretaker had come up behind her and grabbed her, covering her mouth with his hand as he dragged her to the crypt below the church.

Her breathing started to quicken, and her vision glazed. But Sayer moved away and reached for the blankets. "Sleep well."

The space he created made her breathe easier. No one knew, not even Mairi, her best friend, that she had not been able to allow herself to be with a man since that fateful afternoon. She had pretended she had gotten over it. She'd dated, but never once had she been able to allow a man to do more than kiss her. The relationships would then end swiftly, and she'd move on. Most of the men had been understanding, with the exception of Aaron. He'd turned into a stalker, and a horrifying one at that. He'd wanted something from her, but what?

He was still out there, she thought. He was part of this prophecy, and the Dark Times that had come to the Other-world. She was terrified he would find her. When she was alone at night, her room blanketed in darkness, Rowan prayed to the Fates she would never be found. So far, good karma had reigned. She'd been protected here in the court of the Sidhe king.

The door inched open, and Mairi peeked around the cor-ner. "I'm not disturbing you, am I?"

"No. We're done. I'm sorry, Mairi. We didn't learn any-thing new about Carden."

Mairi's expression was somber. "It's okay, Rowan. Just rest. Bran will find Carden. I have someone here who wants to see you."

Rowan's heart sped into overdrive. Keir. Her body lit up, anticipating a glimpse of the rough-hewn Shadow Wraith. He was huge—tall and broad, with a body that looked as if it could snap a person in two; the type she should be terrified of. But she wasn't. Keir did things to her body she had never experienced before. And he'd never even touched her.

"I'm up for visitors," she said, suddenly more animated. Sayer sent her a cocky grin and gave her another quick kiss on the cheek.

"Sleep well," he murmured, with heavy emphasis on "sleep." "And we'll try this again later."

Rowan smiled as she watched him leave. Her expression immediately fell when Suriel walked in. "Hi."

He knew she was disappointed. She saw it in the way his face softened. "Expecting someone else?"

"No."

But he knew she was lying.

Sayer and Mairi took their leave. As the door to her room clicked closed, Suriel pointed to the bed. "May I?"

"Certainly."

Rowan sat up in bed and watched Suriel. Her surroundings looked so normal that it was almost unbelievable that she was actually living in the Otherworld, and the man sitting at the foot of her bed was not a man at all, but a fallen angel.

She shared a strange past with Suriel. He had told her that he was the angel of death and resurrection, and that he had been there that afternoon when the caretaker so brutally raped her. He'd been there to claim her soul, because she was supposed to die. But then, everything had changed. Mairi discovered her healing powers. And she had lived, and the connection linking her, Mairi, and Suriel had been forged.

The power of three in Celtic lore was magical. It represented birth, death, and resurrection. Rowan had always wondered what part she was to play in this trine.

"You've been remembering."

It was not a question but a statement. There was no need to lie to Suriel, when he already knew the truth. "Yes. Sayer . . . got a bit too close, and it provoked . . . memories."

He nodded, and his eyes turned darker. "I remember it, too. Being forced to stand by until it was time to claim you. It haunts me as well. You were so . . . young. And pure."

And after, she had been tainted, in the most heinous way possible. There hadn't been a piece of her that had not been violated. Suriel reached for her and tilted her face up to meet his.

"Never tainted," he murmured. "Nothing could mar this radiance I see. There is innocence still in your eyes. He did not take it all. There is a purity to you, Rowan. Despite what has been taken from you, it still shines."

She flushed and looked away from his penetrating gaze. "I have felt dirty for so long."

"Soon, you no longer will feel that way."

Rowan knew it was true. Soon, she would no longer feel.

"The pain?" Suriel murmured. "How is it?"

"Bearable."

"Does it hurt now?"

"A bit."

Suriel's fingertips glided gently over her temples and forehead. "Close your eyes, and concentrate on my fingers."

She did. The little tingles on her skin made her shiver. Suriel's touch immediately chased away the headache coming on.

"There. All better?"

She nodded and opened her eyes. "Thank you."

His head tilted to the side as if he were studying her. His gaze swept swiftly along her body. "You look very much the same. Are you certain the illness is progressing?"

Rowan flushed. Everyone knew she was dying. Fricking cancer—a brain tumor, to be precise. She didn't know why, but she felt ashamed that her body was giving up, letting the cancer win. To look at her, all boobs, hips, and thighs, no one would think she was dying. People who were dying were supposed to be emaciated skeletons. But she hadn't lost a pound. She was still wearing her size sixteens, which was kind of disappointing, in a sick way. She was expecting to get *very* skinny.

"I'm sure," she murmured at last. "The numbness and tingling are becoming more widespread. Sometimes my legs give out on me, and I can't feel my feet. My headaches are more severe, and occasionally I can't see. All are indications that the tumor is growing."

Suriel nodded, his face falling. Suddenly he reached out and cupped her cheek. "There is luminescence in you. One that belies death."

She smiled. Suriel was good-looking—hot even—but her desire ran elsewhere. What she wouldn't give to hear a certain Shadow Wraith tell her she was luminescent. But then, a dying chick could hardly be a turn-on. Besides, even if Keir shared her desire, she probably wouldn't be able to let him close. She'd panic and shut down. Despite her hunger for him, she wouldn't be able to allow him to touch her.

Gripping the silk coverlet, Rowan strived to keep her tears from falling. She didn't want to die, but her tumor was inoperable. There was nothing to be done for her in the mortal realm, and now there was nothing in Annwyn that could help her, either. So many nights she had feared what the end would be like. Would it bring horrible pain? Would she scream from it? Or would it be swift and painless?

"Swift," Suriel whispered. "I promise."

"Thank you," she replied softly.

"Everything happens for a reason, Rowan. Do you believe that?"

Rowan looked into Suriel's deep, dark eyes and instantly felt a calming peace. Her head no longer hurt, but she was beginning to tire. The restlessness and anxiety that had consumed her only moments before were gone, leaving only exhaustion.

"Rowan," he asked again, "do you believe?"

"I don't know. I guess."

He pinned her with a gaze she could no longer interpret. "Do you believe you are part of God's plan?"

"No. I don't believe in God."

"Yes, you do. You're just angry with Him."

Rowan felt her breath leave her lungs. How could Suriel have known the truth?

"We've all been angry with Him at some point." Suriel turned his head until he was looking out the window into the gardens that backed onto a small maze made up of hedged boxwoods. "We've all hated Him, even."

"'We' as in angels, or 'we' as in mortals?"

He did not look at her but kept his gaze on the garden, his eyes suffering with some unseen memory, his expression distant.

"Me," he whispered. "I have hated Him. I have despised Him for what He has made me do in His name. One wing always dipped in blood—can you imagine it?" he asked, his gaze slowly drawing away from the window, only to land on her. "Can you imagine what that is like, to always be sent to do the dirty work? To be feared? To be hated? To cause such despair?"

"No," she answered, swallowing uneasily.

"You hate Him because of what He has taken from you. Your mother, your father. You hate Him because you think He abandoned you to the nuns who didn't care. You hate Him because He allowed you to be raped. You hate Him now, because you've discovered that you serve some purpose for His plan, and you resent it. You don't want to serve Him, because you don't think He deserves it. You want to punish Him. Am I right?"

"How could you know?" she asked. She'd never told anyone; not even Mairi. No one knew her thoughts.

"Do you think you are the only one to feel this way? Do you think it's easy to never question? To never wonder why you must endure; why you must perform your part in His greater plan? Well, you're not alone. I understand how you feel. I wanted to punish Him, too. And I did. I was one of the seven archangels He first created. I was one of the first to fall."

An archangel. Rowan couldn't help but stare at Suriel, at his soft brown hair and eyes and at his mouth, so perfectly carved and shaped. Yes, she could see him in a long, flowing robe, seated with Gabriel and Michael. She saw the strength in his eyes, the pride. But she saw secrets and pain as well.

"Do you still hate Him?"

"No. I feel nothing. That is my punishment. I'm empty, hollow, except for . . . Never mind." Before she realized what she was doing, Rowan reached out to him, but he pulled back from her, avoiding her touch. "We all have a purpose, both angel and mortal. And though it may not be clear to us, it is to Him. We are all part of God's plan—mortals, angels, the fallen, and the devout. We all serve a purpose. Your conception occurred when the seed of the prophecy was sown. You cannot begin to fathom how much we all need you."

Swallowing, Rowan looked away, trying to let everything sink in. She'd always believed her life was useless. No one had wanted her, not even her own parents. It was kind of hard to take it all in, that now, she might be needed. "You make me sound like I am something special, when I am not."

Suriel smiled and reached for her hand. "You have no idea of your worth, Rowan. In time, it will all be clear. To you. To me. To the others."

"What am I?" she asked him, giving voice to the question she had asked herself all her life.

"A gift."

And then he rose from her bed and bent down, kissing her reverently on her forehead. "We will meet again. And then, we shall know who you are."

"Suriel, why did you really come here?"

He stilled, his hand lingering on her shoulder. His eyes were now guarded, unreadable. Now, she was looking into the eyes of the fallen angel.

"You have something very valuable. And I want to make certain I get it first."

CHAPTER SIX

Rhys rubbed his fingers over the raised cross on the wooden box. It had been hours since he had seen Keir, and even longer since he had come to his office in the guise of doing work.

Instead, he had spent the time gazing up at the ceiling, pondering what the hell was happening. Nothing was normal, and that was saying something, considering his life. Even after hours of introspection, he was no closer to an answer. In fact, he only had more questions—questions that could be answered only by Bran, Keir, or Annwyn itself.

He knew enough of the Otherworld to at least get by. Daegan, although ancient by this time, had been alive when Rhys was a young boy. Despite being turned mortal by the Supreme Goddess, Cailleach, Daegan had had an unnaturally long life. So long, in fact, that Daegan's son and grandson had been forced to hide him in the mansion so that no one would question how a man who was thirty years old when he arrived from Scotland could still be alive a hundred and forty years later.

Long life was a gift to mortals, but for Daegan, it had been just another punishment, because Daegan had been forced to endure nearly a century alone without his beloved Isobel.

Rhys glanced up at the portrait of the couple that hung above the fireplace. Isobel was beautiful, and Daegan had the Otherworldly aura of power and presence.

"You've the look of the Sidhe," Daegan had told him when he was only six. "You're the first of my line to do so. Here, let me look at you."

He had taken Rhys' chin in his wrinkled, gnarled hand and gazed upon him with his violet eyes.

"Sidhe blood runs strong in you. You look very much like me."

Rhys had been horrified, of course, because what he saw was a wizened old man. He didn't want to look like Great-Great-Grandfather Daegan. And the old man had laughed then, hearing his thoughts. "I once was handsome. And you will be, too. Come to me, laddie, and I will tell you of your heritage. For I believe that one day you will have need of the knowledge my stories will bring."

After that, Rhys would find himself in his great-great-grandfather Daegan's room nearly every day. He told him of Annwyn, of all the different places, such as the Summerlands and Wastelands. He spoke of the reflecting pool and all the different races living in the Otherworld. But Rhys' favorite stories were about the goddesses. Even at his young age, he had been entranced by the idea of a group of women, so beautiful and enchanting, yet filled with awe-inspiring power.

One day, Daegan's stories began to change. They became less like fairy tales and more like Survival 101. Rhys had been reminded of Cailleach's curse against the firstborn sons in Daegan's line, but he had also been informed of places where Cailleach's power didn't immediately reach. He'd learned that the reflecting pool would be safe, and Daegan made him memorize over and over how to get to the pool if he passed through the veil that led to Annwyn. He told Rhys about all the different animals and what they represented. He explained that certain animals sometimes allied themselves with humans; if one saw the same animal three times, he could assume the animal had chosen him and would be his guide and protector.

And then he had given him this box, filled with talismans for his journey. He'd never expected to step foot in Annwyn, but somehow Daegan had suspected it was Rhys' destiny.

Opening the box now, Rhys stared down at the small piece of paper and the words written in Daegan's hand. *Remember the animals. They will be your guides.*

From the box Rhys pulled the torc and wrist cuffs, the marks of a high-ranking Celt. The torc was worn around the neck as a status symbol, but also as a talisman against evil.

The ancient bronze was heavy in his hand, but the piece was stunning. At each end of the torc was a carved wolf head. And on each cuff was a Celtic cross with a wolf curled around the base. When Daegan had been banished from Annwyn, he had adopted the surname of his wife. MacDonald had become not only Daegan's name but his clan. When they'd moved out of Scotland, Daegan had given his family a clan animal, and that was the wolf.

It was fitting that Daegan had chosen the *madadh-alluidh* to be the clan's animal ally, for the wolf, like Daegan, was cunning and intelligent. The wolf represented the ability to outthink hunters. It could read the signs of nature and knew how to pass by danger invisibly. It also knew how to outwit those who might do harm and to fight fearlessly when needed. The wolf was a loner that also belonged in a pack. The wolf was the right symbol for the MacDonalds and him.

Rhys wondered why he had felt drawn to the box tonight. Maybe it was Keir and his mysterious disappearing acts these past few days. Maybe it was his own destiny calling him forth. Whatever it was, he felt something was close at hand.

The pretty song of Keir's wren made him look up. She was a drab little thing, her plumage a nondescript grayish brown. But Cliodna had the most enchanting song he'd ever heard. Many times he had seen Keir follow this bird on his divination journeys. But what the bird was doing here, he had no idea. She belonged to Keir.

"I don't know where he is," he grumbled as he picked up the cuffs and placed them on his thick wrists. The bronze was heavy and cool against his skin, but the cuffs felt right, and damn, they looked cool, too.

Cliodna began to sing faster and higher, and Rhys watched her curiously as he placed the torc around his neck. The wolf heads rested against his collarbone, fitting him perfectly.

Rhys waited to feel the magic. Nothing came to him. He wasn't certain if it was supposed to feel like a lightning bolt, or something more subtle, like a tingle of warmth. But the truth was, he didn't feel shit.

Maybe Daegan had really been insane. Those old stories and everything? Maybe it was geriatric dementia talking.

The wren really began warbling out a song, which sounded almost—angry? It couldn't be. But when Rhys looked at her, she flew off the arm of a chair and did a low buzz over his head, pulling some of his hair with her small talons.

"All right," he grumbled. "I'll go with you."

He followed the bird out into the dark hall. It was suppertime, and all the help was busy eating before Velvet Haven opened. The hall was abandoned.

Instead of taking him upstairs where he and Keir lived in the old part of the mansion, Cliodna guided him down the stairs and to the right, which led to the basement.

Suddenly he knew where they were going.

Cliodna's warbling instantly stopped as she hovered by the corner. Her wings flapped excitedly, and he tore his gaze from her and stared at the spot. There was nothing there.

He was about to leave, when something caught the corner of his eye . . . Smoke? No, not smoke, but something resembling vapor, like fog. It hovered, thinning and spreading out as it pressed up tight against the ceiling where it stilled for a few seconds before gathering into a tight mass and funneling down to the floor just like a tornado.

Once the vapor and fog dissipated, Rhys saw Keir transform from shadow to man.

Now, this was interesting. Keir had no reason to transform into a wraith here. Everyone who worked in the club knew what he was—an immortal. He moved freely between Annwyn and the mortal realm; no one questioned it. So why was he hiding the fact that he was going into Annwyn?

And why the hell was he wearing his ceremonial robe?

Pressing deeper into the shadows, Rhys watched as Keir pulled the hood of the purple robe over his head. Keir almost never wore the robe, or the quartz amulet that he was wearing like a necklace.

Rhys knew that each branch of magic had a robe of power

and an amulet. The robes were different colors, signifying their particular magical powers. Keir's quartz amulet and purple robe represented his powers of divination. Both the robe and the amulet were worn during ceremonies, whether magical or spiritual; yet Rhys had never known Keir to don either of them in order to perform divinations. In truth, Keir generally practiced magic naked.

A strange combination of fear and overwhelming curiosity consumed him. Keir was standing at the portal to Annwyn in a ceremonial robe, his head covered, palms raised, and a soft incantation filling the small, dark space between them. What the fuck was going on?

A white light suddenly appeared around the door, and silently it opened, just enough so that Keir could slip through. As the wraith's satin robe slipped beyond the threshold, Cliodna's wings clipped frantically against Rhys' shoulders.

Rhys' instincts were to ignore the mental shove the wren was giving him and to return to his study. But his damned mortal curiosity got the better of him, and he lunged for the door as it began to close. He made it—barely—before the heavy oak door slammed behind him.

He expected it to be black. But the Cave of Cruachan was lit on both its stone sides by black iron sconces that looked like something out of a medieval movie. Symbolic drawings covered the walls. Some looked Pictish, and some Celt. There were animals and trees and other things that looked far more sinister— pentagrams, snakes, the number of the beast, and an inverted cross. He was definitely out of his element here—a stranger in a forbidden, forbidding world.

Rhys took a step, and then another. He heard nothing— not even Keir's footsteps against the stone floor.

A few more steps, and he was at a crossroads. He could go straight, or he could take one of two tunnels—one to the left and one to the right. Both tunnels appeared dark and definitely foreboding.

Knowing Annwyn should be straight ahead, Rhys continued on, cursing that damned wren for first stirring up his curiosity and then promptly abandoning him.

Making his way farther down the winding corridor, Rhys saw a flicker of movement. Keir? But then it seemed to glow gold, and he held his breath, knowing he was at last seeing the fabled golden veil of Annwyn.

Energized, he took another step and skidded to a stop when the hissing sound washed over him. From out of the shadows a snake slithered out into the light, stopping to coil itself only a few feet from him.

It was a small viper, probably an adder. It was poisonous but did not usually release all of its venom in its first bite. But, if it wanted, the adder could kill him if it decided to unload all its venom.

Rhys reached for the lit torch beside him, thinking he'd burn the fucker, but the snake lunged and opened its mouth, preparing to strike.

Jumping back, Rhys searched for something to impale the viper, but there was nothing, and the snake slithered closer to him. It climbed over the toe of his boot, and he resisted the urge to kick it away. It would only come back, and after having been provoked, it likely would bite him.

Still as a statue, Rhys stood, hoping the fucking thing would find nothing interesting in his boots and slither back to the shadows. Instead, the snake began to move, curl around his ankle, and glide up his calf. Oh, Christ, it was twining around his leg and moving up toward his thigh. And then he felt it, the cool reptilian head pressing against his fingertips.

Calm, he told himself. Adders didn't bite unless provoked. And if it did bite, the venom wouldn't kill him. Sure, it would hurt like a bitch, and he'd have some swelling and pain, and maybe even dizziness and vomiting, but he'd live. That was provided the adder gave him only a warning bite. If it wanted to kill, then nothing could stop it.

The adder's head was now pressed into the palm of his hand; then Rhys felt the swaying movement of the pointed tail seconds before it wrapped around the bronze wrist cuff. The next thing he knew, the snake was wrapped around his wrist, and its upper body was curling its way around his bicep.

The reptile's beady black eyes looked into his, and Rhys stared back, wondering what the hell was going to happen.

And then he heard it, from some distant memory in the back of his mind.

"What does the Nathair, the adder, mean, laddie?"

"It is a sign of wisdom, Grandfather Daegan."

"And what does it warn of?"

"That you must be prepared to shed something in favor of something greater and better."

Was this adder ally or foe?

"Very good, Lucifer, you've secured the sacrifice."

The gravelly voice came from behind, and Rhys whirled around, only to find himself bashed in the head. Taken off guard and off balance, he was spun around and was falling face-first onto the stone floor. With a crack, the side of his head hit the unforgiving stone, and a blanket of darkness began to descend.

Fleeing the temple, Bronwnn used the cover of darkness to run from the outer courtyard and into the sacred woods. A cloud obscured the moon, and the leaves of the tall oaks offered excellent cover.

Silently and carefully, she crept farther and farther away from the temple, making certain her footfalls could not be heard. Cailleach had spies everywhere, and Bronwnn had no desire to be caught outside the grounds—especially at night.

The temple had always been a prison to her. But among the trees of the Sidhe forest, Bronwnn found freedom in her nightly rambles.

When she felt she was far enough away, she slowed her steps. Deeper and deeper she made her way through the woods. Cailleach's *oidhche* did not fly into these particular woods, for it feared the wyvern who dwelt in the nearby cave.

Taking a minute to catch her breath, Bronwnn lowered herself onto a smooth rock and inhaled the scents of the forest; pine and yew, the dampness of the grass, and the humidity that clung to the leaves. It was a familiar, comforting scent, and she leaned back on her hands and closed her eyes, allowing herself a few stolen moments of solitude.

This was her favorite spot, for here, on this very rock, her dream lover always came to her. Tonight was no different.

As soon as she closed her eyes, his image sprang to life— tall, with wide shoulders and a narrow waist. His chest was smooth and thickly sculpted. His arms were bulky with muscles, and on his left arm was a band of tattoos. He looked broad, primal—a warrior; an alpha.

There was a thin, black trail of hair that led from his belly, only to disappear beneath the waist of his pants. Her fingers itched to run through the silky-looking hair. Her nose twitched with the desire to scent him, to taste his skin with her tongue.

It was the animal in her that wanted it. The animal that made her newly maturing body heat and stretch with unbearable longing. Lying back against the cool rock, she stretched out until her arms were above her head, and the humidity that dampened the leaves of the tree moistened her gown. The wetness beaded her nipples, arousing her. She wondered what it would be like to feel the heat of his mouth around her nipple. What would it be like to feel him sucking, nipping, pulling her in deep?

On a sigh, she let herself drift away, opening her senses, and willing her dream lover to come to her. In spite of the dangers of falling asleep, Bronwnn could not resist the lure of being visited by him once again. She needed it; needed to feel him. She wanted to be desired; to be possessed—and soon she would be. Cailleach wanted her to mate with the wraith, who was surely her dream lover.

He came to her almost immediately. She felt him behind her, his hot, hard body pressing against her back. His arms felt like iron bands around her ribs, and his breath was sultry and erotic as it whispered against the shell of her ear.

Wordlessly, his large hands rose from her ribs to cup her breasts. She panted, pressing her bottom restlessly against him. She felt him, hard and searching against her thin gown.

Her breath squeezed in her chest as she felt the tip of his

tongue tickle her ear. His fingers had sought out her nipples and were now rolling and gently pinching them. His breathing was faster, and he pressed his hardness against her bottom.

Unable to resist, Bronwnn cupped her breasts and kneaded them, pretending what she saw in her mind was really happening. Between her thighs she was slick, ready.

None of the other goddesses who were reaching their maturity seemed to be this sexually needy. She had heard none of them speaking of dreams or lovers. She doubted that any of her pious sisters touched themselves as she did. But the feeling of it, this primitive, overwhelming need, was unable to be denied.

Slipping her free hand beneath her gown, Bronwnn ran her fingertips up her leg. She was going to touch herself and pretend it was his long, strong fingers as she did so. The image of him came to her swiftly; so, too, did the scent of something new, something dark and earthy she had never smelled before. The scent aroused her, and her lover came to her in a way that showed his hunger. He was frenzied, aggressive, and when his hand ran through her unbound hair, he fisted the long strands and pinned her to the ground, his mouth capturing hers in a hard, drugging kiss. She moaned and clutched at his shoulders. He gripped her hair tighter, as if holding her still so she couldn't push him away, but what he didn't seem to sense was that she wanted him closer, his kiss deeper.

His tongue forced its way between her lips as he caught her breast in his palm and squeezed. He was breathing hard against her, his body taut with tension as his mouth descended lower, along her jaw, her collarbone, only to capture her nipple between his teeth. With his mouth and tongue, he played with her while his hand toyed with her other breast, pulling and tugging at her nipple as she writhed beneath him. Against her hip, he rubbed the length of himself against her. She felt the heat, the hardness—the sticky wetness that coated her skin.

His aggressiveness made her bolder, and she clutched at him, arching, giving him her breasts, and begging him silently for more. Her own panting breaths echoed through the forest, and the scent of aroused male filled her nostrils, awakening the animal inside her.

Her own fingers parted her sex, spreading the wetness, circling the nubbin of nerves that ached. She needed more—him inside her, filling her. She couldn't wait, so she pleasured herself. With a low growl, he suckled her hard and moved his hand down her body until his fingers curled with hers. He growled again as he showed her what he wanted, her fingers plunging inside her. He controlled her rhythm, how fast and hard he wanted her to touch herself—which was fast, forceful, and deep.

He had never been this way with her, this hard and demanding. But she did not fear it—or him. She only wanted more. And when he shoved her hand aside and slid his thick fingers into her, she cried out and accepted him, and the way he filled her.

When he used the pad of his thumb to circle her clitoris, she spread her legs wider, allowing him in closer. Feeling his breath on her skin and smelling the sheen of sweat on his only built up her desire, until she was digging her nails hard into his shoulders.

His beautiful eyes fixed on her, holding her steady with his ravenous gaze; then he pulled his fingers from her, brought them to his mouth, and tasted them. She felt as though she could hear his thoughts. He wanted to watch her take him into her mouth. He wanted her to know his taste, to watch her suck and lap at him.

Bronwnn was on fire. She ran her hands down her body, cupping her breasts, then lower, to her thighs, watching him track the progress of her fingers. She spread her legs wider, hoping he would put his powerful shoulders farther between them, set his mouth to her core, and taste her with his tongue and lips.

In her sexual frenzy, her fingertips grazed too close to the mark on her leg she always tried to avoid. With a gasp of alarm, she snatched her fingers away, but instantly her lover melted away and the other, hated images were upon her.

They were dark and disturbing images of a woman who had symbols carved onto her body. Her nipples were red and swollen, and she was moaning. And then she saw him—the flash of black, the hood covering his features—and she pressed her eyes shut in a futile attempt to stop the vision. But she knew better. She couldn't stop it.

Inside her, she felt the evil, the scent of death and decay. She felt him, the Dark Mage, as surely as if they were the same person. She heard his thoughts, the cruel, biting taunts. And then she saw her dream lover—on top of a stone altar. He was tethered, naked. And there was a blade placed directly over his heart.

She tried to wake up, but it was futile. The vision never left voluntarily. It wasn't hers to command. Covering her eyes with her hands, she rocked back and forth, but it kept coming in waves. Images of blood and ancient Celtic symbols, chanted incantations, and the acrid odor of incense washed over her. And then, the black hood fell back, revealing the mage's face.

With a jolt, Bronwnn woke to her surroundings. She was

breathing fast, the remnants of the vision making her tremble. Unsteady, she rose to her feet, and her eyes searched through the forest. It was quiet and still. Reeling from the vision, and from the sexual need that made her body tremble, she jumped down from the rock, landing far below on a winding path that led to her sanctuary.

The mage had sensed her, too. She was certain of it. There was a connection between them, some cursed bind that allowed her to track his movements, and she was not naive enough to believe that it was one-sided.

She must run and hide. Later, she would try to determine whether her vision had been of the past or of the future. Right now, she must take care of herself.

The change was smooth and painless. She simply had to think of it, and it happened. Now she was safe. The mage would not find her like this, not in this form, for she was no longer a pale-haired goddess, but a white wolf.

Groaning, Rhys felt himself being picked up and hauled up over a shoulder like a bag of flour. His head was swimming, and he felt as though he might vomit. And he hoped he did, right down the back of the bastard's robe.

He couldn't think through the pain and the dizziness and the beckoning darkness. But Rhys knew he had to or else he'd be awakening to the singing of a chorus of angels, his body carved up like a Thanksgiving turkey.

Through the double vision, Rhys saw that they had left the lit corridor and turned left. There was only one sconce to light the path. Shadows played on the walls, and Rhys strived to stay lucid and conscious. In order to escape, he'd need to know which way to go.

His captor's boots scraped against stone. Rhys bounced against his shoulder. They were descending an ancient staircase. Above him, Rhys saw catacombs. It was a crypt of sorts.

Suddenly he heard a noise—a moan. It sounded like a woman—a sexually aroused woman.

"Look what I've brought you, lovely."

Raising his head, Rhys saw a woman tied down to a stone slab. She was naked and marked. Her skin was bleeding, and there were bruises on her body. She trembled, her nerves flickering. "Yes," she whispered as her gaze looked him over. Arching her back, she lifted her hips, showing him what could be his. "I want him inside me," she murmured. "Please," she begged. "The ache. It's growing."

From the darkness beyond where the woman lay, another sound, this one of chains, echoed in the silence. "Not again," came a deep, distraught voice. "I beg you . . . Not another. I cannot bear it."

"But you will," his captor commanded. "Over and over, you will bear witness to my rise. You will watch my power supersede all powers."

What the fuck was this? Where was he? Still under Velvet Haven? Rhys had never fathomed that below the mansion were catacombs. One thing was for sure—he had to find a way out of here before he became this psycho's next sacrifice.

None too gently he was pulled down, his body slammed onto a hard, cold slab. Something shackled his wrists and ankles, and he fought to free himself. Raising his head, he saw the black leather straps that held him down.

"You son of a bitch," he roared as he struggled to pull free of the bonds. But the mage just laughed, a demonic sound that echoed around them.

Next, his clothes were stripped from him. Rhys felt the cold blade glide against his skin as his shirt and jeans were cut away.

"Very nice," the mage murmured as his palm traced over Rhys' chest. "You will make me a lovely skin suit."

"Fuck you," Rhys spat, still struggling. If this murderer took Rhys' body, he would definitely have the upper hand. Keir, Suriel, and perhaps even Bran would fall victim to this psychopath. He would be able to move among them with ease, pretending he was Rhys. He couldn't let that happen.

"What's this?" The mage lifted the end of the torc. "Ah, Celtic. A warrior people. Fearless in battle, and as fiercely spiritual as they are bloodthirsty."

Rhys tried to look into the hood to see the face of the mage. But the hood was deep, and the shadows in the room made it impossible to see.

The mage bent low over him. "Are you spiritual, Rhys MacDonald?"

Rhys tried to bite whatever his teeth could grab hold of, but the mage pinned his head back against the stone with one strong hand on his forehead.

"I know the look in your eyes. It is not fear, but rage. You boil with it."

Rhys opened his mouth to tell the bastard what he truly thought, but he found something shoved in instead. It tasted vile, and he spat it out. The mage laughed again.

"You amuse me. Your strength revitalizes me. You will be

a powerful offering. And because you are so worthy, and you have not once begged for me to spare your life, I will keep your soul—and your flesh."

The hard pit was shoved once more into his mouth, and this time, the mage's hand clamped down on Rhys' jaw, forcing him to keep it inside.

"Thorn-apple." The word was whispered to him. "And incense. No ceremony is complete without them. You'll like it. It's a potent hallucinogen and aphrodisiac."

The room suddenly began to stink of a cloying aroma, and Rhys gagged, both from the stench surrounding him and the taste in his mouth. But in mere seconds he was hallucinating, seeing images through a kaleidoscope of colors and shapes whirling before his eyes. Beyond him, the moans of the woman and the sounds of chains seemed to grow distant as a vision began to coalesce before him.

He felt his body grow warm, then hot, as the picture took shape. He saw himself taking a woman, one hand clutched in her hair, the other cupping and squeezing her breast. She was full and soft, and he wanted to suck her, taste her. Taking her mouth, he plunged his tongue between her lips, tasting her. She moaned, and his cock grew thicker, harder. He needed to bury himself inside the pussy he could smell and feel, so hot and wet between her thighs.

Her hands flew to his shoulders, and he tugged her hair harder, clasping her to him. She couldn't push him away. He wouldn't let her. Claiming her, he kissed her harder, taking her, and then he felt her nails digging into his shoulders; he felt how her body did not strive to get away but instead got closer to him, and his hunger grew more rabid.

Breaking off the kiss, his mouth traveled lower, inhaling her scent, feeling her soft, supple flesh against his lips and tongue. He moved lower, searching for the pink nipples he wanted in his mouth.

His vision swam, a profound sense of sexual need and hunger swamped him, and he bit down, capturing the erect nipple between his teeth, then rolling his tongue around the swelling tip. She cried out in pleasure, her body arching against him. The feel of her, all soft curves against him, made him shove against her, rubbing his cock against her hip.

Consumed now, he tasted her, sucking, nipping, while his other hand played with her breast. He was aware of her hand, lowering between their bodies, then the scent of her sex parting. With a growl, he told her he liked it, that he wanted her to play with herself. But he wanted to be part of it, too.

Wrapping his fingers around her wrist, he used pressure to show her what he wanted, her fingers in her cunt pushing in and out as she thought of his cock pushing deep inside her. She moaned, and he wondered if she would make that beautiful sound when he slid into her.

He imagined it, shoving his cock into her, pounding against her as he held her by her hair and watched her come beneath him.

Unable to wait any longer, he shoved her hand away and sank two fingers into her core. She was hot, wet, and so damned tight that he felt his cock begin to leak.

He couldn't come yet. It was too soon. He wanted more. He needed to feel her for longer; to listen to her sounds that aroused him so much. Whatever poison the mage had given him made him feel as though he could fuck all night and never tire, never stop taking her.

Moving against her, he shouldered his way between her thighs. He was panting, sweating. He could smell the scent of her sex; he wanted to run the tip of his tongue along her seam and circle her clitoris. He wanted to suck on her, to spread her wide, to eat every inch of her. And when she smoothed her hands over her voluptuous body and captured her breasts, shoving them together, he imagined going down on her, watching as she played with her tits as he ate her. Pulling his fingers free, he licked them, tasting her at last as she watched him. She was not afraid of him, or of his desire. He saw that in her eyes. In his mind, he saw her taking his cock and tasting him, too.

The vision was so damned erotic, especially when he knew who the woman was. Experiencing this altered state of sexual excitement was exhilarating. Experiencing it while seeing *her* was beyond anything he had ever dreamt.

What little remained of his conscious thought recoiled at the thought of what was happening to him. How could he be aroused when he was strapped to a stone altar, ready to be carved to bits? But his mind's will to fight wasn't strong enough to counter the effects of the thorn-apple on his body—or the image of the woman lying on her back, her sex pink and glistening, and her nipples little points—waiting to be taken between his teeth once more.

"Good," the mage murmured as he noticed his straining erection. "Now then, let us begin. My lovely little sacrifice is eager to have you."

The scrape of metal against stone made him tense. Rhys saw the blade, glistening in the dim glow of the sconce. It was curved, and the hilt was encrusted with jewels. It was an athame; a sacred knife used in Annwyn; a ritual knife never intended to shed blood.

He felt the cool slide of the blade teasing along his skin. The woman was gone, but he tried to bring her back. He tried to think of where his vision was going to take him next. Images of supple fingers gliding over his skin took root, and he began to imagine his dream lover touching him. He could actually feel her fondling his cock, picking it up, and bringing her mouth down over the swollen head. He pictured himself clutching her hair and holding her there while she sucked him. The image was so arousing and vivid that he barely felt the first scrape of the blade against his skin. Only when the hot flush of blood seeped onto his chest and trickled down his side did he know he'd been cut. But the potent aphrodisiac he'd been given only heightened his arousal. The pain, coupled with the images, made him rock hard.

This was obviously what the mage wanted. He was practicing the Dark Arts—death and sex magick.

Next, he took the tip of the knife and drew a circle around his heart. Incense swirled around him, just like the strange words coming from the mage. The knife came down, cutting in lines, and Rhys knew he had an inverted pentagram carved on his skin.

His body burned; his throat was parched from the thorn-apple and the incense. As the mage leaned over him, working down his chest with the tip of the athame, Rhys struggled not to succumb but to find some reserve and fight. But the knife was cutting into him. His skin burned where the athame drew a straight line down his abs. The sexual need ebbed, leaving his thoughts blank and his vision dark. Even the mage's words became a distant echo in his thoughts. Blackness descended. The burning pain of his flesh receded. He was succumbing to the darkness.

Rhys allowed his head to fall to the side, and he saw his blood dripping along the blade onto a white square of satin. The crimson drop spread out, the satin absorbing his blood. The Death card had been placed in his left hand. Struggling through the fog, he tried to think of the card's meaning. For this was a sacrificial ceremony—everything in it meant something. But he couldn't think; he could barely even feel. The fantasies had left him. Sensation had abandoned him.

"Too much." The blade dropped against the stone. The mage leaned over him and pulled his eyelids apart. "We will wait until some of the effects have dissipated. I want you alive and moaning, and using your considerable imagination to make the spell powerful."

He pulled away, and Rhys heard the sound of the silk robe the mage wore being shed. "I think I will enjoy my little toy once more. You may watch if you'd like."

He didn't want to see; he didn't want to hear. But suddenly, the mage's voice was whispering darkly into his ear. "She's a delightful little morsel, isn't she? Begging for it. Wouldn't you like to get inside her and spend all those erotic thoughts into her willing body?"

Rhys tried to talk, but he couldn't. Then the mage was gone. Rhys saw him, naked, stroll into the dimly lit alcove that housed the altar where the woman was strapped, spread-eagle. She began to moan as he touched her.

Rhys could see only the mage's back and hand; he knew he

was fondling the woman between her legs. "Look how swollen and red you are. Beautiful."

"Please," she implored as she licked her lips. "Again."

The mage's laugh echoed throughout the cavern. "Yes. Again, and again, until the ritual is complete and my powers are stronger."

The woman purred as the mage slipped his fingers between her thighs. Rhys closed his eyes. The noises of their fucking made him think of his vision and of what he had wanted only moments ago—his hand in his lover's hair holding her as he took her hard. But it would never be. Soon the mage would kill him.

Suddenly he felt something slick and cool gliding up his body.

Fighting the heaviness in his head, he opened his eyes and saw the adder. It was coiled around his arm, its beady eyes staring into his.

God, he wished the fucking thing would bite him. Right in his neck, unloading all its venom into his carotid. But it didn't. Instead, it coiled and uncoiled itself around his left wrist, then glided over his body till he felt it do the same to his right.

The moans and cries of the woman and the macabre sounds of pleasure from the mage continued. The magician was lost to his perversions, while the adder began to free Rhys of his bonds.

Be prepared to shed something in favor of something greater and better.

What had he shed? Or had he yet? He didn't know what it meant, only that this snake was helping him.

He was free at last. As he looked into the adder's black

eyes, he felt a small bit of strength, which enabled him to roll over and fall onto the floor.

The mage was riding the woman, crying out a demonic-sounding incantation as she moaned and begged him for more. He wasn't watching Rhys but was completely engrossed in what he was doing to the woman.

Crawling away from the alcove, Rhys followed the winding body of the snake. Its white zigzag stripe made him dizzy, but he focused on it, because it was the only thing he could see clearly in the muted light.

At the stairs, Rhys began to climb. He was bleeding and winded; he needed to stop, but he didn't dare. The mage would be finished soon. The sounds of the woman were growing more frantic, her orgasm coming quickly.

With one small burst of energy and sheer bullheadedness, Rhys got up and ran as fast as he could into the lit passageway. He wasn't steady and he was horribly disoriented, but he followed the slithering adder.

He was bouncing off the stone walls, stumbling and uncoordinated. But he kept up the pace and actually tried to run faster, when he heard a male cry of satisfaction, followed by a shrill scream from the woman. *Shit.* He was killing her, and then he'd be looking for Rhys and would discover him gone.

They rounded a corner, and the hall weaved up and down, making Rhys want to puke. He couldn't go any farther. He stopped and leaned against the wall, his heart racing and his burning body finding some small measure of relief against the cool stone.

A roar of fury reached his ears, and Rhys got his ass moving. Stumbling forward, he tried to stay focused on the snake.

The pounding of feet behind him spurred him on, and just when he thought he couldn't do it, he saw the shimmering gold veil. Lunging forward, he went through the gossamer curtain just as he felt the mage's presence behind him.

All but catapulted through the veil, he came to land on the ground. The mage's roar of outrage reverberated around him, and Rhys stood unsteadily. It was dark, and he was in some kind of forest on a dirt path. He had no idea where he was, other than in Annwyn.

The reflecting pool should be to his left. But there wasn't a path. Naked and barefoot, Rhys began to push through the dense forest. Daegan had forced him to memorize how to get to the sacred waters, and Rhys was moving in the direction of his instinct.

The damned reflecting pool had better be close, he thought, because if he had to go much farther, he'd pass out, and Cailleach would have free rein to fry his ass.

Faltering over an exposed tree root, Rhys cursed and fell to his knees. With his hands in the dirt, he anchored himself, trying to get a grip on the dizziness that slammed into him.

Something cool brushed his knuckles, and he gazed down into the beady eyes of the adder.

This was the third time he'd sighted the snake. There was no denying now that this was an animal guide. But why an adder?

A twig snapped, and he jumped up, crouching to avoid the low-hanging branches. The adder snaked in and out of the long grass, rising and falling over grassy mounds and tree roots until the trees parted and Rhys was welcomed by the glow of the biggest full moon he had ever seen. It was made all the more brilliant by the rippling water beneath it.

The reflecting pool.

On its bank, Rhys fell to his knees, collapsing in exhaustion and pain. His head was still cloudy and heavy. Between his cheek and gum, he felt the round pod that had been shoved into his mouth. He was about to spit it out, when he heard a sound behind him. Glancing over his shoulder, he saw the most beautiful wolf peering out from between the trees. The animal was pure white, majestic, and elegant. It didn't move, but its pale blue eyes watched him warily.

His vision began to swirl, and he reached out—whether to try to fend off the impending attack or to call to the animal, Rhys could not have said. But when he pitched forward toward the ground, he saw the animal stiffen. It sniffed the air, and Rhys knew it smelled his blood.

His last thought was that he needn't have worried about Cailleach; the wolves were obviously going to get him first.

CHAPTER SEVEN

Bronwnn had seen this man before. Despite her wolf form, she saw with the eyes of a woman. This was the man from her dreams. Everything about him felt familiar, from the outline of his prone body to the breadth of his naked shoulders. Even his scent, which was much more potent to her in her shifter form, caused a familiar heating in her body.

Inhaling, she brought his essence deep into her nose and felt the primal instinct of an animal finding her mate.

Quietly, she came out from beneath the leafy canopy of trees. The glowing moon shone on the rippling water, but she had no need of moonlight; she was a wolf now, and wolves saw through the darkest woods, and into the darkest hearts.

Circling him, she studied the hurried, rasping movement of his chest. He was breathing too fast. Beneath him, pools of darkness began to seep out, covering the leaves in a glistening crimson. He was bleeding.

In this form, she could do nothing but lie down beside him and keep him warm. But that would not save him. She had to help him, but to change out in the open, where anyone might see, was too dangerous. She was the only goddess shifter. No one knew of her gift, and she had no intention of sharing it, either.

No, she could not expose herself in that way. Yet everything inside her screamed for her to act; to do something. He was her mate. The animal and the woman agreed on this.

With her muzzle, she rubbed the back of his neck, feeling the black strands of his soft hair tickling her nose. He smelled good. Right. She tasted him then. With a swipe of her tongue, she licked his skin. He smelled like a wraith, but there was something else there; another essence, something harsher, like ceremonial incense, as well as a pungent and earthy odor—the same odor that had accompanied him in her vision.

The man groaned, tried to lift himself up on his elbows, and immediately fell back to the ground. Coughing, he spat something out from between his lips; whatever it was landed atop Bronwnn's front paw.

Thorn-apple.

"Fuck," he growled, trying once more to move. He succeeded in rolling to his back. His face, she noticed, was breathtakingly handsome, despite his expression of pain. His hair was dark and his lashes just as black. His jaw was firm, covered in black stubble. The man before her was naked, and Bronwnn looked her fill, admiring his beautiful, powerful body. From his thick arms, to the black hair on his belly, down to the soft skin of his phallus, he was hard and sculpted, just as a warrior should be.

Bronwnn was mesmerized by his body, by the sheer power and strength it contained. She wanted to touch it, to run her fingers along the firm flesh and hard muscle. She wanted that hard body covering hers. The need inside her grew, until she heard him moan. Worried, she stepped closer, and, glancing up from the part of his anatomy that had captivated her most, she saw how his chest had been mutilated, and how it now bled, the red trails of blood running over his chest and onto his side.

This man—her *mate*—had been a victim of the Dark Mage. Occult symbols were etched into his skin, the same symbols that had been present in her vision. It was true, then, what she had seen! It had just happened. Which meant the dark magician was close, and they were both in danger.

Heedless of anyone seeing her, Bronwnn changed into her human form and quickly bent to her knees, intending to help the stranger up. They must flee this place before either the Dark Mage or Cailleach's *oidhche* found them.

He fought her and she held him closer, trying to keep him from making any noise or hurting himself further. Their skin touched, her breast pressing against his side, and he softened, went lax, and let her bring him up to his knees. Swaying, he steadied himself by putting his thick arms around her waist and pressing the side of his face into her belly. She gasped at the contact. To feel his burning skin against hers so intimately was a shock—but a most welcome one.

Beneath her fingers, the muscles of his shoulders and back bunched up; she rubbed them, trying to stem their trembling. His hot breath caressed her, making her core ache and her nipples bead hard.

She was the one to tremble now. Closing her eyes, Bronwnn tried to pull herself together. She was the only thing between him and the Dark Mage. It was up to her to save this man. Her own desires had no place now. Her own needs were centered on the stranger in her arms, and on her will to keep him alive.

Her vow would not allow her to speak to soothe him. So, instead, she ran her fingers through his silken hair and quieted him with her touch. The tremors that raked his shoulders subsided, and his breathing quickly followed into a steady rhythm. She could feel the way his body intuitively absorbed her energy, taking it deep inside him, restoring his own flagging strength.

This was the way it was with mates. Her spirit recognized this man as her *Anam*—her soul. She was not whole without him, and he would soon realize he was incomplete without her.

Despite her desire to stay locked in an embrace with this man, Bronwnn knew she must hurry and find shelter. She had no idea if the Dark Mage had followed the man into Annwyn, but if he had, it would be only a few minutes before he came upon them. While the reflecting pool was beyond Cailleach's immediate powers, it was too close to the veil that led to the mortal realm. The mage would come here first to look for his victim.

Wrapping her hands around his shoulders, Bronwnn struggled to bring him up to his feet. After a few attempts, he was able to stand and wrap an arm around her waist. Still disoriented and stumbling from the effects of the thorn-apple, he allowed her to guide him along a path that had become overgrown with long grass and wildflowers.

Like a sleepwalker, he followed her. So trusting, she thought, as she looked up at him. His eyes were closed, and his head lolled from side to side. She must get him to her cottage, and there she must rid his body of the poison ruling his mind.

The moon fortuitously slipped behind a cloud, shrouding the path in darkness, and Bronwnn's wolf eyes and instinctive tracking abilities aided them in the dark. Silently, they walked on until she moved off the path and into a densely wooded area. In seconds they were standing before the dilapidated cottage she used for herself.

One night as she explored outside the temple, she had come across the abandoned croft. Besides offering shelter, it afforded her the luxury of privacy, and a place she could truly call her own, where she practiced divination, and the ancient healing arts of her goddess mother. Here she kept her mother's books and studied whenever she could. Her mother had also been the only goddess versed in the Dark Arts. Knowledge of the occult led to greater understanding of all alchemy, so her mother had sought knowledge in the darkness and practiced it for the greater good of all in Annwyn. It was this dark knowledge that Bronwnn knew she would need to call upon tonight, to save this man from the mage's ritual spell.

Here, in her cottage, with all her herbs and spells, she could heal this man—her mate—freeing him from the grip of the mage who sought to rule the mortal world and the Otherworld.

Supporting his weight against her, Bronwnn reached for the rusted latch. He was heavy, and she was tired from bearing the majority of his weight. The hinges groaned as she opened the door, and the man pitched forward, taking Bronwnn with him. He landed on his knees, Bronwnn on her back, the wind knocked out of her.

It was dark in the cottage and quiet. The only sound was the harsh, rasping breath of the man as he leaned over her. With a shaking hand, he touched her face, her cheek, her eyes, then down her nose to her mouth, where the pad of his thumb rubbed back and forth.

His eyes were dark, an indistinguishable shade in the dim light of the cottage interior. But they watched her, focusing on her face even through the glaze that made them shine. She was keenly aware of him, not only of his size above her, but of the way his body seemed to call to hers. She was a wanton to be thinking of her own needs at a time like this. But these desires were too new for her to control.

He cupped her cheek in his hand and leaned down so that his lips were against her ear. "Thank you, *mo slanaitheoir*," he whispered before collapsing against her. *My savior.*

Rhys felt his body being dragged across a wooden floor. He was too tall and heavy for her, he knew, but he was too damned weak to help her. He could barely keep away the call of unconsciousness, let alone drag his carcass to wherever the woman was taking him.

He tried to talk, but his mouth was too dry, and his throat felt as though it might seize up. He could only just crack open his eyes, which was a real bitch, because the brief glimpse he had of the woman as he kneeled over her was stunning. Her hair seemed to glow, and her eyes were a pale blue, a color that reminded him of the icy waters of the Arctic Ocean.

She was an efficient little thing, because he quickly found his body being placed on top of a pile of blankets—no, furs, he realized as he sank into the soft luxuriousness. The woman didn't speak a word, but Rhys heard her walking about the room; then he heard a scratching sound, immediately followed by the acrid scent of smoke. Beside him a roar went up, and the crackle of a log snapped. The flames of a hearth washed over his body, absorbing some of the chills that raked him.

In a way, he was damned glad for the drug he'd been given. It was playing with his mind and giving him a reprieve from the pain in his body. His chest hurt like hell, and he was losing too much blood.

Blackness beckoned, and he fought it, trying anything to stay awake. He thought of Keir, and he tried to reach him, to find a connection, but he was too weak, and his mind too drugged out to do anything effectively.

Lifting his arm, he searched with his hand for the woman. Immediately she was there, grasping his arm. The darkness eased away, and slowly he lifted his head and tried to open his eyes. She was kneeling before him, her body glowing a pale alabaster in the firelight. She looked like a damned angel, but angels, he knew, didn't live in Annwyn.

"Aingeal?"

She shook her head, confirming his suspicions. She was not an angel.

"Mo bandia?"

He frowned. That wasn't what he meant. *Mo* was Gaelic for my. But Rhys saw her nod, even through the blurriness of his vision.

"My goddess."

She was a goddess, he realized. His, if her nod meant what he thought it did. And she was naked. Oh, shit, she was naked and stunning, and everything he could have dreamed of.

Mo bandia . . . The phrase ran through his mind. She had

answered his question with a nod. He had dreamed of a woman. He had felt a deep connection to the one in his dream ...

As he bolted upright, his head swam, but he reached for her anyway, anchoring her with his hand through her hair as he watched the silvery white strands slide through his fingers. Oh shit, his dreams. This woman ...

Had she dreamed of him, too? Did they have a bond that linked them across their opposing worlds and his mortality? Had he been shown his fate when he began to dream of this woman?

Stunned, he allowed her to ease him back down onto the pallet of furs. She was leaning over him, her silky waist-length hair sliding over her shoulders to conceal her breasts. There was no denying who this woman was—*what* she was. His dream lover ... and a goddess of the Sacred Order of Annwyn.

Memories of those dreams came rushing back, and he couldn't stop the way his body responded to her. In his dreams, his body had been hard and aching, but in reality, it was infinitely more acute. He was aware of more than just her physical presence hovering over him. He felt her in his blood, in his soul.

Most mortals would scoff, but Rhys knew differently. He had been raised in both mortal and Otherworld traditions, and he knew in his heart, and believed in his soul, that destinies were preordained, and when the time was right, those destinies revealed themselves.

Like now, this very moment with his *bandia sianaitheoir*— goddess savior—breathing softly above him. This was his fate; this woman. He had been shown her in his dreams, and now he was here with her. Her path was to save him, but what was he to do for her? He was a mortal. She was immortal; a powerful goddess. He could have nothing she wanted or needed; yet he knew that despite his failings, he would not give her up.

The fluttering of her fingertips against his unshaven jaw jolted him. Her touch went deep into his flesh, where he felt it stir inside him. Already, he felt a measure stronger. Fingertips skated from his jaw to his lips, where she touched him tentatively, then down to his throat where the tips of her fingers lingered on his Adam's apple. He swallowed hard, and he heard her indrawn breath.

Rhys knew he shouldn't be turned on. Hell, he'd almost been a sacrificial lamb. But he needed to touch her; to feel her skin, just once. What if he died? He had to touch her before he did.

Reaching out, he placed his hands on her bare shoulders and brushed back her long hair. Her eyes fluttered closed at that innocent touch, and his cock surged at the sight. It would be so easy to span her hips and move her to him so that she straddled him. From there, he could push up into her and watch her as he finally claimed her—just as he had in his dream.

Rhys felt nothing now but desire—not pain; not the blood that had begun to dry on his chest. His vision was crystal clear, and he saw her, a beautiful, voluptuous goddess kneeling before him. Her breasts were heavy, swaying before him, begging to be cupped in his hands.

Slowly, he ran his fingertips along her collarbone, then over to the notch at her throat, allowing her to become accustomed to his touch. Her breathing quickened, causing her breasts to rise and fall enticingly. Slowly, he slid his hand down her breastbone, then cupped one of her breasts, filling his palm.

She gasped, her eyelids flying open at the contact. Slowly, he cupped the other one, lifting it so he could see it full in his hand.

She had beautiful big breasts, just what he liked, and he pressed them together, kneading while watching the pleasure cross her face. Then, with his hand on her back, he drew her lower until her breasts hung above him, and he trailed his tongue over her nipple. Given a slow flick, the flesh hardened, and she swayed into him, her little nails biting into his shoulders, giving him a rush of power and primal aggression.

He surged up against her, making her feel him. The tip of his cock rubbed her thigh, and he moaned as he sucked her nipple. Hungrily, he clutched her to him, her breasts rubbing against his face as he pushed them together and used his tongue and mouth to make her writhe. He wanted his cock there, thrusting up between her breasts. He wanted to watch her take him.

He was getting more than a little excited as he thought of it. Tugging her nipple, he soothed the pinch with the brush of his thumb. She shivered, and he could almost feel the wetness between her thighs trickle against him.

Tugging again, he flicked her nipple, and her lips parted on a silent moan. His touch became more intense as he worked both her breasts. Suddenly, her hand slipped from his shoulder, and she brushed his chest, making him hiss. Instantly, she pushed away from him.

"No," he growled, reaching for her. The pain had been fleeting. The discomfort he felt from his injuries wasn't half as bad as the unfilled ache in his cock.

But she evaded him by jumping up and escaping his hand.

Rhys lifted his shoulders, turning onto his side to reach for her, but he pitched forward when the dizziness took hold of him.

Damn it! Now was not the time for his body's strength to evaporate. With a groan, he realized his moment of lucidity and power was gone, leaving him a weakling mortal on the floor.

Darkness beckoned, and he begged God to give him the strength to resist. But his prayers were not heard, and he slipped deeply into unconsciousness.

Weightless and floating, Keir hovered in the air, staring at the wooden door before him. He felt a strange sensation, a rippling of fear and malevolence, slither over his nerves. Evil—he felt it. He had a connection to it. Rhys?

Closing his eyes, he searched for his mortal's thoughts, but he found nothing. Strange. When Keir had left Velvet Haven, Rhys had been in his office. Perhaps he had fallen asleep.

Trailing down to the floor, his form became solid, and he stood before Rowan's door, torn between the desire to see her and the need to ensure Rhys was safe.

When the door to Rowan's chamber opened, and Suriel exited, Keir's decision was made for him.

This was the evil he had sensed. He knew it. He was always aware of the malicious vibe that seemed to shimmer around Suriel. But the connection Keir had felt? His gaze darted to where Rowan was lying on the bed. Was the connection Rowan? Had Suriel touched her? Hurt her?

"Relax, wraith. I didn't lay a hand on her. Nice robe," he smirked as he breezed by. "Come to do a little magick?"

"Fuck you," Keir snarled.

"Sorry, not into that kinky shit. You'll have to find your mortal for that."

Keir slammed Suriel up against the wall. He didn't take any bullshit innuendos about his relationship with Rhys from Bran, and he sure as hell wasn't going to take it from a fallen angel who understood nothing about the ancient bond between a protector wraith and his mortal.

Keir was about to rearrange Suriel's handsome fallen-angel features when Rowan appeared at the door.

"What's going on?"

"Nothing," Keir growled, sending Suriel a silent warning. Releasing him, Keir wondered just what the hell the bastard had been doing in Rowan's room. She was living in Annwyn, under the Sidhe king's protection. Suriel had no authority here, nor was he welcome.

"I was invited," Suriel snapped. "Your own king asked me to be one of his nine warriors."

"He told me." Keir still thought it was a mistake to allow Suriel in Annwyn and in their business. Suriel had his own mysterious powers; he didn't need to be learning anything from the magick they possessed. Everything inside him screamed that Suriel had a connection to the psychopath they were hunting.

"You trusted me to convince your little mortal friend to stay away from the portal."

He hadn't wanted to, that was certain. "Rhys is a mortal. That's your domain. I had to abide by it, and your God's message."

"I want the same thing you do, wraith. The sooner you believe that, the better off we'll be. The time has come to put our considerable differences behind us. We must all work together."

Keir knew it was the truth, but he couldn't bring himself to fully believe in the angel. "Your business is as a warrior. Leave Rowan alone. She has no part in this."

Suriel laughed. "She's part of this. Accept it."

"I will not allow you here with her."

Suriel's eyes blackened. "You will accept me, wraith, because when it comes time, I will make it painless for her. And I know you understand my meaning."

He did understand. Suriel would make the end bearable for Rowan. Fire and ash . . .

"And if you treat me with some measure of respect," Suriel murmured, "I will make it bearable for you, too."

Suriel left then, leaving Keir to face a bewildered Rowan. She didn't approve of violence. He knew that. He also knew she had no idea what bad news Suriel was. She trusted everyone. That was her one failing. She was too damned trusting.

"Can I come in?"

"Sure." She stepped aside, allowing him inside her room. It smelled of her—of lilies and the faintest hint of woman. It never failed to arouse him, or fill his mind with images of them together in bed. But that would never be. Rowan was ill— dying. *And* she had been brutally raped. A guy as big as he was, covered with tattoos, would not make her feel comfortable and relaxed. His was a body designed to overpower, not soothe.

"What's up with the robe?" she asked, closing the door behind him.

"I thought we might take a journey."

Her gorgeous jade-colored eyes lit up. "A mystical journey?"

He nodded, swallowed hard, and gazed at a spot on the wall above her head. What he needed to do wasn't going to be easy. But it had to be done.

"What's wrong?"

He didn't blink. He tried to hide the spike of arousal—and nervousness—that speared him. He didn't know what would happen—for either of them—when she saw what he looked like. The part that feared her reaction made him rethink what he was doing. The other part, the dominant male side, *wanted* her gaze on him. He wanted to show her his body, like a damned male peacock preening before his female.

All of him wanted her to want what would soon be bared to her.

"Keir?"

His gaze lowered, capturing hers. Mentally steeling himself against her fear and repulsion, he pulled the cloak off, allowing the purple satin to fall to the floor. He had always taken care to hide himself from Rowan. She had seen the tattoos on his hand and forearm, but nothing else. But now he was naked to the waist, his chest completely bared to her.

"Oh my God, they're beautiful," she whispered as she came to him. She touched him with the softest of grazes, and his skin flickered, his muscles jumping as she skimmed her fingers along his chest. "The colors are so vibrant."

He was the only Shadow Wraith in existence who had been born with such markings. They were a cross between Sidhe-type sigils and mortal tattoos. His mother had thought the markings a sign of divinity. Others had seen them as an omen.

"The artwork is incredible. You must have had it done here in Annwyn."

He closed his eyes as her hand wrapped around his upper arm, her fingertip tracing the scrollwork around his bicep. "I was born with them. I recognize certain ancient forms of Celtic knotwork and some of the symbols, but I do not fully understand what they represent, or what my having them means. But they do aid in my ability to divine things."

"I think they're fabulous."

He startled, his gaze searching her face. "You're not afraid?"

"Why would I be?"

A feeling of excitement snaked through his body. "I've purposely hid them from you, thinking they would scare you. They're strange, and not at all comforting to look at."

Her gaze lifted from his chest, to look up into his face. The directness of her stare, the way her eyes glistened, made him want to cup her face in his palms and kiss her hard, taking her and making her his. She wasn't afraid of him. His body lit up with the knowledge.

"Why?"

"I did not want to frighten you with the sight of me."

She softened, and he saw the look in her eyes turn from surprise to something far more alluring. "You don't frighten me. Why would you?"

"A man hurt you. I didn't want to bring up bad memories."

"He didn't look like you, Keir."

The way she said his name made him feel weak. He wanted nothing more than to gather her up and fall onto the soft bed with her. He wanted to show her the beauty they could share as he made love to her. He wanted to hold her and love her and shut out the world—and the future.

"He wasn't anything like you. Nothing at all."

"I wanted you to feel you were safe with me. And like this . . . I look . . . savage."

"Beautiful," she whispered at the same time. She touched him then, his jaw, and smiled. "Why are you showing me now?"

"Because my magick is most potent when I have no barriers."

"And your clothes are barriers?"

"Yes. Among other things."

"And what would those be?"

"Hiding myself from you. Worrying about what you might think of me beneath my clothing. There can be no more barriers between us, Rowan. No more hiding."

"All right," she whispered softly. "Shall I get Sayer, then, if we're performing magick?"

"No."

"No?"

He took a step closer to her, and he was thrilled when she didn't back up in fear. "No Sayer this time."

"But I thought we were taking a mystical journey."

"We are. Just the two of us."

"Oh," she murmured breathlessly.

He touched her, for the first time ever. Keir allowed himself to savor the moment, the contact of his body against hers. His fingertips were on her shoulder, and slowly, he grazed the back of his fingers along her smooth arm. She trembled, and his gaze flicked up from his hand to her face, studying her response to his touch.

"Where are we going on this journey?" she asked hoarsely. He watched as she licked her lips nervously. "Are we trying to find Carden?"

"Yes," he murmured, stepping closer to her, so close that he was forced to lower his head and whisper in her ear. But this journey was something much deeper and more binding than their combined efforts to find Carden had ever been.

With this magick, he was starting a bond that would never sever. It was a form of magic he had never, ever sought.

"Will you be with me?" she asked.

"Yes. Just you and I. Do you want that, Rowan? To be with me?"

He met her gaze, waiting for what seemed like forever for her to answer. "Yes."

He smiled and reached for her, bringing their entwined hands to his chest until she clasped the quartz amulet he wore around his neck. "Then come with me."

CHAPTER EIGHT

Assembling the appropriate herbs, Bronwnn placed them in the wooden bowl and kneeled beside the sleeping man. The minute her gaze fell upon his mouth, she recalled the way he had kissed her with those lips. She touched them, marveling at their velvety smoothness. It had been the most incredible experience to feel her breasts touched and licked. Even now, they ached for more. Just staring at him was reawakening the hunger that had ruled her. She wanted him like a woman wanted a man. She ached to feel him moving deeply inside her, but now was not the time to think of such things.

Taking the pestle, she pressed the hawthorn, rosemary, and elder together to form a paste. The pungent aroma of the rosemary filled the room, soothing her frazzled nerves. She needed to focus on her task of healing rather than on the sexual need she felt running hot through her blood.

Adding mud and a few drops of water from the reflecting pool, she stirred up the ointment and carefully pressed the green paste onto his chest, whispering softly the words of a healing spell. The man, she noticed, did not flinch or grimace. He was unconscious, completely unaware of her. She pressed closer to inspect his wounds. She had cleansed them with water, then washed the dried blood from his chest. The bowl she used was now red with his blood. But the bleeding had stopped, and the wound appeared clean and not overly deep. Now all there was left to do was to apply the salve and offer up an invocation that he would heal. She knew nothing of wraiths, having never even seen one before. Her knowledge of healing extended to her own kind, of course, and to the Sidhe and the other species of Annwyn under Cailleach's power. She hoped what she was painting over his chest was not going to kill him.

The remnants of the ceremonial incense and the thorn-apple were washed away as well, leaving another scent that Bronwnn could not identify. It was completely foreign to her, resembling nothing she had ever come across before.

Bending over him, she pressed her nose to his neck and inhaled. The smell was strongest over his pulse; unable to resist, she licked him with the tip of her tongue. He tasted of salt, and virility. Yet that elusive scent continued to confound her. She had never smelled anything like it, but it aroused her, drew her in, and made her long to be covered in his scent.

Drawing away from him, Bronwnn noticed his torc. It was not surprising to see a warrior such as he wearing one. But what was fascinating—and thrilling—was that his torc and his wrist cuffs were decorated with images of wolves.

He was, indeed, her mate. If she had had any doubts, they were gone. He carried the image of her shifter self on his cuffs and the torc. She knew now that their fates were intertwined. She was his, and he was hers.

Continuing with her exploration of his body, Bronwnn carefully tended each wound with the herbs and an incantation. He slept deeply and peacefully. Depending upon how much thorn-apple he had been given, it could be hours or even a day before he awakened, free of the effects.

Settling down beside him, she watched the slow rise and fall of his chest. The firelight flickered along his body, and she studied the shadows, the way they played over his ridged abdomen, and below, his sex, which was large and thick, even in his current state.

Bringing her legs to her chest, she rested her head against her knees, watching him and wondering about him. She thought of when he awoke, and what he would say to her. What would he think of her? Bronwnn had a moment of flickering insecurity. What if she wasn't what he desired in a female?

As soon as the feeling came, it left. They were fated to be lovers, she reminded herself. They had been physically intimate in her dreams, and he always came to her, eager to touch her. Their union was written in the stars. He would want her. Just as much as she desired him.

The crackling of the fire, the warmth, the excitement of what had happened and what was yet to come, took their toll on her, and she drifted to sleep, heedless of the dangers of what might very well come to find them.

Rhys awoke, his throat excruciatingly dry, his eyes gritty and sandy, and his body stiff and sore. It was dark in the cottage. The fire had died, and the room had begun to cool.

He was naked, he realized, and his chest had been covered in something green and pasty. Trying to get his bearings, he raised his head from the pallet and squinted. Through the grimy window, he saw the faint glow of the sun rising in the distance. He had no idea what time it was, or even what season it was in Annwyn, but with the sun so low over the horizon, he figured it was early morning.

He'd survived the night, thanks to his little goddess.

Carefully he sat up, eager for a glimpse of the woman. A powerful rush of protectiveness and curiosity ran through him when he thought of her. He couldn't believe that his dreams had been entwined with a goddess and his fate tied to hers.

He tried to speak, but his voice didn't want to work, so he sat up. At first, his head spun, but then it cleared. He half expected to find her lying beside him, and he looked to his right and saw that *something* was there. But it wasn't his goddess. It was the white wolf he had seen peeking out at him from the trees when he'd first fallen by the reflecting pool.

A moment of fear impaled him, but then rational thought prevailed. If the wolf wanted his throat, it would have had it by now. Obviously, this animal was a guide.

Rhys smirked as he ran his hands through his hair. This was the second time he'd seen the wolf. One more time, and it would be his ally, just like the adder. It was damned strange how these animals all of a sudden came to him. He was no shaman—he wasn't even a Sidhe—but there must be something about him that attracted these animals. Perhaps he really did have a purpose in Annwyn.

Rhys ran his hand through the wolf's thick, luxurious fur.

Slowly, its eyes opened, revealing the most astonishing pale blue eyes he had ever seen.

They stared at each other carefully. Taking care not to make any rash movements, Rhys gently raised his hand to the wolf's muzzle. He knew enough about canines to understand this was the best way to befriend them; to let them sniff. But the wolf cocked its head and looked at him as if he were mad. Just as he was about to pull his fingers out of reach, the wolf surprised him by sniffing his fingertips, then licking him.

He smiled and petted the animal behind its ears. This was no savage beast. It was tame. Rhys wondered if the wolf belonged to his goddess. It seemed the right kind of animal for her to have. There was an ethereal majesty to the wolf, the same sort of angelic beauty his goddess bore.

Lying back down upon the pallet, Rhys turned on his side and studied the wolf. Swallowing hard, he tried to talk once more. "Where is your mistress this morning?" he asked, his voice deep and gravelly.

The wolf blinked, its eyes widening as it turned its head to look out the window. In a flash, the animal leaped up and ran to the door, which was slightly ajar.

"Don't leave!" he called hoarsely. The last thing he wanted was to be left alone in this cottage—in Annwyn—without any sort of ally. The wolf was the closest thing he had to a friend and guide.

The wolf turned and gave him a last look, its blue gaze unblinking. Either Rhys was insane or he heard the beast say "Stay" before it lunged out the door.

Fuck! Collapsing back onto the warm pallet of furs, Rhys

groaned. He didn't like being weak and not fully able to defend himself. He was also exhausted, just from that small amount of movement, which told him he'd be easy prey if anyone found him here.

What he needed was to regain his strength and get the fuck out of here. And for that, he needed to find Keir.

Closing his eyes, Rhys tried to focus on the wraith, but he kept seeing a pale-haired goddess leaning over him, her face awash in pleasure. She was an alluring woman, so damned tempting that he abandoned trying to locate his wraith and instead allowed himself to indulge in a few private and sexy thoughts about his goddess.

He was safe enough for now. And his dream goddess beckoned, so he followed her like a damned disciple.

Bronwnn crept quietly into Cailleach's solarium. The Supreme Goddess was awake and dressed, and she was dining on bread and cheese. When Cailleach saw her, she motioned her over to the table and pointed to the empty chair beside her.

"Be seated."

Bronwnn obeyed silently. She had no idea if Cailleach knew about her walk in the woods last night. She prayed she did not.

"You appear tired. Have you not been able to sleep?"

Bronwnn shook her head in denial, but Cailleach glanced at her skeptically.

"Your time is close upon you. It can cause disturbing dreams and disrupt sleep. It is normal."

Nervously, Bronwnn clasped her hands together. With a nod, she acknowledged that her sexual maturity was not simply coming, but had, indeed, arrived.

"You have no mother to guide you through this change, or tell you of the Shrouding. I will guide you when the time is right."

Bronwnn raised her gaze to the goddess. She had never before acted as anything other than her superior. Bronwnn had never known the love of a mother. She actually knew very little about the woman who bore her; all she had were her mother's books.

"I wish for you to take a mate. I have decided upon an appropriate male. One who is strong and worthy. One who will empower you. He is a strong male. Highly magical."

Bronwnn thought about the man she had left in her cottage. She could still feel his magick running along her body. Her nipples still tingled where his mouth had suckled her. She wanted him. She could hardly wait for nightfall so that she could return to him.

"You will obey me in this."

She nodded, eager to obey this edict. She wanted this mate more than anything.

"He is a Shadow Wraith. A most powerful one. An alliance between the goddesses and the wraiths will protect Annwyn."

Again she nodded and attempted to look passive and accepting. It was difficult, since everything inside her wanted to jump for joy. Not only was she going to sleep beside the man for the rest of her existence, but she was going to leave the temple, and Cailleach's grasp.

The goddess sat back in her chair and whistled. The white

oidhche flew from its perch and landed on the sleeve of Cailleach's gown. "There is a disturbance within Annwyn. I felt it last night. It is not the Dark Mage, but something else. Have you seen anything?"

Bronwnn swiftly shook her head. Cailleach frowned and turned her attention to the owl. "I sent him out, but he came back empty-handed. He saw nothing. Yet even this morning, I still feel it. Something—*or someone*—is here." When Bronwnn raised her head, she met Cailleach's pointed gaze. "I would like you to look for me."

With a nod, Bronwnn rose from the chair to return to her chamber.

"In here," Cailleach demanded. "Before me."

Bronwnn stumbled but swiftly regained control. She didn't want to perform a divination here, in front of Cailleach. She didn't want the goddess to hear or see anything that Bronwnn had taken such great pains to hide. But there was no remedy. Cailleach would not bend, and she would only grow suspicious if Bronwnn kicked up a fuss.

With a nod, she reached for the book that contained her visions and her images of the prophecy. What she had never put in writing was that she had a way to connect with the Dark Mage.

Opening the book to a blank page, she reached for the quill and allowed her fingertips to rub against the soft feathers. She needed to ground herself in order to see. It was a little more difficult with Cailleach seated on her throne, watching every move she made. But after a few seconds, Bronwnn successfully put Cailleach out of her mind and began to focus on the dark clouds. Through the solarium's window, she focused on the gathering storm. It would rain soon, and the scent of her lover would be washed away. Perhaps she might even persuade Cailleach that her instincts had been wrong and that it had, in fact, been the Dark Arts she had sensed last night.

Thunder rumbled across the sky as she thought of a way to dissuade Cailleach from searching Annwyn for the "disturbance." Even though Cailleach wanted this union between her and the wraith, Bronwnn could not help but feel she needed to protect the man in her cottage from the goddess and her far-reaching power. There was some hidden motive to this alliance that Bronwnn sensed but did not understand. Her instincts were always correct. She had learned to survive on her instincts, and they were telling her now that her lover needed her protection.

The gathering storm soothed her, and as she watched the swirling clouds thicken and darken, her lashes lowered, her trance beginning. She had a fleeting image of her lover, but she forced it aside, fearing she might say something while under the spell. He must be protected at all costs.

"Well, get on with it," Cailleach muttered irritably. It was not like the Supreme Goddess to show any emotion other than perfect composure. Something was most definitely wrong.

Closing her eyes, Bronwnn focused on the gathering winds. She could hear the sounds of Annwyn, the leaves and the trees, and every living thing that moved and crawled. At last, she was one with the elements, and as her breathing slowed and her mind stilled, the vision came upon her.

The number three appeared. Mindlessly, she picked up the quill and wrote what she saw. The next images were of three women, their faces heavily veiled and their bodies shrouded in white gossamer gowns. Bronwnn had seen their image before—the Sacred Trine. Now she heard the words, "Oracle, Healer, Nephillim." They kept repeating the words, over and over.

Just when she thought there would be no more to her vision, a new image appeared—one of a man, tall and majestic. His hair was dark and his skin pale. She had never seen him before, but she felt an instant connection. On the left side of his neck was a mark—a brand of sorts—and she drew it in her book, trying to sear the image in her mind.

"Camael," her mind whispered as she wrote the symbol, running over it with the tip of the quill several times to darken it.

That was all. The spell broke.

Cailleach came behind her. "The Sacred Trine," she murmured. "Yes, we must find it and protect it at all costs."

The goddess' finger scrolled down the page until she reached the symbol. With a shaking hand, she touched the Φ that Bronwnn had drawn.

Cailleach visibly trembled, then whispered, "He's returned."

Bronwnn turned in time to see Cailleach hurrying from the solarium. "Send a missive to the raven," she called. "I must meet with him and his warriors. There is no time to lose."

Rowan stared at the man who stood before her. Never in a million years had she expected to see Keir half naked—and in leather pants of all things. Despite the cancer eating away at her, her ovaries still seemed to be in perfect working order, because they shot a surge of estrogen that flooded her blood and made her want to fan herself. Lord, she was hot just looking at him.

Keir was beautiful. She'd always known he was. But this— the bulk and hardness, the tats—defied anything she had cooked up in her nightly dreams. He was too perfect for words. And if she didn't stop staring at him like a fool, he was going to know how she really felt about him.

Friends. She cleared her throat and found the courage to gaze up into his mysterious gray eyes. She loved how they were rimmed in violet. She once thought they were contacts. Now she knew they were the real deal.

He reached for her, and she shivered, anticipating his touch. The touch she had wanted for a long while now—well before she knew what he was.

"Are you afraid?"

Only of you not wanting me. But she shook her head. She could hardly say that. She was dying. It was unfair of her to tell him such a thing. It would put him in an awkward position. Besides, he was gorgeous and had women hanging all over him whenever she had seen him in Velvet Haven. The chances of his liking a plump chick like her were zero. Even worse, he was so nice that he'd take pity on her and kiss her just because she wanted him to. She didn't want to be a pity fuck.

"If you're not frightened, then why do you shiver?"

No way was she going to answer that. Even if she did admit to him what she wanted, she doubted she could let herself go enough to allow him to make love to her.

"It's cold," she answered instead.

He stepped closer and slowly wrapped his arms around

her waist, bringing her up against the hot, solid wall of his chest. She gasped at the contact, at the feel of him surrounding her.

"I'll warm you up."

She was burning. It was a little scary at first, feeling all that muscle surrounding her. It instantly made her feel vulnerable, until he lowered his head to her ear and said, "Take a deep breath."

She did. And then she took another until the alarm receded and she felt nothing but Keir around her. Closing her eyes, she pressed the side of her face against his naked chest. She listened to his breathing, smelled his skin, and allowed herself to savor this moment she thought she would never experience with him.

He held her still and tight, letting her get used to his height and size. But then he moved his hand up her back, a slow, gentle glide along her spine. His touch was so incredible. She felt it all the way through her shirt as if she were naked. Then she realized Keir was naked. Where his leather pants had gone, she had no idea, but she knew—she felt his nakedness against her. One shift of her thighs, and his cock would be nudging between them. At the thought of that, her legs threatened to give out on her, and he caught her more firmly around her waist.

"Step onto the robe."

She followed his command and allowed him to help her to stand on the satin. She absolutely refused to look down, although she wanted to—badly. She wanted to see if the rest of his body was as amazing as the top part.

"This is the best way I can do this. My magick is always strongest when I'm naked." It kind of sounded like an apology, and Rowan bit her lip. He didn't want to be naked with her. He had to, for magick's sake.

"We both need to stand on the robe. It's the grounding force for my divination magick."

"Okay," she said around a hard swallow. He was pressing closer to her, so close she felt his heat and smelled his skin. Her mouth watered as she wondered what he would taste like.

"Touch me," he whispered against her. "Ground yourself to me."

His voice was deep and dark, like black velvet; his suggestion heady. She didn't know where—how to touch him, but he took the guesswork from her. He placed her hands on his chest, then took her fingers and made her hold on to the quartz necklace once again.

"Is this going to work?" she asked skeptically.

"Yes, and even better if you would shed your clothes and stand naked against me."

She almost choked. Naked in front of Keir? She wasn't ready for that. Hell, she might never be ready for that.

"Magick must flow between us. Skin to skin. My energy mixing with yours."

"I can't," she said, her voice rising in panic she couldn't hide.

"Shh," he soothed, pulling her close. He held her still and allowed the panic to subside. "It's okay; we'll do it like this. It'll work. I'll find a way to make it work."

Suddenly she felt let down. Part of her wanted him to insist she let go of her fears and strip for him. She wanted him to fight for her, to make her do as he asked. She wanted to be wanted by Keir, even if it meant he wasn't gentle but downright demanding. Perhaps she wanted to throw caution to the wind and have Keir take her, because she was too damned scared to take him.

"Rowan," he murmured, "let your mind go."

She tried to forget about how much she wanted him, how he felt holding her; it worked, too, but the minute she felt herself loosening up, the old fears came rushing back.

"Shh," he soothed as she whimpered. "I'm here."

Rowan felt his hands moving along her back till they made their way into her hair. He rubbed her scalp and pressed his mouth to her temple. The tip of his cock nudged against her jeans, and she almost melted at feeling him grow against her.

"Wh-what are you doing?" she gasped as she felt his lips against her cheek.

"Relaxing you."

Oh, God, her heart was beating too fast and she couldn't catch her breath, and it was not because she was remembering, but because she wanted this. She wanted him.

"Will you give me something?" he murmured. His deep voice sent tremors through her.

Anything, she almost cried, but instead she nodded, slowly. A little unsure. Pressing her closer, he brushed his mouth against her ear. His breath was moist, hot, and it made her belly flip.

"Give me your trust, Rowan. I would never, ever hurt you. I want only to take you somewhere."

"Where?"

His palm slid down her back until his fingers rested low on the waistband of her jeans. "A place only for us."

Oh, God, was it possible he was thinking what she was thinking? Pulling away from her, he brought her down to the floor so that she lay on the satin. She was on her back, gazing up at him, her heart pounding and her blood rushing in her ears. "There's something I've wanted to ask you to do for a long time." He smiled and brushed his hand along her shoulder.

"To take this journey?"

"Yes."

"Where are we going?"

"I don't know. I've never done this before."

Instantly, Rowan's enthusiasm deflated. He wasn't here for what she foolishly thought—obviously. Because there was no way Keir had never done *that* before.

"Oh," she muttered, shifting her body on the robe. Evidently her idea of a mystical journey was a lot different than his.

"You have powers, Rowan; I know you do. We just have to tap into them. You can't get at them because of your fears, which are understandable, of course. But I believe we can access them together."

"If I do have powers, what do you want with them?"

He looked startled. "Nothing."

"Then why bother?"

"It will tell us about your past."

She shook her head. "The past is not happy, Keir. I don't need powers to tell me that. Nor do I want to rehash a whole bunch of drama from my childhood."

"But you do know you're not fully human?"

"Suriel. Now you. What is it with you? What interests you about what I might or might not be?"

His hands gripped hers, and he lowered himself to the carpet. His wide shoulders were between her knees, and Rowan had the mad urge to run her hands through his dark hair.

"I am hoping there is something in your past that might change your future." Rowan watched him swallow hard. He never blinked, keeping his gaze trained on her face. "I want to help you. I want to *save* you."

She couldn't help herself any longer. She ran her fingers through his hair and marveled at how silky it felt. "I'm beyond saving. You know that."

"I don't think so. I believe I know a way—through magick. Will you let me?"

How could she refuse a face like that? With a quick nod, she accepted.

Reaching for the quartz that hung around his neck, he lifted it and showed it to her. "This is a talisman. In meditation, you need something to hold on to. Use this—and I'll always be able to find you, wherever you are."

"Why quartz?" she asked, smoothing her finger over the glossy surface.

"Quartz is the gem that rules divination. It is a balancer between beauty and peace. When worn, it aligns mental, emotional, and astral bodies. When you wear this, and clear your mind, you can call upon me, and I can come to you."

"Do you mean like astral projection?"

"Yes. But spiritually as well."

Rowan bent her head as Keir removed the necklace and placed it on her. The warm quartz nestled between her breasts, and Keir let his fingers linger over the stone. Holding her breath, she waited for him to touch her; to brush his fingertips over her breasts. But the touch never came.

"Have you ever heard of scrying?"

"No."

"Let me show you something." With a wave of his hand, a mirror magically appeared before them, and he helped her up so that they stood before it. She gazed at them in the mirror's reflection. He stood behind her, dwarfing her despite her voluptuous proportions. His arms snaked around her waist, and he pulled her back to him.

"Scrying is a method of divination. One simply gazes at or into an object to still the conscious mind in order to contact the psychic mind."

She couldn't tear her gaze away. What would it be like to watch him in the mirror as he touched her? To see him making love with her?

"What are you saying, Keir?" she forced herself to ask, although she was barely listening to him. All she could hear was the sound of their passion. Would he moan? Did he whisper during lovemaking, or would he talk to her, arousing her with dark words and heated innuendos?

She would want him to talk, she realized. To tell her all the things she needed to hear; all the things she'd heard him say to her in her dreams.

"By calming your mind," he whispered into her ear, "you might be able to see the future, or to have visions of past or present events."

"Can't you do it yourself?"

She saw in the mirror's reflection how Keir's gaze strayed to the quartz nestled between her breasts. "What I want to do, I cannot do by myself. I have come to believe it may be possible to walk through dimensions, say to the past, and thus change that past. What if, by traveling back in time, we could undo our sins, and change our fate?"

The look in his eyes was now haunted. There was a flicker in the reflection. She glanced up and saw that Keir's eyes were no longer silver but an odd shade of white, the irises replaced with a brilliant light that drew her in.

"Will you help me?" he asked, hypnotizing her with that brilliant gaze. "Act as my portal and help me find what I'm searching for. Perhaps through me you will learn to have control over your powers. And then together we can find a way to save you."

She felt her will was suddenly not her own as she stared into the mirror. "Keir," she said nervously, her nails digging into his arms, "I don't want to do this."

"What do you see?" he asked, ignoring her protests. "What do you feel?"

"Frightened."

He squeezed her and lowered his head to her ear, keeping his gaze locked on hers in the mirror. "I've got you," he murmured. "I won't ever let you go."

But she knew at some point she would die, and any friendship they had would be gone. Who was she to deny him this one favor? He'd done a lot for her, and that was something she wasn't going to ignore.

"For me, Rowan? Please. Just try it once."

"Tell me what to do."

"Keep looking into the mirror. Allow your fear to go and know that I'll keep you safe. Wherever you go, I'll be there with you."

Looking into the mirror—at him—wasn't the problem.

It was letting her fears go. She wasn't one to drop her guard, but she wanted to do this for Keir, and maybe, then, she would discover something about herself. Hopefully it wouldn't be depressing.

Holding Keir's gaze, she absorbed the feel of his strong arms around her. Slowly she began to match her breathing to his and let her mind empty of her racing thoughts. The quartz nestled between her breasts began to heat and glow.

Without conscious thought, Rowan held out her arms and placed her palms on the glass. Her body jolted, and Keir held her tighter, whispering into her ear, but she didn't hear a thing. The mirror seemed to pull her in, and she let it. This was the journey she had agreed to take. And true to his word, Keir was right behind her, holding her, anchoring her to him.

As if having an out-of-body experience, Rowan saw herself step into the mirror and through a vortex that was a kaleidoscope of bright colors.

Once the spinning stopped, she found herself in the middle of a forest. The trees were leafless, and the sky above was the deep steel gray of winter. Before her, a man lay prone. His face was pressed into a thin blanket of snow that covered the ground. His bare hands were outstretched, as if he had fallen flat on his face. He was wearing jeans, black boots, and a long black wool coat. He wasn't moving.

She looked back, toward the portal through which she had entered this world, and saw herself with Keir. His arms were still around her, and he was peering intently into the mirror. She saw her own body, held securely in his arms. It was then she understood what had happened to her—astral projection. She had no idea she was capable of such a feat.

She turned back to the man on the ground and gently toed his hand with the tip of her shoe, searching for any signs of life—nothing.

She took a step back and nearly screamed as his hand suddenly grabbed her ankle. He was awake. And oh, God, he was moving toward her, using her ankle as leverage as he dragged himself closer.

The man made no sound as he heaved his upper body up from the cold ground. Slowly, his dark head rose, until she caught a glimpse of strong lips and a masculine jaw. The wind gusted, blowing his long hair away from his face.

She swayed, swallowed hard, and took a step back, just as he got to his feet and unfurled his tall body. He was now standing before her, a little unsteady, but his gaze clear. She gulped, taking in his face and the beautiful eyes glistening down at her.

She had never seen anyone like him. The entire left side of his face was tattooed with strange symbols, the sprawling marks covering his forehead, his eyelid, his cheek, all the way down to his mouth, where the corner of his lips bore the same strange marks.

She glanced at his face and felt her body tremble at the sight.

It was as if someone had drawn an imaginary line directly down the front of his face, purposely destroying half his beauty, while leaving the other side unmarred, a side he would have to confront every time he looked in the mirror. A side that silently whispered, "*This is how I used to be.*"

He said nothing, just continued to look down into her face with those mesmerizing eyes of his. A shadow shifted against the trees, and her gaze darted to it. There were wings. The man's shoulders shifted, and so, too, did the shadow behind him.

Rowan reached out to touch him but pulled back at the last moment. The clouds above parted, allowing the smallest bit of moonlight into the forest that surrounded them. Its glow revealed what Rowan secretly feared; the marks on the angel's face were the same symbols as those on Keir's body.

"My God, who are you?" she asked.

He took a step toward her, reaching for her. "You have the look of her."

"Who?"

"Your mother."

Rowan swallowed hard and allowed his long fingers to graze her cheek. "And wh-who are you?"

The vision began to fade, and Rowan felt her body pulled back toward the mirror. He reached for her, and their hands and fingers just missed each other. But she heard his voice, whispering all around her.

"I am your future."

She shook her head. No, it couldn't be. Would this be the angel to take her when she died? A butterfly, its wings a startling combination of white and electric blue, flittered between them. The angel caught it in his palm and uncurled his fingers, showing her the beautiful creature.

"You hold the key."

"I don't know what you mean," she whispered, glancing at the butterfly's flickering wings. "I have nothing. I don't know anything about a key."

"The key to the Sacred Trine. The Healer, the Nephillim,

the Oracle," he said to her. "Two born of the same womb, but not of the same man. Keep this knowledge safe."

The vision ended, and Rowan was sucked backward, straight through the mirror, where her soul slammed back into her body.

"Welcome back," Keir whispered.

"Oh my God," Rowan gasped as she saw the blue and white butterfly seated on her shoulder. "What the hell just happened?"

"I believe we have just discovered a powerful ally in this prophecy."

"The angel?"

"No. You."

CHAPTER NINE

Rhys had no idea what time it was, because he'd slept for hours after the wolf and his goddess had left him. He was thirsty and sore, and more than a bit curious about the world he now found himself in.

He'd managed to sit up, and thankfully his head had stopped spinning and his stomach stopped lurching. He was hungry, but there was nothing in the cottage to eat or drink. Hell, he had no idea what they even ate in Annwyn. Berries and leaves? He laughed to himself. With the size of Bran and Keir, Rhys doubted there was nothing but berries on the menu.

Did he dare try to get himself outside? His gut told him no. Soon his goddess would come back to him. Then he would question her, and he would have his answers. She would not save him, only to promptly abandon him.

Propping himself up by the massive stone hearth, Rhys glanced down at his body. He was naked, his thighs streaked with dirt and dried blood. His chest, however, had been washed, and some green putty-type shit was covering his wounds. He had to admit that the stuff felt good, and, as he began peeling it off, he saw how his skin was beginning to heal beneath the paste.

Bringing a chunk of the paste to his nose, he inhaled. It was organic, the smell of pine and plant and earth. That didn't surprise him. The inhabitants of Annwyn practiced the Druid ways, and the Druids believed that every living thing, from the smallest leaf to the largest animal, held its own living spirit. The Druids used herbs in their healing, their ceremonies, and their magic. Rhys had been told of the ancient ways but had never seen them in practice. Now he was a recipient of those ways.

Speaking of magick, Rhys wondered where the hell Keir was. Rhys had been certain the wraith would have appeared on the cottage doorstep eons ago. He had even sent out a mental search for him, but there was nothing—no connection at all; just quiet.

Sighing, Rhys rested his head and closed his eyes. He was royally fucked if the goddess had decided to abandon him. He could tell the cottage wasn't used very often, and the likelihood that someone would stumble across him wasn't very good— someone who would help him, at least. Cailleach, on the other hand, might very well appear before him, ready to kill him.

He was close to dozing off again when the latch on the door clicked. His skin flickered, and he prepared to fight the intruder as he watched the door slowly creak open.

In the threshold stood his goddess. Her gaze, alarmed, flew from the empty pallet to the wall, where he saw relief flash in her blue eyes.

"I'm still here," he said quietly. "But I began to wonder if you would come back."

She said nothing, just turned and closed the door. On her shoulder was a bag, and she walked to the worn wooden table and set it down. Opening it, she set the contents on the table.

Rhys watched her work. This was the first time he had seen her through clear eyes, without the drug clouding his mind. His erotic hallucinations were not exaggerated. She was beautiful, and her body was stunning, all fine curves and high breasts. Her hair was up today, exposing the back of her neck, which, of course, made him think of coming up behind her and running his lips over her downy skin.

"What is your name?" he asked as he moved his hand lower to cover his cock. There was no need for her to see him in this state—at least not yet.

She didn't answer, and he asked in a louder voice, which still got no reply. But she did turn to him, her hands full of food and a flask.

Kneeling before him, she ignored his nudity and held out a loaf of bread to him. He noticed there were cheese and fruit as well.

It wasn't a double Big Mac combo, but it would do. He was starved. "Thank you."

She nodded and looked at him expectantly. Rhys didn't know how he was going to eat with an erection. He was also starting to get a little uncomfortable with the one-sided conversation.

She nudged the bread at him, and Rhys accepted it, spreading the cloth it had been wrapped in on his lap to cover himself. Then he broke the bread apart and began eating. It was warm and soft, and nothing had tasted better. Grabbing a piece of cheese, he devoured it, then the berries. She passed him the flask, and he took a big drink of the cold water.

She watched him for a few seconds, then began to assemble some bottles and jars she had placed on the dirt floor behind her. She worked quietly and methodically. Chewing the bread as he silently watched her, he wondered.

Finally, he asked, "Do you not speak?"

She shook her head that she did not.

"But you hear?"

She nodded. Rhys was disappointed, because he would have liked to have heard her voice, but it didn't lessen his desire for her or his certainty that they were meant to be together. They would just have to find other ways to communicate.

As he ate, she began tending his wounds. With a warm cloth, she washed the remainder of the paste away, leaving the reddened and raised scars on his chest. Carefully she touched one wound—an inverted pentagram—and looked up at him, questioning him with the tilt of her head.

"Artwork courtesy of the Dark Mage. I had the misfortune to run into him in the Cave of Cruachan."

He saw in her eyes that she understood. She went back to work on his chest, cleaning and rubbing his wounds with lotions that had him smelling like a pine forest. The medicine stung for a few seconds, but the stinging was quickly replaced with a cool tingling that neutralized the burning he felt from the wounds.

"Do you know the Sidhe king?"

She paused and looked up at him. Then she nodded slowly, which led him to believe she knew *of* Bran, even if she didn't know him.

"Can you take me to him?"

She shook her head violently, then pointed to his chest.

"I'm better. Thanks to you. But I need to get to Bran."

Again she shook her head, and Rhys reached for her wrist. "I can't stay here. I need to leave."

Rising up, she twisted her wrist, freeing herself from his weakened grip.

"If you won't take me, I'll go searching myself."

She shoved him back down, then promptly left him on the floor. Damn if the woman wasn't stubborn.

"I'm healed," he called after her as she walked out the door of the cottage. Damn it, he hoped he hadn't offended her. It probably wasn't the right thing to do with a goddess who had just saved your ass.

Slowly Rhys stood up and smoothed his hands over his face. The food had given him strength, and the medicine that covered his chest was tingling nicely, cooling the fire of his skin. In all, he felt pretty good for nearly being a human sacrifice. And he owed it all to the woman who had just left him—again.

Rhys made his way to the door and opened it, prepared to step out and see where she was. But the snarling sound made him freeze. Before him was the white wolf, and its teeth were not something Rhys particularly cared to experience digging into his leg.

"All right," he muttered, stepping back. The wolf moved forward, forcing Rhys back into the cottage. Rhys didn't know whether to put his hands in the air in surrender or to cover his genitals, which were pretty much eye level with the wolf. Damn it, he really needed some jeans.

The wolf forced him back until Rhys was standing in the

spot by the fire. Their gazes were locked, and Rhys reminded himself not to make any sudden moves.

Lowering his tall body onto the fur pallets, Rhys slowly brought his arms down. "All right, I'm here. I'm not going anywhere."

The wolf whimpered and immediately sat back on its haunches. Rhys suddenly saw the intricate blue design on its left hind leg. He went to touch it, but the wolf snapped. A warning only—its teeth weren't anywhere near his skin, but the sound of clamping jaws had the intended effect. Rhys backed off.

"Where did she go, huh?" he asked the wolf. It cocked its head and studied him. Its eyes were gorgeous; so icy blue—a lot like the color of his goddess' eyes, he thought.

The animal let him put his palm on its head and rub between its ears. "There, see, I'm not going to hurt you. But I do need to get to the Sidhe king."

"Soon . . ."

He heard the word, whispered in a woman's voice. He jumped, afraid it was Cailleach, but as he looked around the cottage, he realized no one was there besides him and the wolf.

As he stared into the animal's blue eyes, Rhys began to feel sleepy. His exertions had cost him, and now he was feeling weak and exhausted. *Pansy-ass mortal.*

Even though he didn't want to show his weakness, he couldn't help but recline on his side. The furs felt good beneath him. The animal followed, curving its body into Rhys' front.

"Don't you leave me, too," he mumbled as he let his arm drape over the wolf. "And don't decide to rip out my throat when I fall asleep."

The last thing he saw before sleep claimed him was the wolf's eyes. They really did remind him of the goddess' baby blues. Man, he thought with disgust, he was really fucking losing it.

When Rhys was asleep, Bronwnn slowly rose. His arm was still draped across her body, and she was loath to move it. It felt good. He felt good. But she knew she must.

The change into her woman's form was swift and painless. She stood beside him now, gazing down upon him. He was so handsome, and his voice was the color of the night, black and sultry. It washed over and made her skin prickle with awareness. Perhaps she found his voice so arousing because she no longer had one of her own. He hadn't appeared to be disappointed by her not speaking to him. She had fleetingly wondered if he would. They were to be mated, after all. They would have a lifetime spent together. And if she didn't talk . . .

Bronwnn's gaze roved along his hard body. There were other things to do than talk, she thought.

Turning, she went back to the table and set about her task. She had wanted to bathe him, to soothe the ache that must have settled into his body after lying on the hard floor all day, but then he had fallen asleep.

She would take care of him now. Taking the cloth and bowl of water, she returned to his side and kneeled. The water was warm, and she dredged the cloth through it, wetting it, then brought it to his face. Carefully she washed him. He sighed but did not wake.

The thorn-apple was a powerful drug. The lethargy and mental fatigue he was suffering could last for days.

She had wanted to continue hearing his voice, to study his beautiful violet eyes, but this was nice, too—the quiet and being able to watch him unguarded and asleep. She could peruse his body and allow her gaze to linger on parts she hadn't dared to stare at while he had been talking to her.

His body, so hard and big, was a work of art. Bronwnn let her fingertips trail along the contoured ridge of his thigh. He was as hard as granite, but warm. She continued washing him—his arms, then his legs. She avoided his chest, allowing the witch hazel ointment to work.

She had no idea how long she kneeled beside him in the pretense of bathing him. His body was clean, and the water had cooled. She was done. But she could not force her hand to stop touching him. She wanted more—to straddle him and feel his body beneath hers. She wanted to touch him intimately, to take his staff and feel it grow in her hand.

She was a virgin, but she was not innocent of sex. She was the goddess of sexuality and fertility. She knew the ways of pleasure. They were instinctual to her. Sex was nothing to be ashamed of or to fear. She embraced it—would embrace it with him.

Boldly, her fingertips left his thigh and trailed over to his hip, then to his cock. She had heard many species use this word to refer to that part of themselves. She liked the sound of it; she wanted to hear it uttered in the man's deep voice.

Her finger traced the length of it, and the man moaned, and she watched as it grew, thickened. She reached out and curled her fingers around it, feeling its satiny smoothness and thick veins. He was broad and long, and the need to smell and taste was overpowering.

She held him, feeling it pulse in her hand. He was warm, the veins growing, filling. And then she jumped as she felt his fingers curl over hers.

"Yes," he purred sleepily.

Using his hand, he pumped up and down, and she listened to his moans of pleasure as she studied the rhythm he liked. His skin was flushed, and his abdomen was tense and rigid. His free hand moved to cup the sac between his legs. He rolled it and squeezed as the pressure of his hand on hers increased, encouraging her to quicken her strokes.

His breathing was fast, his cheeks stained red. His cock was now so thick, her fingers could no longer curl around the staff. The musky scent of his body aroused her, and she felt her nipples bead and her thighs quiver. Her mouth actually moistened as she studied the way he looked in her hand.

Then, he was reaching for her, his strong fingers wrapped gently around her nape, and he brought her down, till the wet tip of his cock brushed against her mouth.

He tasted of salt, sweat, and the unidentifiable scent that aroused her so much.

"Take it in your mouth."

Her body felt hot, alive. His voice was even more arousing when heated with pleasure. His voice in the quiet made her wet, reckless.

She was innocent; yet instinct guided her where inexperience could not. In all her dreams of him, she had not done this, but as she had watched over him last night—their first night together, staring at his body, touching it—she had wanted to taste him.

She lowered her head and sucked him deep, listening to his low groan. She took pleasure in the way he fisted his hand in her hair—just as he had in her vision, when he had been rough and primal. The animal in her stirred, recognizing its mate. The animal was not gentle, and it overtook the woman in her.

Sucking him, she pleasured him with the tip of her tongue. First, she used tiny flicks; then, deeply she drew him in, sucking him and tasting his skin.

"If this is heaven, then thank God for death," he whispered as he bucked his hips forward. He grew thicker in her mouth, and she used her tongue to lave the smooth skin, then the wrinkled edges of his shaft. As he moaned and grew more forceful, she felt her body turn soft and her thighs grow slick.

Moving her hand between them, she discovered her core was wet and aching. Then her hand was brushed aside, replaced with his hot, hard palm.

"Wet and waiting," he murmured huskily. "You want me."

She whimpered, the only sound she permitted herself, and it turned him into something more feral—something to match the animal in her.

Before she knew it, before she could understand his intent, or how he had the strength, he removed his shaft from her mouth and pulled her body on top of his until her thighs straddled his hips. His hand sought her folds, the stroking and rubbing of his fingers making her want to scream in pleasure.

He watched her; she felt his beautiful violet eyes roving along her nakedness. His eyes darkened as his gaze fixed on her breasts. He licked his lips, and she pressed forward, allowing her breasts to dangle before him.

"Nice," he whispered. "Now let me taste them."

Bronwnn brushed her nipples across his lips, teasing him. He captured one, bit gently down, then circled the hard tip with his tongue. His hand was now clutching her, kneading her bottom. She arched, tossing her head back so that her breasts were fully before him and his hand was squeezing her.

"You have the finest tits and ass I've ever seen."

The words aroused her, even though she didn't quite understand them. She knew they were said to arouse, and they did. She was wet, and she was rubbing herself against his swollen shaft.

"Come," he commanded. His hands fixed on her hips, and anchoring them on either side of her, he flexed up, meeting her, connecting with her wet sex.

"Rub on me," he whispered as he brought her down and kissed her cheek. His breath was moist against her, his words hot in her ear. "Let me feel your cunt."

Her whole body was quivering now, and he held her tighter as he rubbed his cock against her, the length of him sliding between her slick folds. She was moving faster now, and his breathing was quicker as it whispered against her.

"Fuck, I want to be inside you."

She wanted that, too, but it was too late. She was shuddering on top of him, mindless of anything but the pleasure that centered deep in her sex and spread out to her limbs. She would have cried out, but she was mute, her body fractured from her mind. And then she collapsed against him, her breasts pressed against the hard wall of his chest.

His fingers ran along her spine, soothing her. His touch was soft, reverent. He kissed her cheek, then the crook of her neck.

"That was better than my dreams," he whispered, and Bronwnn nodded her agreement.

Her dreams had been nothing like this. Nothing could have prepared her for the exquisite feel of his hand, his hard body, the primitive need she felt binding them.

"*Mo bandia*," he murmured, before kissing her.

My goddess.

CHAPTER TEN

"I've dreamed of you, you know."

Rhys gazed down into the face of the woman lying in his arms. She was beautiful, especially now, her skin flushed in the afterglow of passion.

"For weeks you've come to me." Her blue eyes peered up at him. "Has it been the same for you?"

She nodded, and a sense of relief and elation flooded him. She had dreamed of him, too.

"We're connected. Fated." His hand grazed along her back, and she shivered. He held her closer, basking in the feel of her. "You're mine."

She agreed. He might be a mortal, but Rhys knew how things worked in the Otherworld. He had mingled with immortals all his life. He knew of their ways, their beliefs. Dreams figured heavily in their culture, and Rhys knew that he and this woman were now deeply intertwined.

"That's how you knew to find me."

She nodded, then kissed his chin, using her fingertips to

trace the outline of the torc. He had forgotten he was wearing it. He smiled, thinking of the wolf head at either end of it—a fitting animal. Somehow Daegan had known he'd make this journey. He had also known a wolf was in his future.

"I have to get to Bran," he murmured as he nuzzled her hair with his lips. "I've seen things I must tell him. It's important."

She shook her head and held him tighter. She wasn't letting him go. While he appreciated her concern, Rhys knew he couldn't stay in this cottage forever. It wasn't his nature to hide and be idle. He needed to do something. And that he had firsthand information on the Dark Mage was vital. No one had been so close to the killer and lived to tell about it.

She was still clutching him, and he held her close, reveling in the newfound softness inside him. He hadn't even been inside her, and already there was a connection between them. He felt it, coursing through him. He would protect her with his dying breath. She was his, and he would keep her safe—and satiated.

"If you're not going to let me leave, then what are we going to do?"

The hunger in her eyes made him instantly hard. This was a woman who could satisfy all his needs. She was lusty and eager, and he liked that. She was also strong and independent, and capable of keeping him in check when he didn't want to admit he was too weak to do something.

He kissed her, a soft and lingering kiss, and when he pulled back, her eyes were still closed. He smiled, then lowered his head once more to kiss her again. This time he used the tip of his tongue to brush along the seam of her lips. She gasped, and he clutched her tighter.

He wanted to make this right, to cement their bond. He was going to be inside her this time when she came.

"I don't even know your name," he murmured against her mouth. It obviously didn't matter to her, because she pressed up against him and deepened the kiss.

He wanted her. Badly. But Rhys couldn't help but slow things down. This was what he wanted, to be inside her, to make love to her. Except he wanted to make certain his beliefs were what she believed.

"I've dreamed of you, and you've dreamed of me. I believe you're mine. That we're destined to be together. Is that what you believe?"

She pulled back just enough so she could gaze up into his face. Her slow nod made his body light up.

"Then you agree to this? You . . ." He swallowed hard. "You accept me as your mate?"

Her smile was big and warm. He gathered her close and began kissing her, but not with the slow, lazy kisses he had teased her with before. Now he was kissing her hard, his mouth open over hers and his tongue delving deep into her mouth.

Rolling on top of her, Rhys rested his weight on his elbows and allowed his fingers to curl into her hair. It felt like silk, and she smelled so damned good to him.

She was restless beneath him, her voluptuous body curved into his hard one. Jesus, he was the luckiest bastard in the world to be able to claim a woman like this. She was beautiful and responsive, and she was his . . .

Something he couldn't recognize snapped into place inside him. All of a sudden, his feelings were stronger, more acute. He felt possessive, but something else? Love? Was it even possible? Had he started to care for her in his dreams?

Shit, this feeling was so foreign to him. Maybe it was just a hard-core case of lust. But when his hands left her hair so his thumbs could brush along the bounding of her pulse, he knew it was something much stronger and more long-lived than a simple case of a hard-on and a willing woman.

Her heart was beating fast, but so was his. Her pale skin was flushed pink with sexual excitement, and her breathing was rapid, irregular—aroused.

Lifting up from her body, he gazed down at her. She was gorgeous, her breasts full and pink tipped—perfect. Cupping her breasts, Rhys ran the pads of his thumbs over her nipples, watching as they beaded. She moaned then, the first sound she had made. It was beautiful, and he fell onto her like a starving man.

He suckled her, blew hot air across her nipples, nibbled at them, while her legs slid over his ass and her fingers clawed at his hair. Her pussy was wet; he could feel the slickness of her folds against his cock. He wanted to penetrate her, but he wanted to taste her, too.

Sliding down her body, he spread her sex and licked. She cried out and reached for his shoulders, lifting her hips to meet his mouth. He took his time licking, tonguing her. She was wet, sweet, and he brought her up slowly, making her burn.

When she was ready, when he felt her fingers in his hair pulling him up, he loomed over her, caught her gaze, and slowly rubbed his cock against her.

"Do you want this?" His breathing was heavy and his words gruff with passion. She reached for his ass and gripped him, lifting herself to him.

He teased her by circling the tip of his cock against her clit; she purred, the sound like some wild animal. It made him feel primal, and he slipped into her, stretching her wide.

She was tight, and he was careful. He knew she would be a virgin. Goddesses who wore white were chaste. After they had taken a mate, they wore various colors. This goddess, he thought with satisfaction, would know only him, and soon she would no longer be chaste, but his.

Plunging deep, he broke her, forging through her and stretching her to fit him. She did not cry out but clung to him, nipped his neck, and bucked her hips back against his, taking him deep.

Slowly he rocked against her as their chests rubbed together, and they looked deeply into each other's eyes. Never had he felt anything so damned good. He'd had sex—lots of it—but never with a woman he knew was to be his, and never alone. Keir had always been there, either in form or shadow, feeding off Rhys' energy. It had never been just Rhys alone with a woman he desired.

He would never share this one. The thought slammed into his head as he deepened his thrusts—claiming her. Keir would have no part of her, no energy from their union. He couldn't allow it—wouldn't. They'd have to find other ways for Keir to feed, because what was happening between them right now was for them alone.

"*Mo bandia*," he whispered as he thrust harder. "Come with me."

Her eyes closed, and she shivered beneath him as he played with her clitoris, still wet from his mouth.

"Come," he whispered again, afraid he wouldn't be able to

hold back much longer. And then she did, shivering in his arms, holding him close and clamping around his cock.

"You're mine now."

She smiled a womanly smile—one that said she didn't take any offense to his mortal possessiveness.

Keir shut the door to Rowan's chambers and leaned against the wall. He still couldn't believe it had worked. She had taken him with her on her journey. But through the euphoria of knowing there was another way to connect with her, his conscience poked at him. He'd lied to her, not because he deliberately wanted to hurt or deceive her, but because he knew she wouldn't understand what he wanted to do.

Rowan was new to magick and Annwyn. She saw things as only black and white, good and evil. What she couldn't comprehend yet was that magick had many faces. Some might condemn him for what he was thinking of doing, but he was doing it with an honest heart, and a love that wouldn't die.

In his soul, he knew who he was—Rowan's *Anam Cara*—Soul Friend. They *could* be together, if he used the right magick, and if Rowan allowed him to break through the barriers of her past. There was a future there. He had seen it; he had seen her.

There was so much more that he could do, now that he had confirmed that Rowan was indeed not fully mortal. But one thing did weigh on him—the angel in the vision. Keir wasn't certain what his presence in Rowan's future meant. But he would find out. Rowan held a key to the prophecy. That had been an unexpected finding. He was happy to have something new to report to Bran, but that hadn't been the reason for his visit. He'd wanted to know if Rowan could trust him; if he had the power to make her forget and experience something new. And she had. And that knowledge sent him reeling.

He would go back to Velvet Haven and use a divination to see what he should do next. There was a way to keep her alive through magick, and Keir would do it. But first, he needed to find Bran, and maybe even that pain-in-the-ass fallen angel.

Looking down at his palm, he studied the symbol he had drawn, the Φ etched on the angel's neck. It was a strange symbol, one that looked both divine and demonic. It was different from the symbol the Dark Mage had used when he had murdered the mortal outside Velvet Haven. That symbol denoted the angel Uriel, as well as Gwyn, the god of the dead in Annwyn, and the ruler of the underworld.

So, who was this angel, and what was his role? Keir wondered. "*Destroyer* . . ." whispered the word in his mind. Was this angel the ninth warrior? Would he deceive them all?

Closing his fingers over his palm, Keir decided it was time to learn of the Sacred Trine. They had been so focused on the Dark Mage, and on finding Carden, Bran's half brother, that they'd ignored that part of the prophecy. And that was a mistake. Now more than ever, they needed to understand it and how it brought both the mortal and immortal realms together. Only then, once the prophecy was fully understood, could they defeat the faceless Dark Mage and put an end to the Dark Times in Annwyn.

Stepping into the shadowed hall, Keir froze. A black adder with a white zigzag stripe was curled up, hissing at him. As a shaman, he knew that seeing the reptile was not mere coincidence. The snake was here for a specific purpose.

The nathair was long associated with wisdom, reincarnation, and cunning. The appearance of a snake on a mystic journey was a sign of something great to come. But one had to be prepared to shed something to obtain something greater.

Why was this snake before him? What must he shed?

The adder lunged at him, mouth open and fangs prepared to strike. Keir instantly dissolved into shadow, and the snake plunged through. Keir thought he had evaded the snake, but the stinging on his calf told him otherwise. He'd been bitten. Adder venom was not lethal to wraiths, but it was useful in divination.

Hovering as a shadow up by the ceiling, Keir watched as the adder slithered along the hall. Below him, Keir saw a card, facedown, directly in the spot where the adder had been curled up.

Forming into his body, he dropped down and winced as his calf burned. Ignoring the pain, he bent to pick up the card. It was from the tarot, and when he turned it over, the image of Gwyn riding his white horse during the Wild Hunt greeted him. It was the Death card.

Glancing up, he gazed down the long corridor, now empty of the snake.

The Death card meant more than Death. It meant rebirth and transformation. It was a card that implied the separating of one's self from the past to start a new future. Since it had been combined with the presence of the adder, Keir was certain the divination he had just been given was a good omen. He was on the right path. He had deceived Rowan, true. But it was in order to save her.

Clutching the card, he made his way from the Sidhe king's

castle back to the veil. He needed to get back to Velvet Haven.
He had left Rhys alone for too long.

Rhys pointed to the word Bronwnn had written on a sheaf of
parchment.

"Your name is Bronwnn?" Her face lit up as he pronounced
it perfectly. Thankfully, his study of Gaelic was paying off. "It's
a beautiful name."

She kissed him, then reached for the quill and paper. *Yours?*

"Rhys."

I like it. She looked at him shyly. He reached for her, bringing her onto his lap, but she scooted off and was back to writing
something.

Are you in pain?

"No." At least not that kind. Shit, he wanted her again.
His body and cock ached for her. It couldn't still be the effects
of the drug. Could it? Maybe it was just a case of lust. What did
it matter? he wondered as his gaze raked over her luscious body.
He wanted her and would likely never tire of having her.

Hungry?

Just for her. He shook his head and reached for her, but she
tapped his hand with the quill and wrote something else.

How did you know what I am?

He shrugged, then grinned at her. "With a body like yours,
there's no doubt you're a goddess."

She blushed and looked away. She wasn't ashamed of her
body, or the way she sat naked beside him. It was the compli-
ment that flustered her. Lowering his head, he captured her gaze.

"You're beautiful, smart, courageous, and you perform the healing arts, and it's made me wonder what goddess you are."

She looked at him, her pale blue eyes wide. Yeah, he'd been preoccupied with sex and having her, but that didn't mean he didn't notice things.

The quill scratched against the parchment, and he couldn't hide his huge grin as he read what she had written.

I am the goddess of sexuality and fertility.

Well, wasn't he a lucky bastard. The goddess of sexuality. He'd certainly won the mother lode when she picked his sorry ass up from the ground.

Say something.

He could almost hear the anxious sound of her voice translated into those two frantically scribbled words. With a smile, and a gentle caress against her cheek, he leaned forward and kissed her.

"Thank you, Goddess of sexuality and fertility, for saving my life, and gifting me with your body."

Her smile undid him, and he touched her again, enjoying this conversation and this closeness taking root between them.

You're welcome. And I think you're beautiful, too.

He laughed and brushed her hair over her shoulder. He wasn't beautiful, but the woman sitting beside him—his future mate—was stunning. All the other women he had known were obliterated from his memory with just one glance at this woman, as beautiful on the inside as she was outside.

He watched as his fingertips slid down the perfect alabaster skin of her shoulder. She was smooth, soft, so warm against his calloused fingers. "I really need to find the king."

Too dangerous.

"It's important, and I'll come back to you. I promise."

There was no way in hell he was leaving and not coming back to her. Already he could feel her creeping into his heart. This wasn't just a case of mind-blowing sex mixing up his brain. This was Annwyn and fate, and the idea of a lifelong mate, a person one could feel in one's soul—a mate who not only made a person feel loved and desired, but also complete.

Beware Cailleach.

He laughed. "You don't have to tell me. I know she's been after me ever since she learned of my birth."

Bronwnn cocked her head and stared at him. She was obviously puzzled. But then she shrugged and looked away.

"When is it safe to leave? I have to get to the Sidhe king. There are things he needs to know—important things."

It's never safe. The Dark Times have come, and Annwyn is under their pall.

"*Mo bandia,*" he whispered, "I have to find Bran. It's the mage I must speak to him about. It's important, or I wouldn't ask it of you. I wouldn't risk you at all if I could find him myself."

Tonight I will take you.

Nodding, he reached for her and brought her down beside him. She was naked still, and he couldn't help but admire the view or the fact that she seemed right at home in her own skin. "Thank you."

She nodded and wrapped her arms around him. She brought her face to the crook of his neck, and he swore he heard her sniffing his skin. He wondered if he smelled bad. He hadn't showered, and he'd been in that crypt . . . but then she sighed and let her nose trail across him, and he figured he smelled all right to her.

"You're beautiful, you know."

She pressed into him, and he kissed her temple. "I love the color of your hair, your skin, the feel of you in my arms."

Curling into him, Rhys held her close while his hand began to wander. "Your skin is soft, smooth. Like rose petals."

She stretched on his lap as his palm skimmed over her breasts and down her belly. "But you're softest here," he murmured as he parted her folds and rubbed her with his fingers. "And you get so wet for me."

She squirmed on his lap, awakening his cock. He wanted her again, but it was probably too soon. She had been a virgin, and it was little more than an hour since he'd claimed her. He should probably just hold her and talk with her some more. They had much to learn about each other, and he wanted to know everything, but he couldn't seem to resist her.

She didn't seem to mind, though, and when he raked his finger up the seam of her sex, she moaned and sighed. Slowly he circled her, thumbing her clit as he dragged his tongue up her neck. "Spread your legs; let me see you."

Her head tipped back as his thumb circled her and his fingers slipped inside her. She moaned, making a deep, husky sound that echoed in the quiet. He glanced down her body and saw his dark hand between her pale thighs. "You're perfect, Bronwnn, perfect."

He watched as he rubbed her, her golden curls shimmering in the firelight. It was growing dark, the moonlight filtering in through the grime-covered window.

Slowly he pleasured her, watching every nuance of her face, the way her body moved and her breasts tightened. Her nipples were still reddened from his mouth, and he used his tongue to taste her, to flick. She moaned against his throat and cupped her breasts in her hands, offering them up to him. Damn, she was perfect.

He suckled her deep into his mouth, the rhythm matching the movement of his fingers. She was wet, his fingers glistening with her desire. Spreading her legs wider, she told him without words what she wanted.

"Deeper?" he whispered. "Harder?"

She nodded, then gasped as he filled her deep. Her thighs opened wider, and a shaft of moonlight splayed on her. It was then that he saw the blue tattoo that ran the length of her inner left thigh.

Leaving her pussy, he brushed his wet fingers against the intriguing design. To his shock, she screamed, and her body went rigid in his arms as if she were having a seizure.

"What's wrong?" he shouted, though she couldn't answer. He tried to let go of her and lay her down on the floor, but she held on to him like a dying man hanging on to a rope.

Her eyes rolled back, and then her body went slack in his arms. Panic seized him. He was out of his element here in Annwyn. He didn't know a damned thing about medical shit. Helplessly he realized he could do nothing until she came out of it. Until then, he would hold her and keep her safe.

The vision was upon her now. She had been foolish to expose herself in such a way, but she had been too wrapped up in the pleasure that Rhys was giving her to remember to hide the script that ran up her thigh. Never had she been so careless.

He had nearly touched it when she had been in her wolf form, she reminded herself. Rhys was devastating, not only to her body but to her mind. She would need to find a way to guard herself. But she was here now, in the midst of a vision she did not want, and could not stop.

It was black as pitch, and quiet. She could hear breathing close to her, but she could not see. Even with her keen wolf vision, she was blind in this obsidian darkness.

She was in a cavern of sorts; she could sense that much. The rhythmic tapping of water hitting rock sounded in the distance. The scurrying of a rodent across the stone floor made her shudder. Where was he? she wondered as she rubbed her hands along her arms. He was always in these visions. The tattoo on her leg was her cursed link to him.

Her heart was racing as she took a cautious step forward.

"Go no farther."

She froze as the disembodied voice reached her. By the goddess, she wished she could see. Bronwnn possessed a fair amount of steel will and courage, but this was unnerving. The darkness, the uncertainty, and the evil she felt in this cavern were beyond what her courage could withstand.

"He will find you, and when he does, he will sacrifice you."

Bronwnn turned in a slow circle, her hands outstretched in an attempt to connect with anything. Suddenly her wrists were seized, and she was pulled forward. A light flared, and she found herself looking into the face of a nightmare.

She nearly screamed, but the creature's filthy blackened hand covered her mouth. His eyes . . . By the goddess, they had been removed, leaving only black sockets. His face . . . One half was tattooed with angelic script. And on his neck, he bore the mark revealed in the divination she had done for Cailleach.

Camael . . .

"No noise. He waits for you beyond the darkness. You are what he needs."

She tried to talk, but no words would form. She was terrified, trembling. But he pulled her closer so that he could whisper in her ear.

"Protect the Sacred Trine. Protect it at all costs, for it is what he wants most. The trine has more power than even the flame and the amulet. The Oracle, the Healer, and the Nephillim—protect them all, and you will have what you need to defeat the mage."

He brought her closer, and the sound of chains clinking together made her realize how heavily bound he was. Softly, she traced the contours of his face, and he held her hands, his fingers shaking. What was he?

"Bring back the nine warriors to release me, and I vow to you I will aid your cause."

The door opened, and a shaft of flickering candlelight shone upon them. A hooded figure stepped forward. Bronwnn could feel his eyes upon her, his laughter slithering over her as he approached.

"Ah, my little voyeur. Always hovering just out of my reach."

His steps were slow, purposeful, allowing her fear to rise.

"How long I have waited to meet you."

Standing, Bronwnn steadied herself. The creature who held her pulled her closer and whispered into her ear. "An angel with no flame is no longer immortal."

The Dark Mage pulled on a chain that circled the man's neck, choking him. He released her as the mage dragged him down to the stone floor where he landed by his boots.

"My little abomination has no need of your stories, Camael."

The mage stepped closer, and Bronwnn felt her body begin to tense. He knew it, because he laughed, sensing her fear. What did he know of her? Nothing—he couldn't.

"I can taste it," he murmured, "your fear. You smell like your mother."

That caught her attention.

"Oh yes, I knew her. She taught me the ways of your Black Arts. I pleasured her for a time, in exchange for her knowledge. Foolish bitch."

Camael groaned behind the mage, which seemed to amuse him. "My brother believed he was in love with your mother, but love is such a fleeting feeling, isn't it? She gave him up for me. Of course, he's spent the last millennium planning his escape and his subsequent return to her. But there is nothing to return to. I sacrificed her. Her knowledge made me very powerful."

Bronwnn seethed with hatred. The mage was no more than two feet away from her now. She still could not see his face, but she could smell him, a putrid, rotting stench that made her want to vomit.

"Indole," he murmured. "An element present in all the delicate white moth–pollinated blossoms. It is the only common element in perfumes created to arouse the senses. Although it has the distinct aroma of putrefaction, it's an aphrodisiac. Sexually stimulating while giving a taste of the sweet elixir of sin. My sacrifices are bathed in it, a radiance born of darkness and death. Wait till you have sex magick, my lovely. You'll die of the pleasure it can bring."

She shook her head, unable to fathom what he was saying.

"So lovely and innocent. You look just like her, you know." A pale hand reached out, and she jumped back, avoiding his touch. He laughed and called over his shoulder. "If only you could see her, Camael! She is the spitting image of Covetina. All innocence and etherealness just waiting to be corrupted." He leaned in, his voice dropping. "Do you know why you are here?"

She shook her head and took another step back, even as he advanced on her.

"You're here because we're connected. But you already know that. While you may look like your mother, I'm afraid that is where the similarities end. You are your father's daughter. And all good girls do their father's bidding."

No, it couldn't be. She refused to believe that someone so evil had any connection to her. But somewhere deep inside, Bronwnn knew it for the truth. This . . . *creature* was her father.

Blinding hatred and rage filled her, and she turned, lunging at his throat, which was hidden by the black coat. Darkness blackened her thoughts; her only need was to kill.

She was the wolf now, and she was going to rip him to shreds.

CHAPTER ELEVEN

Keir paced the perimeter of Rhys' office, stopping to stare into the empty box on top of the desk. The torc and cuffs were gone. Cliodna, his wren, was perched on his shoulder, silent, but watching as Keir rifled through the room.

From what he could ascertain from the club staff, Rhys had not been seen for at least eighteen hours, maybe even longer. He hadn't been out on the floor last night, nor had he been present for the close of the nightclub. This morning, when Maggie, the housekeeper, went in to make his bed, she discovered that his bed had never been slept in and that the supper tray she had sent up the night before was untouched.

Struggling to calm his thoughts, Keir tried to piece together a time line. Time moved much more slowly in Annwyn, and Keir never forgot that, but he had to admit he had dallied too long with Rowan, leaving Rhys unprotected. How long had he been in Annwyn? That might tell him how long Rhys had been missing. But try as he might, he couldn't recall. He'd been too caught up in Rowan and the divination.

Fuck! Slamming shut the box, Keir picked it up and threw it against the wall. Where the hell was Rhys? Surely he would not have gone into the Cave of Cruachan. He'd been warned. Rhys knew what would happen to him in Annwyn if Cailleach discovered his presence. And the Dark Mage? Keir shuddered to think what that sadistic motherfucker would do to Rhys if he ever found him.

"I see you've managed to lose my kin."

Keir glared over his shoulder at the Sidhe king. "He's not lost."

Bran fisted his hands on his waist. "How long has he been gone?"

"I don't know. At least eighteen hours, but probably longer. I've been in Annwyn and lost track of time."

Bran's gaze was hooded when he replied. "I sensed he was gone. That's why I'm here. The mortal fool never was one to take orders."

Keir didn't particularly care to hear the king's thoughts on Rhys. Yeah, he was a stubborn ass, but he was most likely in trouble. Whatever the king felt didn't matter. Rhys was the issue here. And finding him was first priority. Rhys likely had ignored both his and Suriel's warnings. MacDonald was far from stupid, but he felt he needed to prove himself, not only to Bran and the others, but to himself.

Bran's mismatched eyes lifted to meet Keir's gaze. "Any chance he left the club and went into the city?"

"What does your gut tell you?" Keir snarled, feeling the fear well up once more.

"It's not *my* gut that's connected to him."

Keir did see red then. "It's not as if we're always in each other's heads. We do allow each other some time off."

"Can't you just search your feelings and find him?"

Keir whirled on him. "I can't get a fucking connection with him!" Punching the desk, Keir unloaded all his fury and fear into the wooden top, watching with satisfaction as the thick oak cracked down the middle. He hated telling Bran anything, but he hated showing his terror and worry even more.

Bran swallowed uncomfortably. He had never hidden his distaste for the unique bond Rhys and his wraith shared. "Has this . . . inability to connect with MacDonald happened before?"

The relationship between mortal and wraith was what it was. Rhys needed Keir's protection, and Keir needed Rhys' emotions for fuel. Normally, emotions were plenty for a wraith to live on, but as time went on, Keir found he needed *more*. It was through the passion of sex, when Rhys found release, that Keir preferred to feed. It didn't matter what the fuck the king thought of them. The only thing that mattered now was finding Rhys.

"No," he grumbled, hating talking of what they had to-gether. "Our emotional bond is strong. I can usually hear him . . . and feel him. But now I can't." Keir glared at Bran as he paced the room. "I don't know why he's not answering me."

"Maybe he's not answering you because he can't."

"He's alive. I can sense that much. But I can't tell where he is. I can't even hear any of his thoughts."

"Maybe he's unconscious?"

"The brain still sends out waves in that state. In fact, it's easier to hear him and find him when he's sleeping, because he's unguarded."

For someone who claimed to hate his great-nephew, Bran

certainly looked worried. "You warned him away from the cave as I commanded?"

"Of course."

"And the portal? It's still enchanted?"

"There's no way Rhys or any of the staff opened the door."

"Positive?"

"Rhys has zero magical abilities. He's tried, and none of his attempts have been successful."

Keir glanced at the empty box on the floor. Rhys might not have any magick inside him, but maybe the torc did. Unfortunately, Bran followed the direction of his gaze, and his expression turned murderous.

Bran looked once more at the box, then to Keir. "He's impetuous, hotheaded, stubborn, and pissed-off with being a mortal. He could only have gone one place—Annwyn."

Bronwnn came awake in Rhys' arms. The metallic taste of blood filled her mouth, and she gagged as she struggled to break free of his grasp. Her mind was reeling with the knowledge that she shared the same blood as this evil magician who was terrorizing Annwyn.

"It's okay," he murmured as he smoothed his hand over her hair. Her body was shaking violently. "You've bit your tongue. That's where the blood is coming from."

Shaking her head, she wrestled out of his hold. She had to wash. She had to get the mage's blood away from her skin. It sickened her—the taste of it and the knowledge that he was inside her.

Memories of the vision replayed in her mind. She had lunged at him, breaking the skin of his throat with her fangs. But the instant she had bitten down, the vision had ended and she was returned to her body.

"Look at me, Bronwnn," Rhys soothed. "Let me wipe your mouth."

She looked frightened and wild when she saw herself in the reflection of Rhys' eyes. What she had witnessed and heard in that vision horrified her—first what the mage's captive had said, and now this. The revelation of who she was and the understanding of her connection with the mage—it was all too much.

How she wished she could speak to Rhys and tell him what she had seen. But there was safety and comfort in her silence, and she was not yet ready to put into words what had been revealed in that black crypt of evil.

Frantically she pulled away from Rhys and reached for the quill and parchment she had used to communicate with him. *Vision. Mage. To Bran.*

Rifling his hands through his hair, Rhys glanced at the paper, then back at her. "You had a vision of the mage, and you need to get to Bran?"

She nodded, then stood, her legs unsteady. Rhys caught her and wrapped his arms around her waist. "Easy; I've got you."

Sinking into him, she turned in his arms and pressed her cheek to his chest. She had never had anyone to comfort her before, and the feeling was extraordinarily nice.

Beneath her cheek, Rhys' heart pounded in a soothing tempo. His skin was warm, his unique scent a reminder that he was hers, and that he would keep her safe. For all her existence, her safety had been her own responsibility. It had been up to her to soothe her aches and pains, to fill her loneliness and need. But now she had Rhys, and she wrapped her arms around him, holding him tight because she feared he would evaporate into the air.

Nothing was going to take her mate from her. *Nothing*.

She knew she was getting the mage's blood on him and tried to pull away, but he tightened his hold and kept her close to him. "Not yet," he whispered to her, chasing away the tremors in her body with the palm of his hand. "Let me hold you."

They stood like that for a long time, and Bronwnn allowed herself to absorb his strength. All her previous visions of the mage had left her frightened, scurrying to hide for fear he could see her. And she had been right to think that, because he had known she was there all along. He had felt her. He had seen her.

But this vision left her horrified. So much had been revealed, yet so much left unanswered. She needed answers. She needed the king, who had vowed to protect her. She didn't dare go to Cailleach, because she would have to take Rhys with her, and she knew deep down inside that Rhys was not safe from the Supreme Goddess.

"I've seen someone else have a vision while having a seizure," he whispered into her hair. "Her name is Rowan."

Instantly, Bronwnn felt envious. Who was this woman? Did she mean something to Rhys? She hoped not, for she had no wish to kill, but she would if the woman thought to take Bronwnn's mate from her.

"She's here in Annwyn, at the king's residence. I wonder if she could help."

Bronwnn wanted to be nowhere near another woman for

whom Rhys might have feelings. She knew she was being foolish to think Rhys hadn't had any previous lovers. He was far too
skilled for that. But Bronwnn hadn't thought about seeing the
women he had taken to bed, let alone being introduced to them.

Suddenly, Rhys stiffened, then pulled her away from his
chest. He was gazing down at her, but she refused to look at
him. She was filled with envy, and her mouth and chin were
covered in blood. But he forced her chin up with the tip of his
fingers.

"Did he see you in your vision?"

Reluctantly she nodded.

"Did he speak with you?"

Again, she admitted he had.

"Then is it possible that he has visions of *you*? That he can
see where you are?"

It was Bronwnn's greatest fear. Gazing up into his eyes,
she nodded.

"All right. We're leaving—now."

Bronwwn knew he was right. They had to tell Bran. Her
connection with the mage must be acknowledged. She only
hoped and prayed that Rhys would still want her after he discovered who, and what, she was.

Keir paced Bran's study just as he'd paced Rhys' office. He
couldn't sit. He couldn't focus. He'd been trying to locate Rhys'
thoughts and still couldn't.

"Sit," Bran ordered.

"I can't."

Mairi, the king's mate, came over and took his hand. Her presence did not calm him as she intended. "Why don't you go and see Rowan?"

He couldn't—not when he was unraveling like this. He might do something stupid. He wasn't thinking clearly.

A quiet voice interrupted the conversation in the room. "May I come in?" No one had noticed Rowan appear in the doorway. "I've had a vision. I think I know where Carden is."

Bran shoved back his chair and jumped up. The two warriors who flanked him followed suit. Melor was a black-haired phoenix with the ability to be reborn. Because of that, necromancy was his magick ability. To Bran's left was Drostan, a griffin shape-shifter who was also a summoner. "She's a mortal," the griffin sneered as his golden eyes narrowed on Rowan.

"And so is my queen," Bran growled.

Drostan's razor-sharp claws retracted. But his eyes were still golden and filled with fire. "And whom does this one belong to?" he asked as his lusty gaze raked over Rowan's voluptuous body.

"Me."

Drostan's gaze slowly left Rowan to fix on Keir. Keir didn't like the look in the griffin's eyes. He respected no boundaries. He took what he wanted, and he cared for nothing but his own selfish pleasures.

The griffin wisely chose to keep his mouth in check, but Keir placed a protective arm around Rowan's shoulders.

"Tell us your vision," he said softly.

Nervously she swallowed and looked at him, Mairi, and then finally Bran. "I fell asleep and awoke in a beautiful garden. At first, I thought it was a dream, but then I knew it wasn't.

It felt so real. And when I could smell the flowers, I knew it couldn't be a dream."

"And Carden?" Bran asked quietly.

"I traveled through a tunnel. There was water in it, like a little canal. It wasn't deep, only up to my knees. I didn't know where I was going, but I followed the winding path, and it ended at a bank of stone steps. There were doors, and I . . ." She trembled and stepped closer to Keir. "I knew I had been there before."

Mairi reached for her and held her hand. "It's okay, you don't have to go on."

"I think I've finally figured out the riddle," she said, her body steeling itself beside him. "'A house of mourning, a garden of pain, a path of tears.'" She stared at Bran. "It was a cemetery. And I saw a statue of a gargoyle. In his hand was a torch, which was lit—like a lamppost. But the light within it flickered, like a flame. Maybe the flame you've been looking for?"

"What is a cemetery?" Melor growled. "And why would you trust this human?"

"A cemetery is hallowed ground where mortals bury their dead," Keir snapped in reply. "And we trust this human, because she's never been wrong, and her intentions are the purest of us all—unlike your dark thoughts and past, Melor."

"Enough," Bran barked. "We will put aside our differences. Mortals and immortals alike are both affected by this prophecy. It will take all of us to discover the identity of the Dark Mage and destroy him and his apprentice. There is no room in our alliance for petty squabbles."

"Rowan," Mairi asked quietly, "have you any idea which cemetery?"

"No, but I feel most strongly that it is within the city. The surroundings definitely felt familiar to me. I need more time, though, to try to dissect the words, and to have more visions. Maybe I will see something familiar, such as the name of a church or something attached to the cemetery. I will keep trying. I know this riddle and my visions are the only clues to Carden's whereabouts."

"Thank you," Bran said. "Your help in this is crucial."

She nodded and, for the first time, Keir felt her fatigue as she pressed into him. He held her up with his arm, his heart feeling heavy. She looked exhausted, and there were dark circles beneath her eyes.

"You had a vision because of a headache, didn't you?"

She nodded, her face flushing. She was looking at Drostan and Melor, and Keir knew she wanted her illness kept private.

"Rest," Bran ordered her. "There is still time to find my brother. I would not have you exhaust yourself."

Mairi was reaching for her friend when Cliodna flew into the study and landed on Keir's shoulder. She began to sing in a high-pitched song that sounded a little frantic.

"What is it, friend?" he asked.

Her tiny wings were flapping furiously, and he picked her up, holding her in his palm. His little wren wanted him to see something.

Keir had always preferred to practice his magick alone. But when Rowan entered his life, he had been forced to perform his divination magick before her and Sayer. He still didn't like it, but he was becoming used to it. After the divination spell with Rowan, he felt slightly more at ease to do magick before others.

Letting his mind still, he focused on the bird's black eyes.

Beside him, he felt Rowan's body pressing into him. Normally, it would have been a distraction, but this time it felt good to have her with him.

His vision narrowed, and his body became lighter as he focused on the bird. Then suddenly his spirit was lifted, and he was transported to another place.

Keir found himself standing before a ramshackle cottage in the midst of a thick forest. Firelight flickered from behind the filthy window. Inside, he felt Rhys and heard his thoughts. The mortal was edgy, fear tainting his thinking. Keir tasted that fear on his tongue.

The wren flew before him, and his concentration broke. The divination was over, and his spirit was once more reunited with his body.

When his vision returned, he saw seven faces staring expectantly at him. "I know where Rhys is."

Rhys knew he wasn't crazy. He'd seen enough magical, unexplainable shit in his lifetime to understand and believe that the Dark Mage could very well find Bronwnn through her vision.

He had to get her out of there, before the bastard found her. Both of them had suffered run-ins with the murderer. But it was Bronwnn he worried over. She was pale and shaking. His capable goddess was terrified.

"We're leaving—*now*."

She didn't try to stop him. Instead, she ran to the table and wiped her face with a damp cloth, then pulled a white gown from the bag she had brought. She slipped it over her head, and, as the garment's fabric slid downward, Rhys watched as it hugged her curves. The long hem slid over her thighs, covering the blue line of the tattoo.

He had touched her there, seconds before she had gone into her trance. That tattoo, he thought, was not simply a tattoo, but a portal of some sort. She saw that he was looking there, and she hurriedly covered her thigh.

"That's how you had the vision, isn't it? I touched you there."

She nodded, then glanced away from him.

"How does the connection work?"

Shrugging, she avoided his gaze and packed up the bottles and jars into her bag. Then she pointed to the door.

Fine. They would leave, but this conversation definitely wasn't over.

Reaching for the door, he inched it open and peered into the darkness. Trees surrounded them, and the first rays of dawn were too weak to penetrate through the tall trunks and thick canopy of leaves.

He listened for a second, then proceeded to take a step. He was blocked by a massive chest.

"Going somewhere?"

His heart stopped, then immediately started firing again when he looked up to find Bran, the king of the Sidhe, glaring down at him.

Keir was behind him. So were Sayer and two other men Rhys had never met. Gazing out over the gathered crowd, he saw Rowan and Mairi at the back of the pack, their eyes wide and their cheeks pink. *Shit!* Instantly, he placed his hands over his genitals.

"Drostan," Bran commanded. "Summon a pair of pants for our friend. He seems to have misplaced his."

The blond-haired warrior stepped forward and looked at him from head to toe with a distasteful grimace. "My summoning magick is for greater things than this. Besides, he's a mor—"

"Do it," Bran snapped.

Rhys found his lower body encased in black leather. Personally, he was a jeans type of guy, but leather would do for now. He nodded his thanks to the warrior, who continued to look at him with disgust.

"What took you so long?" he asked Keir. "I've been searching for you for days."

"I couldn't hear you."

Keir had his arm around Rowan. No wonder Keir hadn't heard him. He'd probably been too busy listening to Rowan's sighs of pleasure.

Reaching for Bronwnn's hand, Rhys pulled her out from behind him and heard Keir gasp. Rhys knew the wraith had seen her in Rhys' dreams. Their gazes met, confirming what Rhys suspected. "*We'll talk later,*" they mentally conveyed between them.

"We need to leave this place," he announced as he stepped out into the night with Bronwnn in tow.

"You may both come back to the castle." Bran's gaze drifted over Rhys' chest. "But what has happened?"

"The Dark Mage," Rhys said. "We have information about him, but not here. This place isn't secure."

"Then let us be off."

"Not so quickly, Raven."

Rhys whirled around as the woman's voice came from

the forest. Behind him, Bronwnn clutched his forearm. Then, a woman wearing a long white gown and a white robe stepped out from between two trees. Her golden blond hair hung to her waist. She looked like a medieval princess as she glided over to them.

He knew who she was the minute her gaze turned upon him.

"Rhys MacDonald, descendant of Daegan, you are not welcome in Annwyn."

Keir stepped between them, and Cailleach glared at him. "Your bond has no power here, Shadow Wraith. The mortal is mine."

Rhys heard Bronwnn gasp at the same time she squeezed his hand. He squeezed back, letting her know everything was going to be okay.

"Rhys MacDonald, your life is forfeit, the punishment for trespassing in Annwyn."

"Cailleach, you will stay where you are," Bran commanded.

"Alas, your orders do not pertain to me, Raven. This is my curse, and I will deal with it as I wish."

Keir stepped between them again, and the goddess raised her hand. "I could kill you, wraith."

"I am prepared to die for him."

"But not in Annwyn. Not this night. You are needed elsewhere, and so you will turn back and leave us be."

Keir started to say something, but Cailleach pressed past him. He reached for her, but she sent him a lethal glare, then fixed her gaze upon Rowan. "Is he the only one you would die for, wraith?"

Rhys sensed Keir's shock as well as the pain and rage that

lanced through him. If he was fully prepared to sacrifice himself for Rhys, he was a thousand times more determined to protect Rowan from Cailleach.

"Leave us," she commanded the small group. "He is mine." She turned on Rhys and raised her hands, which started to glow. Rhys wondered how bad her zap of light was going to feel as it pierced his body.

"Now, Rhys MacDonald, you will die for entering Annwyn."

There was a deep growl behind him, and then his wolf lunged at Cailleach, landing at her feet. It snarled and snapped, and the blue ink on the left hind paw glimmered in the moonlight. Rhys knew then he was looking at his goddess.

"Bronwnn, no!"

Cailleach narrowed her eyes, hatred shining in them. "You've been hiding things, I see," she said to the wolf.

Cailleach raised her arm and pointed her fingers at him, but the wolf lunged, snapping at the goddess once more.

"You fool," she taunted. "You do not know what you're doing."

The wolf—Bronwnn—circled the goddess, growling low in her throat. Cailleach watched her warily; then her gaze widened, as if she had just realized something important.

"Do you think this man is your mate?"

The wolf growled, then glanced over her shoulder at Rhys, then back at Cailleach, who was beginning to laugh as she glanced between Keir and Rhys.

"Stupid girl, your protection is ill placed."

Bronwnn—the wolf—snapped at Cailleach, whose face turned dark with anger.

"You think he is the wraith. But you have no clue, do you?" Cailleach replied, her voice dripping venom. "He is nothing but a mortal, cursed by my own spell."

The questioning glance in the wolf's eyes made Rhys step forward. There was hurt in those blue eyes—and pain. Had she not realized who he was? Bronwnn swung her head in Keir's direction and sniffed the air; then her gaze fixed on each man, all except the king, and Cailleach laughed.

"Silly little fool," she snapped. "You've given yourself to the wrong man. You've defiled yourself for a lowly mortal."

Suddenly the wolf vanished, replaced by a naked, kneeling Bronwnn. Rhys ran to her, but Bronwnn held out her arm, halting him. And a piece of him shriveled up. Did she no longer want him because of his mortality? Who—or what—had she believed him to be?

Her bowed head slowly lifted to look into Cailleach's chilly eyes. "Supreme Goddess," Bronwnn murmured, her voice lilting and beautiful—a sound that would haunt him forever. "I wish to offer you an *adbertos*."

CHAPTER TWELVE

Bronwnn waited anxiously for a response from Cailleach. She could feel the curious stares on her back, but mostly she felt the hard glare of Rhys, whose anger clouded the air. She could almost taste it as it wrapped around her.

Closing her eyes, she fought back the tears that had started to form. He was a mortal, not a wraith. He was not her mate, yet she had dreamed of him . . .

Cailleach circled her, and Bronwnn fought the urge to feel shame and humiliation. She had given herself to Rhys because of her dreams. Because inside herself she had felt Rhys was her mate. Why she had dreamed of Rhys and not the wraith, she didn't understand. But it did answer the puzzling question about his scent. It was a mortal's scent. And it covered her own flesh like a blanket. She never wanted to be washed of it. Yet she knew the connection they shared was at an end. Her fate was tied to the wraith—not to a mortal.

"You've broken your vow of silence," Cailleach uttered in a cold voice. "You must have great feelings for this pitiful creature to come to his defense and to break a vow you have held for so long."

"I can defend myself," Rhys snapped, and Bronwnn glared at him. Cailleach was already livid. Rhys' insolence would only enrage her further.

"What is it you'll sacrifice to me for this mortal's life?"

"May we please have this discussion in private?" she whispered. What she had to say, she did not want Rhys to hear. She did not want to see him, because if she did, she might no longer possess the will to do what needed to be done. She would save him at any cost, because he had become her ideal. In her heart, he was more than a lover. The past two nights had been more than sexual pleasure. In her soul, he was her mate. And a woman did not allow her *leathean* to be slaughtered by a vengeful goddess. She could resign herself to living without him, as long as she knew that Rhys was alive, and living in his world.

Cailleach paused to stand over her. "All right, then. I will grant you your request. We shall speak of this in private."

"If you touch one damned hair on her head," said Rhys as he took a few steps forward, "I will not tell you, or your nine warriors, what I know of the Dark Mage. And after my run-in with him, I know a lot more than anyone else."

Cailleach whirled around then, her rage palpable as it radiated through the air. "Who do you think you are?"

"The great-great-grandson of Daegan MacDonald."

"You have none of his powers. You're a pathetic mortal, and no match for me, or anyone in Annwyn."

"You once thought Isobel MacDonald was no match for you, either. But her love for Daegan proved you wrong."

The goddess did seethe then. "Your arrogance will be your undoing," Cailleach stormed.

"My pride is the only thing that kept me alive while I was suffering under the mage. My mortal soul and drive prevented me from becoming his next victim. Humans, Cailleach, are different from you, but we are not inferior."

"Rodents, all of you," she snapped. "I have the power to crush you with the flick of my hand. Do not tempt me to use that power."

"But then you won't know what I saw. And thinking you can torture the information out of Bronwnn would be a mistake, because I've not burdened her with my ordeal. I am the only one who knows, Cailleach. And I can be just as stubborn as you."

"You will share what you know, or you will die, mortal."

Rhys stood tall, his chest filling with indignation. "I'm not afraid of death. If my destiny is to die with dignity while standing up to you, then so be it."

"There will be no dignity in your death," Cailleach taunted. "How well do you think you would hold up against my torture?"

"No!" Bronwnn launched herself toward Cailleach, falling to the goddess' feet. "I will do whatever you want, Supreme Goddess. Anything. Just . . . spare him."

"Don't," Rhys beseeched her as he gave her his hand to help her up. "Don't do this. I can handle whatever she tries to do. You don't have to lower yourself before her for me."

Shaking her head, she tried to convince Rhys to let her be. He didn't understand Cailleach's powers. He could have no way of knowing how powerful her magick was—or how she never backed down from a challenge. "I know what I'm doing," she whispered. "Let me save you."

"Not if it means you'll be taken from me. No. I'll face her."

"Raven," Cailleach commanded, her expression as dark as the clouds that now covered Annwyn. "Take your warriors and this mortal back to your realm. I will speak with you later."

"The hell you'll order me around like I'm a fucking kid," Rhys snarled, his fingers curling into fists.

With a blinding flash of white, Rhys was gone, and Bronwnn's scream echoed through the forest.

Within the blink of an eye, Rhys was thrust forward, landing on his ass inside a castle. *Fucking magick.*

He really hated it, especially when he had none of it.

"Rise and look upon me."

Bronwnn did as she was told. With a wave of her hand, Cailleach draped Bronwnn's nakedness in a drab gray gown. She was no longer virginal, no longer fit to wear white. She had forgotten that she was naked all that time, but the look of disgust in Cailleach's gaze reminded her of her shameful conduct before Rhys and the others. A goddess was to be serene at all times. She had acted like a virago—and a wanton. She should be ashamed, but Bronwnn felt only relief that Rhys was safe—for now.

"Your mother was forced to wear this color also—gray for impurity."

Her poor mother had been corrupted by the vilest creature in existence. It was not her mother's fault that she had been seduced. Surely the impurity was only one-sided.

"Whatever possessed you to share your body with him,"

Cailleach demanded, "when I told you that you were to be mated with the Shadow Wraith?"

Bronwnn looked Cailleach directly in the eye, holding her stare. She could not be meek and mild now. Rhys' life was still in danger, and she was the only person who could save him.

"I have dreamed of him for many weeks now. When I saw him in Annwyn by the reflecting pool, I naturally assumed he was my mate. He . . . smelled of wraith," she whispered. "He was very badly injured, and . . ."

"He smelled of wraith," Cailleach sneered, "because he is part of my curse. He is the great-great-grandson of Daegan, and when he was banished from Annywn to live his life with his mortal lover, I cursed the firstborn son of their union, and every firstborn after that. It was my desire that no bastard halfling be allowed to come back and claim the throne of the Sidhe. No mortal would ever corule Annwyn. But Daegan had just enough magick left in him to perform one last spell, and that was to give each firstborn male a Shadow Wraith for protection. None of the others have ever dared venture into Annwyn, until this stupid mortal."

"He's not stupid," Bronwnn snapped. "He's very brave and strong. Stronger than many warriors I have seen in the temple."

Cailleach glared at her. "Mortals are the very essence of evil. They strive to overtake everything—to rule that which is not theirs. I will not tolerate his presence here."

Bronwnn studied the goddess. "It is his wraith that you intended to bind me to, isn't it?"

"Of course. Keir is special. I've sensed that from the beginning. He is more magically gifted than any wraith I have ever known. With his powers combined with yours, a great alliance will be forged."

Rhys would not tolerate that. He would not allow her to go to the wraith. She sensed his possession, still feeling it as she remembered the way he held her, claiming her body with his. "If I am to mate with the wraith, then why did I dream of Rhys? Why did I sense him as my mate when he is not magical, or immortal?" she wondered aloud.

Cailleach looked outraged. "The mortal is nothing to you any longer. The wraith will still have you—I'm sure of it. And you will take him. There is no question about that. Now—your powers." Cailleach narrowed her eyes. "You are the only goddess shifter in our history. Tell me about your powers and when you received them."

"I won't until you agree to my *adbertos*."

Cailleach's eyes turned frosty. "How dare you!"

"I'm not afraid to die, either, Cailleach. And you should know that I have further knowledge of the mage, and powers that far surpass those of any of the other warriors. You need me in this fight. And I will not fight for you until you agree."

"You will not mate with *him*."

She knew that. She knew Cailleach's wrath and vengeance would not allow her to go that far. Pride resided where her heart should. Lifting her chin, Bronwnn steadied her bounding heart.

"In exchange for sparing Rhys MacDonald's life, I will mate the wraith, forging the alliance that you so desire, and I will aid the king and his warriors in any way I can. But . . . you must allow me to say good-bye to him. And you must promise never to do him—or his children—any harm."

Cailleach's nostrils flared with indignation. "And if I don't agree?"

"I will run where you cannot find me—*ever*."

"There is nowhere in Annwyn that I cannot discover you."

"I will make Rhys take me to the mortal realm."

That made the goddess seethe. She was bound to Annwyn. She could not leave this world. "You ungrateful little bitch! After everything I've done for you after—" She started for her, then stopped, her eyes widening in fear. What she saw looking back at her, Bronwnn had no idea, but suddenly the anger went out of the goddess, and weary reluctance replaced it. "Very well," Cailleach murmured. "I accept your *adbertos*. You may return with me to the king's court, and there you may say good riddance to the mortal."

"Settle your feathers," Keir demanded. Angrily Rhys flung the wraith's hands off his shoulders and prowled the length of Bran's study.

"Don't tell me to be calm. That bitch could be killing her."

"Cailleach needs this particular goddess, MacDonald." Bran sighed. "She isn't going to kill her."

"This is bullshit," Rhys barked. His frustration and fear for Bronwnn were escalating. "She's out there alone with that— that witch."

"Bronwnn is the Supreme Goddess' handmaiden," Bran reminded him. "She will know how to manage Cailleach's moods."

Rhys stopped his pacing and glared at them. "What the hell is an *adbertos*?" Bran and Keir shared a hooded glance. "I've never heard the word."

"That is because it was never allowed to be spoken. Daegan forbade it."

Then it must be bad news, Rhys thought. Great. What else was happening that he didn't have a fucking clue about?

"An *adbertos* is a sacrifice," Keir explained. "It is not something to be done lightly."

"No," he said, shaking his head. "No way." What the hell had Bronwnn been thinking? What was she sacrificing? Herself? Oh, hell no! He'd haul his mortal ass before the Supreme Goddess and kill himself before he allowed Bronwnn to do such a thing.

"You had better get yourself under control, MacDonald, before Cailleach arrives," Bran ordered. "Your life expectancy is getting perilously shorter, and this mood of yours will not ingratiate you with the goddess."

"Nothing could, because I'm Daegan's descendant. She already hates me."

"When one lives as long as a goddess does, revenge always comes at last."

Rhys whirled around to find Cailleach standing beside Bronwnn, who was dressed in a hideous gray gown. Their gazes met, and she glanced down, away from him. He wanted to go to her; to ask what had happened; to see if she was okay. But Keir stood beside him, blocking his way.

"My handmaiden has offered me an *adbertos*, which I have accepted. As her wish is to speak with the mortal in private, we will first talk of the mage, and what you know. Then, you may speak to my handmaiden. Do you agree, mortal?"

Bran shot him a glare, and so did Keir. He was raging inside and only wanted to take Bronwnn aside and ask her what the hell she had offered the witch.

"Do you agree, Rhys MacDonald?" Cailleach asked.

"Yes." But he ignored her look of warning when he strode over to his mate and hauled her into his side.

"Are you all right?" he whispered. She trembled but looked up at him and nodded.

"Now then, you have seen the mage," Cailleach prompted.

Rhys dragged his gaze away from Bronwnn's face, which suddenly looked so sad. "I have. He dwells beneath Velvet Haven, in the Cave of Cruachan."

Everyone in the room sucked in a simultaneous breath. "And how the hell did you find your way into the cave?" Bran demanded.

Rhys stole a look at Keir. "Cliodna brought me to the door. Keir went through, and I followed."

"That fucking bird," Sayer snarled.

"Watch your mouth," both Bran and Keir demanded. Then Keir spoke to him. "I thought you were still in your study. I didn't feel you behind me." Keir's gaze then found Rowan, who was seated by the fire. "I've been distracted lately."

Rhys took pity on his wraith. "*Later,*" he mentally told him. "*I'm alive, and there're no hard feelings.*" Keir's eyes met his, but Rhys saw there was a new darkness in them. His wraith was consumed with Rowan and her impending death. Nothing could penetrate that wall, not even Rhys.

"And then what?" Cailleach demanded as she took an empty chair beside Bran. Rhys looked away from Keir and settled his gaze upon Cailleach.

"When I was young, Daegan told me stories of Annwyn, and how, if I were to ever find myself there, I should head directly to the reflecting pool where your powers do not immediately reach. He said the reflection of the water acts as a shield and temporarily weakens you."

Cailleach's expression turned murderous, but Rhys carried on, not particularly caring if he was spilling the goddess' weaknesses to everyone in the room.

"He told me how to get to the veil and how to find the pool. So, when I went into the cave and didn't see Keir, I followed the lit corridor to Annwyn. But then, I was stopped."

As if by magic, the adder suddenly slithered beneath the oak door and snaked its way into the middle of the room. Everyone quieted as the beady black eyes fixed on Rhys.

"You know this animal?" Keir asked wonderingly.

"I do. He stopped me in the corridor. It allowed the mage to hit me over the head and drag me to his underground crypt."

"Kill it," Mairi squealed as she jumped onto a chair. "Oh my God, it's huge. Bran!" she shouted as the snake started to sway.

"Muirnin," Bran murmured as he took his queen into his arms. "The adder is a sacred animal. It represents wisdom and reincarnation."

"I don't care if it marks the coming of God! Someone get rid of it."

Rhys bent to his knees, and the snake slithered over to him, climbed up the length of his arm, and wrapped around his bicep. When he glanced up, Keir's eyes were as big as saucers, and Cailleach was now standing. Only Rowan and Mairi looked alarmed. Bronwnn, he noted, was smiling. He had a way with animals—always had. Like with the snake, and now his wolf as well.

"The snake is a representative of sin and evil throughout the mortal realm. It is a symbol of the fallen angel Lucifer."

Rhys nodded, acknowledging Cailleach's claim. "I thought so, too. The mage even called him Lucifer."

"There are two worlds here," Cailleach reminded them all. "Two very different doctrines. The mortal is fortunate this particular snake was an ally."

"Or an agent of the mage," Sayer stated from his spot in the corner of the room. Rhys had barely noted the Selkie's presence. But as always, Sayer lurked in the corners, observing.

"How did you escape?" Bran asked quietly.

"The mage fed me a drug and tied me to a slab. I was hallucinating, and he was performing some rite on me. Behind him, there was a woman tied up. And beyond her, in the darkness, was another—a man—although I never saw him. But the mage spoke with him, and he answered back."

"And the woman?" Bran asked. "What did she look like?"

"Blond. Mortal, I believe. I can't tell you more. By this time, I was nearly unconscious, and I was losing blood." Rhys swallowed hard. "He gave me too much of the drug, and I remember that he left me. He wanted me awake. Wanted my screams. When he left me, he went to her."

Bronwnn pressed into his side, and he took comfort in her embrace. While he wasn't a suck ass, he was haunted by that woman's scream and his inability to help her. "He ... ah ..."

"Performed sex magick," Keir supplied, "and you heard it." "Yeah."

"And she was killed."

Rhys pressed his eyes shut. "Yes."

Cailleach's gaze flickered to the snake, then to him. "What significance does this animal have for you?"

"It released me from my bonds and showed me the way out of the cave. When I went through the veil, it was the adder that led me to the pool."

Cailleach glanced at Bran, then back to him. "An animal ally."

"There is no denying the snake saved my life."

"You are a shaman," Keir said to him, "as am I."

Rhys shook his head. "No. I merely knew from Daegan's stories that animals could befriend a person."

"The adder has seen something in you," Bran provided. "And to be chosen by the most sacred of animals is something to be revered. It cannot be ignored."

Rhys gazed down at the adder wrapped around his arm. It was now sleeping. Never in his life had he dreamed that he'd have a reptile twined around his arm, but there it was.

Suddenly, the scales began glistening an iridescent pink, then gold, then finally silver. When the glistening was gone, a silver amulet in the shape of the snake was wrapped around his arm.

Cailleach walked to him then. "You have shed something in favor of something greater. The adder is yours now. Your guide. Your protector."

Rhys looked deep into her pale green eyes. "He doesn't do me any good in the mortal realm."

She refused to look at him. "Raven, you will keep the mortal here, in your castle."

"A prisoner?" Rhys challenged.

"Yes," she murmured as she looked up at him. "For now."

The goddess evaporated, and Rhys was left with all eyes directed at him.

"What I don't understand," Bran said, "is why only you were targeted. All of us have walked through that cave and have never seen or heard anything. Certainly we have never been attacked."

"He wanted me."

Keir's gaze met his, and instant understanding lit up his eyes. "*He* knew you would ignore Suriel and my warning. *He* sent Suriel to provoke you. It was your destiny all along."

Rhys nodded. He had much time to think of things while he had waited for Bronwnn to return to him. In that time, he reflected on everything that had happened and had reluctantly come to the conclusion that God wanted him in this fight, even though he was only a lowly mortal.

"Suriel asked me if I had faith, and I told him I did. I believed that I was intended to go. And I did. The mage was waiting for me, because he wanted my soul for his magick, but, more importantly, he wanted my body. He was going to use it to infiltrate the nine warriors. You would believe it was me, and the mage would have access to all your plans. That is why I escaped and could not save the woman. I was close to death and not strong enough to save both of us. So I saved myself, because in the end, it was saving all of you."

Bronwnn hugged him, and he allowed himself to absorb her warmth. He wasn't proud of what he had done. He felt like a damned coward.

"The adder came to you because you are worthy," Keir said to him. "His wisdom is now your wisdom, and what you have seen will aid us more than a month of reconnaissance work ever could."

"I can't tell you more than that. He lives beneath the corridor to Annwyn. When you leave Velvet Haven, it is the cavern to the left. That's all I saw."

"There is a man there, chained," Bronwnn murmured. "I saw him."

Bran waved in her direction as he spoke to everyone in the room. "This goddess is a seer. She is the writer of the prophecy."

Bronwnn finally lifted her face from Rhys' chest and looked upon those who stood before her. When her lashes lifted, revealing her fully, Rowan and Mairi gasped.

"What is it?" Rhys asked as Bronwnn stiffened beside him.

"Look," Keir whispered as he helped Rowan to stand. She came forward, out of the shadows and into the candlelight.

It was Bronwnn's turn to gasp. It wasn't possible. In this light, she and Rowan looked remarkably alike. Why had he never noticed it before?

"How can this be?" Bronwnn asked. "You are a mortal woman."

Rowan looked to Keir. "My journey," she reminded him. "Do you recall what the man said to me?"

Keir nodded, repeating the lines. "'The key to the Sacred Trine,'" he said to her. "'Two born of the same womb, but not of the same man. Keep this knowledge safe.'"

"'Born of the same womb,'" Rowan whispered.

Bronwnn's beautiful blue eyes turned a turbulent shade of gray. "'But not of the same man.'"

CHAPTER THIRTEEN

"What is this about a journey?" Bran barked.

"A divination," Keir replied as he reached for Rowan's hand. "We were searching for Carden and discovered something far different."

"What precisely was that?" Sayer asked, suspicion in his voice as he looked between both Rowan and Keir. "And when was that?"

"When? None of your damned business. What did we discover? An angel with a tattooed face who spoke of a Sacred Trine."

Bronwnn was immediately shocked. This woman, this *mortal* woman, had seen the same man she had? They were connected. *Sisters?* "I have seen the same angel in a divination. He is being held captive by the mage. He is bound by chains and begs us to release him. He will join us if we do."

"An angel?" Keir questioned her. "Are you certain?"

Rowan and Bronwnn both held out their hands, showing the symbol they had each drawn on their palms. It was remarkable how they were so connected, two people from two different realms.

"But whose symbol is it? It's not the one on the wall that was left at the site of Trinity's murder," Bran growled.

"We're at a roadblock if we can't locate Suriel. From what I understand, he's gone back into hiding. Convenient excuse, if you ask me," Keir grumbled.

"Where the hell is he?" Bran thundered. "Damn it, that angel is trying my patience."

"The fallen are never dutiful, or trustworthy," Rhys reminded the king, who glared at him in response.

"Suriel," Bran roared, his voice echoing off the ceiling. "Show yourself."

"My love, I hardly think he'll hear you."

"Mairi, your *friend* is probably hovering about the door as we speak."

As if to prove the king's point, a deep voiced drawled, "You called?" It was followed by a flash of light, and the magnificent sight of black feathers, which furled back to reveal a leather-clad Suriel. "Although I prefer e-mail to crow song."

The king glared at the angel. "Where have you been?"

"Oh, just here and there. I do have a boss to answer to, you know."

"Like hell," Bran thundered. "Your boss cast your ass out, and now I'm the only one you have."

Suriel glared at Bran. Gone was the ease, replaced by a tightly held anger. Then his gaze searched the room until he found the king's mate. "Hello, Mairi."

She smiled and went to him, hugging him tightly.

"How is my *Anam Cara*?"

Bran growled low in his throat. He hated to be reminded that Suriel and Mairi shared a sacred bond.

"I'm fine, Suriel. But I think you're provoking my husband."

Suriel released her. "For you, then. Now, what is it you want from me? I'm supposed to be avoiding Gabriel."

"There," Bran commanded as he pointed to Rowan's and Bronwnn's hands. "Tell us the meaning of that symbol."

Suriel glanced at their palms, his face tight.

"Camael," he whispered. "He's alive, then, is he? I thought him long gone."

"Who is Camael?" Bran demanded. "Bloody hell, this grows more vexing and confusing."

"Does Cailleach know?" Suriel asked her, ignoring the Sidhe king's glare. Bronwnn nodded, making the fallen angel smile. "She won't like that."

"Who or what is Camael?" Bran thundered.

"Camael is an angel of murky associations. He was an archangel, an angel of war, but more notable for his obsession with God's new creation. It was he who told us of the delights to be found in the flesh. When I followed him from heaven, I expected to be taken to Earth, but then I discovered he had been frolicking in Annwyn with a goddess named Covetina."

Covetina had been her mother. Had she also been Rowan's?

"How did you get in?" Bran demanded.

"Cailleach let us in. Camael, Uriel, and me."

Bronwnn couldn't believe her ears. The Supreme Goddess? The angel's dark eyes turned to her, his eyes lit with mirth. "Cailleach fancied Camael, but he had eyes only for her handmaiden, Covetina." Suriel looked at the woman named Rowan. "You have his eyes, that lovely jade color."

Rowan collapsed against the Shadow Wraith. "That's not possible. My mother left me at Our Lady of Mercy and in the care of the nuns. I never knew my father. She was just an ordinary woman . . ."

Bran cleared his throat and placed an object wrapped in white silk on the wooden table. "When Sayer, Keir, and I went to your store a few weeks ago, Sayer enchanted you so that I could discover information about Mairi."

"Bran!" Mairi gave him a slap.

"Just precautions, *muirnin*," he murmured. Then he focused his attention back to Rowan. "While Sayer was asking you questions, I came upon this."

Opening the silk, he revealed an ornate athame encrusted with gems, including a large moonstone, the gem that represented the order of goddesses. On the blade was angelic script.

"You told us the nuns found this in your bag. It was the only thing of any value."

"It's just a blade."

"No," Bronwnn murmured, "it is not. It is a sacred ritual tool used in the Shrouding ceremony of a goddess and her mate."

"That's angelic script." Suriel pointed to the engraving. "And I see Camael's sign on the etching."

Rowan's eyes were big and wide as she looked at Bronwnn. "We're sisters?"

Bronwnn nodded, feeling happy to have found a sibling, but desolate, too, because the angel in question was not her father. The evil mage was. Obviously Rowan had been created out of love, and she had been conceived in darkness.

Awkwardly, Rowan embraced her. Bronwnn immediately felt her beauty, the purity of her spirit. "*Nephillim*," the word whispered to her. Her sister was part of the Sacred Trine. Did she know it? Did the others?

Pulling away, Bronwnn smiled at her sister. "You're not mortal at all, but angel and goddess."

Rowan blushed and looked over her shoulder. "I can't believe it."

"I can," Keir murmured.

"We must act soon," Bronwnn announced. "In my divination, the mage has seen me. We've spoken. When I see him, he can see me. But we have an advantage. When I see him, it's in the present. I know what he's doing, what he's planning."

"How?" Suriel questioned, his suspicion aroused. She wasn't ready to divulge that. First she wanted to tell Rhys, and then she would let the others know.

"I have my ways."

"Everyone is an open book here, Goddess."

"You shut your mouth, Suriel," Rhys snapped. "Leave her alone."

"Or what, flesh bag?" Suriel taunted.

"Enough!" Bran barked. Everyone stopped bickering and looked to the leader of the group.

"It's late, and Rhys and Bronwnn are exhausted. Nothing more can be done tonight. I suggest we digest what we've learned and convene here tomorrow morning. Wraith, take Rhys to the east wing. Mairi, show Bronwnn to her room, please."

"We're not being separated," Rhys snarled.

"It's not my decision, but Cailleach's." Bran's gaze traveled over her. "I have to honor the *adbertos* and Cailleach's will."

Bronwnn was tugged out of Rhys' arms, but not before he whispered into her ear, "I will find you. Expect me tonight."

Goose bumps covered her body. One more night with Rhys was all she asked for. She would give him her heart and soul and all the pleasure she could pour into one night.

"I'll be waiting," she whispered back.

The gray vapor poured down from the top of the door. Rhys watched it, mesmerized by its swirling, writhing elegance as it spilled over the dark wood and onto the floor.

The wraith was here at last.

Shadow followed the vapor, then swirled with it, becoming Keir. He stood before Rhys, glaring down at him. "I ought to choke the life out of you for that stunt you pulled."

Rhys stood and met the wraith, eye to eye. "You can't blame me. You were popping in and out of Velvet Haven, coming and going in wraith form. It wasn't like you, so naturally it got me wondering—and worried."

"You didn't have to worry."

"No?" Rhys demanded. "Then why did I feel your thoughts? Your anger, and fear. It was building, and you wouldn't let me in."

Keir glanced away. "It's nothing you needed to know."

"Well, that hurts," he snapped. "I'm an open fucking book, and you get to pick and choose what you want me to know? After all this time, Keir?"

He glanced back over his shoulder. "I've been distracted."

"By magick?"

Keir shrugged. "By the cards, by spells, by Rowan and her impending death. By a fucking dream in the night where I hear a woman pleading for mercy."

"You're still having that dream?" Rhys asked. "Is it Rowan?"

"I don't know." Keir dragged his fingers through his hair. "I think so. She's dying, and in pain, and she's begging for someone to end it."

Rhys reached out and touched Keir on the shoulder. They hadn't really talked since that night they took the woman in the club. They certainly hadn't touched. Theirs was a complicated relationship. They had a tight bond, kind of like twins. But twins didn't share what they did, and that was what confused things. They weren't lovers, and they weren't brothers. They were more than friends, but they were different species.

"Don't try to figure it out," Keir warned. "It'll give you a fucking migraine."

Rhys smiled. "I already have one."

Keir snorted and made his way to the window. Gazing outside, Rhys saw the wraith's eyes stray to the end of the castle where Rowan lived. He knew better than to ask him how she was.

"How are you?" Rhys asked instead.

"Pissed."

"Because you can't save her?"

Keir nodded, then raised his arm against the stone sill. His gaze never strayed from Rowan's room. "She's going to die, and there is nothing my immortal soul or magick can do to change it."

"But she's a goddess and an angel. How can she die? She's not mortal."

Keir whirled around, his eyes flashing with anger. "I don't know what she truly is. I don't know if she's immortal. I know only she's dying and I can feel her slipping away, and feeling that is killing me. It's making me fractured. I'm not doing right by you because I can't see past my pain for her. I'm fucking up all over, and letting you slip into Annwyn proves just how much."

Rhys strode over to Keir and hugged him gruffly. "You know I'll be there for you when the time comes. You know that. I'll help you through it." Keir struggled against him, but Rhys held him tighter. "I don't know what this prophecy means. I don't know what the future holds for any of us, but there is one thing you can count on, wraith, and that's me by your side, bugging your ass. For as long as I live."

Nodding, Keir pulled away from him. "I'm sorry," he said on a deep breath. "This is all my fault. If I had told you, none of this would have happened."

Rhys knew and felt they were no longer talking about Rowan, or about his stupid trek into the cave. "You saw her, didn't you? You knew she was going to be your mate."

Keir moved away, putting more than a physical distance between them. "I did. I saw Bronwnn in the cards. Cailleach wants us together because we are both practitioners of divination. She believes we will enhance each other's gifts."

"But you knew I was dreaming of her."

"I did. At first I thought it was because of my thoughts. But then I began to learn of your desire for her."

"And you didn't say anything because you wanted to spare my sorry ass?"

"No," Keir growled. "Because I thought I could wait

until . . . after Rowan was gone. I can't . . . I couldn't be with the goddess before that. Even knowing it was Cailleach's wish, I knew I couldn't obey. Not until . . ." He swallowed and dropped the thought. "After, I planned to share her—with you. I thought it would work until"—Keir met his gaze—"until I realized you felt more for her than desire."

Rhys felt his body stiffen. The thought of Keir with Bronwnn made him crazed. The thought of sharing her . . . He couldn't even go there.

"I won't take her from you, Rhys, I promise. She isn't my mate."

Suddenly, Keir was at the door, holding it open. "We're wasting time. Cailleach's *oidhche* will be here in a matter of hours, checking on you. Go," Keir ordered.

"Cailleach will kill you if she discovers your deception."

Keir shrugged. "I'm halfway there."

Rhys sent him a hard glare. "No, you're not. And I won't let anything happen to you. Got it?"

Keir nodded, but Rhys realized, too late, that the wraith wasn't looking him in his eye. For the second time in their long association, Rhys could not hear or feel what the wraith was thinking.

The ugly gray chemise tore easily in Rhys' hands, and, without thought or guilt, he ripped it up the center, revealing Bronwnn's pale body in the moonlight. Breasts, round and full, rose and fell with deep breaths as she stirred in her sleep. Hungrily his gaze raked over her voluptuous curves, drinking in everything he had longed to see. There was enough moonlight to illuminate her body and the V between her thighs as she spread them for him. She was wet, glistening, and he wanted to taste her; to finger her.

Cupping her breast, he stroked her nipple, watching as it puckered beneath his thumb. Already aroused, he felt himself swell further, and to relieve some of the ache in his groin, he brushed his cock along her milky white thigh. None of his suffering was abated, however, and he stroked himself along her smooth skin over and over, watching the tantalizing visual of his cock rubbing her leg.

God, he wanted her. She was his, regardless of whatever she had offered Cailleach. They were fated to be together.

She stirred and sighed huskily, still slumbering dreamily while he fondled her breasts. His gaze slipped to her face, and he watched her lips part when he pressed her breasts together. Damn but he needed to feel those lips on his cock.

Raising himself to his knees, he nudged her thighs wider and kneeled between them, resting his weight on his hands. Pressing forward, he trailed his mouth between her breasts, then down her belly where he circled her navel with his tongue. Gooseflesh erupted on her skin, fanning out along her midriff. She stretched, then reached for him, clutching his hair in her fingers.

"Rhys, I feared you wouldn't come to me."

"Of course I came. Bran's not much of a jailer."

She sighed, and he looked up along her gorgeous body to her face. "Talk to me, Bronwnn," he whispered, "I love your voice. The way it moves along my body. Say something . . . Tell me something."

"I ache to have you inside me," she said, catching his gaze. "I desire you like no other man. I want your cock pushing inside me, filling me."

"Keep going," he murmured. "You've made me rock hard." Just to prove it to her, he pressed his cock against her, and she reached for him, but he evaded her touch.

"This is for you, *mo bandia*. Just lie back and let me hear those little cries of yours."

Tonguing her belly again, he listened for her sighs and felt her hips shift on the bed as he lowered his mouth to the damp curls. Spreading the soft folds, he raked his tongue up her length, arousing her with his mouth. She was wet and writhing, her fingers curling in his hair while her hips moved in an intoxicating, erotic rhythm against his probing tongue.

"Rhys." She sighed, rubbing her sex against him. Her voice in the quiet turned him on. The way she said his name lit him on fire. "Please," she said with a keening cry as she tensed and tightened, but he stopped just before she came. He wanted her wild for him.

Sliding along her body, he licked the valley of her breasts and slid his now-rampant erection between them. He showed her how to press her breasts together to increase his pleasure, and he groaned, watching his cock slide between her breasts.

"Suck me," he demanded. He watched as her pink tongue crept out and licked him slowly, teasingly so that he nudged his cock farther into her mouth.

"That looks so damned good," he moaned. Fuck, she was good. And gorgeous, and everything he could have ever desired.

"Show me more," she whispered, meeting his gaze and

flicking her tongue along his erection. "Show me what you want."

Needing no more encouragement, Rhys moved away from her and brought her to her knees. Kneeling before her, his cock soaring in the air, he entwined his hand in her hair and motioned her forward so that her mouth was poised over his tip.

"Take all of me. I want to watch you on your knees."

And then she slipped the tip of him past her lips and put his whole shaft in her mouth. With gentle pressure of his hands in her hair, he guided her into a rhythm painstakingly slow and erotic. He told her how to suck him and how to bring the tip of his cock to her lips without letting him slide out of her mouth. He described how to build his passion slowly, glimpses of her tongue curling around his shaft and her hand working his length as he watched.

She mastered the skill in minutes, and soon he needed only to groan or fist his fingers in her hair for her to know what he liked. As she worked her magic on him, he reached for her breasts and filled his hands with them, his fingers becoming more insistent as his desire escalated. Watching her loving his cock aroused him more than he thought possible. He'd always loved the sensation of a mouth on him, and Bronwnn certainly knew what to do with hers. She was a Siren like this and so very good at fueling his need. Already he was close to coming, and, wanting to draw it out, he moved away from her, settling himself against the headboard and motioning for her to come to him.

When she crawled on her knees to him, he was already gripping his cock in his hand and stroking himself shamelessly.

Damn it, she was working him up, and he needed this release, this climax with her. With a soft purr, she lowered her mouth to his wet tip, and he circled her lips with the head of his erection. Her eyelids fluttered closed as her tongue flicked out, as he teased her with his cock, and she moaned, as if savoring the taste of him.

Slowly her tongue swirled around his shaft until he could not bear it. Pulling out of her mouth, he reached for her and brought her legs around his waist. "Lean back on your hands and rest your feet on the bed," he rasped as he parted her thighs and stroked her swollen pussy. As she leaned back, her sex was exposed, slick and wet. Taking his cock in hand, he rubbed it against her folds, teasing himself by watching and listening to Bronwnn's escalating pants as he pleasured her.

Her hips were rocking as well as her breasts, meeting him stroke for stroke. It would be so easy to take her like this, to drive into her and watch the whole act. Giving in to his desire, he brushed her opening and grinned as she looked up at him through a veil of hair. Teasing her, he traced her slit, watching her passion-glazed eyes widen.

"Do it." She sighed, the sound husky and breathless. Nudging her hips forward, she forced the tip of him inside. She was scalding hot and drenched with arousal.

"What would you like me to do, Bronwnn?" he teased, slipping a fraction deeper inside her. She gasped, and he watched her toss the hair from her face over her shoulder. He could now see all of her—full breasts with pink nipples that were pebble hard and lush thighs that were open wide for him. "What would you like?" he asked again, watching as he slid deeper into the curls.

"Take me."

He reached for her hips and brought her toward him. "Only if you watch." And only then, when he was sure she was watching him inch inside her, did he take her, not in one swift movement, but in slow, straight strokes. When he was certain he had aroused her enough, he looked up from their bodies and commanded that she look at him. Eyes locked with hers, he slid deeply inside with a forceful thrust. She gave a little gasp, but then he felt her thighs go tight around him; guiding him with the inside of her legs, she brought him forward, urging him on.

"Harder? Deeper? Tell me how you want it, Bronwnn."

"I don't know. Just don't stop," she cried.

His strokes were fast, furious; his passion spiraling. She clutched at the sheets as her orgasm built. His was building, too, and when she came, he poured himself inside her, then pulled her down on top of him.

"Rhys?"

"Hmm?" he murmured as he kissed the top of her head.

"I just want you to know that mortal or not, you make my body sing."

He smiled into her hair. "Mates," he murmured. "My body is supposed to do that to yours, just like you make me completely insane with desire."

She snuggled next to him and started to breathe softly and rhythmically. "Go to sleep, *mo bandia*, because I'm planning on waking you up later. I want to hear your body sing again."

CHAPTER FOURTEEN

Cailleach stared at the man who had dared to enter her chamber. She was in bed, her hair down around her naked shoulders and the sheet pulled tight over her naked breasts.

"You have some explaining to do."

The man was not really a man. He was an angel—a fallen one.

"I owe you nothing," she hissed.

He moved so fast that she startled and pressed herself against the headboard. She had sent her *oidhche* out into the night to spy on the mortal. She was alone, and never had she feared the darkness as she did now, with her old nemesis looming above her.

"You always were such a stubborn female."

Lifting her chin, she gazed deeply into Suriel's black eyes. "I would not bow to you then, and I will not now."

Clasping her chin in his hand, he forced her to look at him. "I should have just taken you. Fucked you and showed you who was the greater power."

"Your coarseness sickens me."

"You shiver, but I doubt it's from sickness."

Flinging his hand from her, Cailleach pulled the sheet tighter to her body. "What do you want, Suriel?"

"What we both want. The flame and the amulet."

"That's not all you desire."

He smiled, that beautiful fallen face lighting up with mystery and menace; sensuality and sin; pleasure and pain. "You know what I want, Cailleach."

"I do not trust you. You're evil, Suriel."

"And you're not?" His long, tapered finger stroked her cheek and skimmed down her jaw to her shoulder, where he let it trail along her arm. "I know what you did, Cailleach."

Alarm seized her, and she met his onyx gaze. "You know nothing."

"You parted them."

"You do not know what you speak of."

He laughed as he brushed his fingers back up the length of her arm. Her traitorous nipple hardened, and his gaze slipped down, focusing on it as it pressed against the sheet.

"Two tragic, tortured souls," he whispered.

"Get out," she commanded. She was weakening. Her always-strong resolve was slowly unraveling.

"You led Covetina to Uriel. You fed her to the bastard."

"I did not!"

"Because you wanted Camael for yourself." He pressed against her, his fingers teasingly resting at the edge of the sheet she clutched to her breasts. "You wear the white of a pure goddess. But you're not."

"You know nothing!" she sneered, hating this angel. Of

the three, he had always been the most lethal and dangerous; the most difficult to control. Whom was she lying to? She had never controlled Suriel. Even Uriel, with his dark pleasures and his ambition to learn the Dark Arts, was not as dangerous as the angel before her. There was something so very primal and black inside Suriel. She felt it—the hunger for power; for revenge; for all-consuming satisfaction.

"When you discovered that Camael loved Covetina," he said, moving closer so that his breath whispered across her shoulder, "you flew into a rage. In a jealous, impetuous rage, you tore them apart. You banished her. You knew Uriel was no good, that his heart was impure, and still you led him to her. You knew what he would do to her, but you didn't care. You wanted Camael."

Her heart was racing; her breathing fast. He was too close, looming over her, breathing against her.

"She was your handmaiden. You knew her secrets, that she had mastered the Dark Arts. You knew and didn't care, because all you desired was Camael. You didn't care that Camael mourned her. You didn't care that Uriel would rape her."

She couldn't listen to any more. Tearing the sheet from the bed, she wrapped it around herself and walked away from him.

"The past has no bearing on what is happening now."

He stalked her, pressing her into the shadows, against the wall. "You don't think so? All misdeeds must be atoned for at some point. Yours. Mine. In Annwyn. In heaven. In the mortal realm. It doesn't matter where or when. Only that it will happen."

"The flame and the amulet will be found, and none of that will matter."

"When was it you discovered you needed Covetina's amulet, Cailleach? Was it after you fed her to Uriel, or was it later, when her child—Uriel's—told you?"

"I don't know what you're talking about."

He reached for her, pressing his long, tall body against hers. "You sacrificed Covetina, and then you stole her child."

Her body stilled, and Cailleach looked up into Suriel's face. "She betrayed me. It was against our laws. Our order."

"Because she slept with an angel—or because she slept with the angel you wanted?"

To hear the truth from Suriel was more than Cailleach could bear.

"You took her child from her. You assumed that with the combined powers of Covetina and Uriel, the child would be of use to you. Either that, or you feared the child might have skill in the Dark Arts, and you wanted to make certain no one else could use her against you."

She shook her head, denying it all, but Suriel smiled, enjoying her discomfort. "But what you didn't know was that Covetina had borne Camael's babe. In secret, of course, before you banished her."

No. Cailleach felt her expression freeze in horror. No, it couldn't be.

"I didn't know, and I certainly did not take Camael and Covetina's child."

"No," Suriel said with a dark smile. "I did. But he'll believe me when I say it was you."

Cailleach sagged against the stone wall as Suriel looked down at her. "The child has lived and died a hundred times in the mortal realm, and each time her soul is transmigrated to another living being, I watch over it, protecting what is mine—what you need. Do you know whose body Camael's and Covetina's daughter claims?" Cailleach shook her head, her mind reeling with the implications that the amulet might be forever out of her reach.

Suriel bent lower and pressed his lips against her ear. "Rowan."

Cailleach stiffened beneath him. "Why?" she asked, still puzzled that Suriel had even known about Camael and Covetina. She had thought him too busy pursuing his own pleasures to take any interest in what she or the others were doing. "Why did you take their child, and into the mortal realm?"

"To have my revenge on you, of course," he whispered darkly in her ear. "When you spurned me as a lover, you made an enemy of me, Goddess. I knew that Covetina had given the child her amulet, enchanting it so that it would always follow the child's soul. And I knew that one day, you would need that amulet. That's why I wished to possess it—to keep it from you."

"You bastard!" she snarled. "You would ruin my world—and all the innocents of Annwyn—because I would not mate with you?"

"Why not? You ruined mine. I left heaven because of you. Because I wanted so desperately to taste your flesh. But that was a thousand years ago, and I no longer lust for this body." His hand moved insolently along her curves, touching, pressing. "It holds no more allure for me. I no longer think about what it would be like to sink myself inside you, or what you would look like sated and languid, your high-and-mighty Supreme Goddess sneer wiped away with my kiss. No, that has all been replaced by my vision of destroying you."

"You have no powers here," she hissed. "Your threats are empty."

"True, I don't. But I have power over the mortal who is destined to make rise to the prophecy. You can have no idea what power she holds. I can make her obliterate your beloved Annwyn. I can make her walk the path of my choosing."

"How?"

"Because I am the most commanding angel on Earth. Because I have the power to bring death or resurrection. Because I know what her fate is."

"That is why Gabriel wants you," she whispered. Finally, everything was coming together. "Gabriel wants the knowledge you possess."

"Gabriel won't get it. And neither will you."

Cailleach narrowed her eyes. "What is it you want from me?"

With a smile he pushed away from her. Darkness engulfed him, and he stepped back into the shadows. "I'll let you worry about that for a while longer. Think on all the frightening possibilities, Goddess, and then make your thoughts a hundred times worse. That's what I want from you."

The shadow swallowed him up entirely, and then he was gone, leaving Cailleach alone, and for the first time ever, truly frightened. Sliding down the wall to the floor, she clutched the white sheet to her body.

He must never discover the truth about the prophecy. He had been close to the truth but had not quite uncovered it.

Resting her head against the wall, she closed her eyes and thought of Covetina. She had been her handmaiden, her confidante, her best friend. And in a fit of jealousy, she had ruined both their lives, and the lives of two innocent children. Her envy had set the prophecy into motion. Her betrayal of her one true friend had cast a darkness in her heart that Cailleach had never been able to shed.

No one knew of her part in setting about the prophecy—except Suriel. What would he ask for in return for his silence? She shivered. There had been a promise in those dark, obsidian eyes of his. He would be back for her, and she, the Supreme Goddess of Annwyn, dared not refuse whatever it was he wanted—not if she wanted her secret safe.

Rowan rapped quietly against the door for the third time. Obviously Keir was sound asleep; either that, or he wasn't in the room. She was about to leave when the door opened a crack and Keir peered out. Seeing her, he opened the door a bit more, revealing his gorgeous half-naked body.

Rowan felt her eyes go wide at the sight. She would never, ever get used to seeing him shirtless—all those tattoos and the big, bulging muscles. Her mouth went dry as she looked her fill. Then she reminded herself that Keir was a friend. And that was all he was.

She looked away from the six-pack abs and up to his face, and her heart started racing. The five o'clock shadow he was sporting made him look different, lent him an added air of danger and virility. This was a side of Keir she was certain no one ever saw. He always kept himself calm and in control, but now he looked a bit wild, and oh so gorgeous.

"Are you okay?"

She appreciated the worry she saw in his eyes, but at the same time it irritated her. She was dying, but she wasn't dead.

"I, ah . . ." she said, wetting her lips, trying not to make it appear that she was checking him out when she obviously was. "Rowan?"

Even his voice was deeper, more enticing, alluring. Oh, how she wanted him. Despite her past; despite never having been able to enjoy the touch of a man, she wanted him. She wanted so badly for him to be the one to push past her fear and break down the barriers.

"Can I come in?" she asked at last.

His beautiful violet-rimmed eyes flickered with emotion. "I—I don't think so. Let me get my shirt, and I'll come out."

"No, wait"—her hand shot out to hold open the door— "I'd really rather do this in private."

With obvious reluctance, Keir opened the door and stood back, allowing her into his room—or perhaps "tomb" would have been a more fitting description.

The door closed behind her, clicking into place, thrusting the room into a darker shade of black. The candle flames flickered with the movement of air, and Rowan blinked several times, trying to accustom herself to the darkness.

"Have a seat."

Keir tossed a stack of books onto the floor, freeing up a chair beside the bed. She cast a glance at the bed and saw that it was a huge antique four-poster. The coverings were black, as were the curtains. The walls were painted black, and even the dozens of burning candles were black.

As she sank down onto the chair, she watched Keir shrug into a white shirt, which he didn't bother to button.

"You're nervous."

"No, I'm just—"

"Nervous," he said again.

She laughed uneasily. "Just a little. I don't know why."

"It's the black. It affects you."

"I suppose," she muttered, looking around the room. "There certainly is a lot of it." Jeez, it was like something out of a gothic novel, with all the candles and the silk and the black.

"It helps me think," he said, passing her a glass of water he had just poured from a carafe on a table beside the bed. "There is no distraction, nothing to intrude on my thoughts."

"What were you doing?"

He waved to a circle on the floor. Tarot cards were spread out in the shape of a Celtic cross. He bent down and picked up a card, passing it to her. "The Empress."

"And that means?"

"You. She is a powerful psychic; yet she keeps a part of herself hidden—like you." He glanced at her, then back at the tarot spread. "All the cards are there. Everything about the prophecy; it is there, just waiting to be interpreted—discovered."

"And which is you?" she asked, her voice suddenly hoarse. He passed her the card and watched her face.

Death.

The card dropped from her fingers, landing faceup on the carpet.

"It is not what you think. This is the card of rebirth, a time of change. A time for something to end, but also for something to begin. It is the phoenix rising from the ashes. Death is not the end; it is only the precursor to resurrection. It's a powerful card."

She stood up, needing to control her thoughts, but he reached for her and stroked her arm.

"I've frightened you. I'm sorry. Many consider the tarot an invitation to evil. But much can be learned from the cards. I do not use the cards for the Dark Arts, but to shine light in the darkness."

Rowan slowly looked at him. It was now or never. Her time was drawing to an end, and she needed some answers. "Is that why you isolate yourself, why you come here to this black room?"

She heard his breath catch and saw him turn away from her, his face a beautiful mask concealing his thoughts and feelings. "I don't isolate myself."

"It's only you and Rhys. And when you're not with him, you're alone."

He glanced at her over his shoulder, his eyes dark and stormy. "Have you ever noticed how a house can be full and bursting with life, yet one can feel utterly alone in it?"

"Yes." She had felt that way, too, especially now, staying with Bran and Mairi. People surrounded her, people who cared for her; yet she felt utterly alone.

"You and I are very much alike. Few people, I think, would even acknowledge such a thing."

Rowan nodded and glanced about the room. "Perhaps that is what draws us to each other. We are alike."

His eyes turned violet, and his voice dropped to a bone-melting purr. "Is that the only thing that draws us to each other?"

Her stomach did a little flip, and a million butterflies were suddenly set loose inside her. She couldn't answer his question. It was too personal. It was too risky to tell him the truth. Instead, she let her gaze wander around the room as she thought of an answer.

On a table beside the bed, a square of shiny black satin lay beside a candle. On the fabric was a lock of blond hair. Crumpled beside it was a piece of paper.

Keir suddenly stood in front of her, blocking her view. "What is that?" she asked.

"Nothing."

"Keir—"

"Nothing that concerns you, then."

Rowan felt her heart crumble to dust. Did Keir have a lover? Was it Bronwnn? The blond hair was light enough. Oh, God, was Keir with her ... sister? It was possible. Rhys and Keir shared things—all things—or so Sayer had told her. Maybe they were sharing her.

And why wouldn't they? Bronwnn was gorgeous—and thin, which was something Rowan was not. Figured. She *would* discover she had a sister, and that she was the ugly one, all in the matter of an evening.

"What brings you to me tonight?"

It was a question, but his words and the huskiness of his voice made it sound downright seductive.

"I—I don't know." She glanced away, unable to meet his gaze. "I suppose I needed someone to talk to. And Mairi ... Well, ah ..."

"She is with her mate," he supplied. Taking her glass, he set it behind him on the table. "What is it you wish to talk about?"

He advanced upon her, and she backed up. He followed her, not allowing her any space.

"I ... ah ..." She tried to think of something to say, anything but the truth, but it flew out of her mouth before she could stop it. "I couldn't stop thinking about you."

His eyes grew darker and his chest broader as he continued to swallow up the space between them.

"Tell me these thoughts."

"Tonight," she whispered, licking her lips nervously. "Bronwnn. What I am."

"No. The other thoughts. Of me. Of you."

Of course, she had thought of them together. But now she wished she hadn't, because she didn't know how to go on. She wanted him. But she needed him to make the first move.

"Tell me," he demanded, his voice darker, more commanding. "Let me into your thoughts. You thought of us together, didn't you?"

"A journey," she blurted out. "You know, to learn more about me. What I am? Don't you want to learn more about me?"

He was forcing her back, and she wet her lips once more, her body responding to the aggression she felt pouring off him. "Yes, I want to learn more."

She smiled in relief, which faded when she felt the bedroom door press against her back. Rowan was forced to look at him as he loomed big and male over her.

She tried to speak, to ask him where he wanted her for the divination, but he held a finger up to her mouth to silence her.

"I've wanted to learn how you would feel in my arms. Taste on my tongue. I've wanted to learn your body, what you like, what makes you wet and moan. I want to know what it's like to be so deep inside you that I can feel you pulsing around my cock."

She could hardly think as he reached out and touched her,

pulling the quartz necklace from beneath the neckline of her dress.

"I want to know what it's like to have you naked beneath me, your eyes focused on me as I show you how much I want you."

She gulped and saw his gaze drop to the fluttering pulse in her neck. He inhaled and pressed his eyes shut.

"I already know your scent; it clings to me. But what I don't know is how you will smell when you're aroused. When I've marked you with *my* scent."

"Keir," she whispered, afraid to touch him, afraid that this last minute might have been a dream, and any second now she was going to wake up alone in bed, her body weak and chilled, her head hurting from the growing tumor.

"All this time I have kept myself apart from you because I believed you feared me. I was afraid I would hurt you. My desire . . ." He lowered his head and nuzzled her ear. "My desire for you is so strong. It's grown, and I'm so hungry for you, Rowan. Tell me, do you feel the same way? Have I guessed wrongly that the real reason you're here tonight is not for a divination journey, but another sort of journey altogether?"

She was literally trembling all over. Yes, he was right. She had come to him in the hope that he would show her passion. She wanted—needed to know—if he felt anything for her.

"Have you come to share your body with me?"

She blinked, and then she nodded like a mute idiot. She couldn't speak. She was so damned nervous.

"How long?" he whispered, and she heard the door lock behind her. His hands reached for her shoulders, and he smoothed his fingers down her arms. "How much longer will I have to wait to learn everything about you?"

"Please," she pleaded, and she hated the bit of fear she heard in her voice. She wanted him. Her body was crying for his, but her past would not give up its claim on her.

His head lowered till his mouth was resting against her ear. "How long since you had a man inside you?"

Rowan closed her eyes and allowed herself to drown in the sensation of his face pressed into her hair. "Keir," she said huskily as his fingers brushed her hair over her shoulder, baring her neck.

"Have you ever had a man kiss every inch of your skin?" He pressed his warm mouth against her neck. "Have you ever had him explore every part of you with his hands, his mouth, his tongue?"

"Please," she whimpered. But was it a plea for him to stop or to continue?

She felt him reach around her hips for the hem of her dress. He pulled it up slowly, teasing her with the movements of his fingers and his breath against her neck. Her legs shook as he slid the lace from her shoulders and kissed his way down her arm until the dress fell silently to the carpet. She stood before him in her panties, watching as his gaze roved over her body. Instinctively she covered her chest with her arms.

"Don't."

His command was harsh—dark—and her nipples beaded tightly.

"I'm going to look at you. Feel you. Taste you. And I can tell you right now that I'm going to love everything I feel and touch—and the taste of you"—his gaze lifted to her face—"is going to be ambrosia."

Nervously, she allowed him to pull her arms away from her body.

"Perfect."

One word, said in his dark, passionate voice, was more powerful than any she could imagine. The hunger, the desire she saw in his eyes made her stand a little straighter, a little prouder of her body, away from which he seemed unable to look.

"How long since a man has tasted your skin? Felt between your thighs, and made you come?" Never, she wanted to scream, but she could not. She could only gasp as Keir's large hand cupped her breast. His hot palm pressed into her soft flesh as he rubbed his hand along her nipple, making it hard and beaded as it strained against his hand.

"Tell me how long, Rowan."

She turned her face to his and watched as his hot gaze passed over her face, then down to where his hand cupped her breast. He used his fingers to feel her and send her nipple and areola puckering. Sharp stabs of need shot through her, straight to her belly, and suddenly she felt the desire to curl her fingers in his hair and guide his mouth to her breast.

"Don't be afraid, Rowan; don't," he whispered softly, gazing up into her eyes. "I won't hurt you. I only want to be with you. To give you pleasure. To have you take it from me."

As if aware of her desires, Keir lowered his head to her breast and closed his eyes, running the tip of his tongue along her searching nipple. The sharp spark of desire ignited deep in her belly and made her knees weaken. She reached for him, her fingers biting into his upper arms—arms that felt so solid and strong.

She watched as he curled his tongue around her nipple, then slipped it gently between his lips, sucking her. She had never seen anything so damned hot, and arousal swept through her, making her moan. She reached for his thick, silken hair and ran her fingers through it, clutching it tightly as he built the pressure up inside her. Not even her own fingers tugging at her nipples felt this arousing. Keir's mouth was pure decadence, and she encouraged him further with little moans and whimpers.

He lifted her up as though she weighed nothing, then turned her so she was kneeling on the bed and his mouth was level with her breasts. He was pushing both her breasts together.

"So beautiful," he rasped as he cupped her and brought her breasts together in his hands. "I want to do so many things with these. I could look at you forever. I could feast on you forever."

"Yes," she said in a long rush of breath and whispered words as he ran his tongue along both nipples. He released her, nuzzling the scented valley of her breasts before capturing one nipple between his teeth and nibbling gently so that she called out and was forced to smother the sound in his hair.

His hands slid down her waist to grasp her buttocks, and he cupped her, pushing her forward so that he took her breast into his mouth and suckled her fiercely as he kneaded her bottom. His finger found the cleft of her sex through her panties, and he pressed his finger against her, wetting the fabric. "Have you dreamed of me kissing you here?"

She nodded, and with a wave of his hand, she was divested of her panties. "I've thought of it, too," he whispered. Then he slid the pad of his thumb between her swollen folds until he found her clitoris. She sucked in a breath as he passed his thumb lightly over it. "I've thought every day about going down on you, tasting you. I've imagined you naked, but nothing compares to what I see now."

"Keir, you're saying all the right things," she gasped.

"All true," he whispered as he kissed his way down her chest. "I've wanted you since the first time I saw you in your store. I've had you every night in my dreams."

"Then why did you wait?"

"Because I was afraid that I would hurt you. That you would see my tattoos, and that they would remind you I was not . . . human." He met her gaze. "I want to be with you, Rowan. But I'm not a mortal man."

"I see only you now. I feel only you. Right now, it's just you and I." She was amazed at the words that fell so easily from her mouth. But they were the truth. Right now her past was forgotten. It was only Keir with her.

"I'll make this right for you, Rowan. I swear it."

She moaned as he slid down her body and put his mouth to her sex, blowing hot breath against her swollen, sensitive flesh.

"You need it, don't you? My mouth down here, tasting, licking . . . *eating*."

"Oh, God," she cried as she felt his mouth pressed against her. She felt the firm, wet tip of his tongue thrusting between her sex until he could flick her clitoris, and she wanted to beg him to press his face into her so she could feel that hot, hard tongue on her skin. Thrusting her hips back so that his finger could enter her, he groaned and cupped her pussy, rubbing her with his palm as his finger sank into her.

"You're so wet." His eyes had darkened to a glittering silver. The violet edge was now a dark purple. She saw that his fingers were wet and glistening, and that he wiped the moisture from his hand onto the black satin square.

"What are you doing?" she asked.

"Shh," he whispered. "Don't think. Just feel."

Then his jeans were off, and he was naked—and how he took her breath away. He was big and gorgeous, and his cock was huge, the tip glistening wet.

Rowan thought she should be terrified, but she wasn't. She wanted him inside her. She wanted to feel him.

Reaching for him, she curled her fingers around him, stroking him. His eyes sparkled as he leaned into her. "This is going to be so damned good." And then he brought his mouth down slow and soft against hers. Fisting his hand in her hair, he angled her head so he could taste her, and Rowan opened her mouth to him, allowing him to search between her lips with his tongue. He kissed her long and slow, his tongue moving with hers, his hand fisting and loosening in her hair.

It was a kiss with no ending, and soon she was so needy, so reckless, that she was clutching him to her and rubbing herself against his hard body.

"Lie back and spread your legs for me."

She was completely naked, and a little unsure of baring herself to him. But she did what he wanted and was rewarded with the hottest, lustiest growl she had ever heard.

"I knew your pussy would look this good. Damn, I can't wait to get inside you."

She smiled. "You are a talker. I'd wondered."

His eyes flashed to hers. "Is that all right?"

"What you say makes me feel alive, and beautiful."

"You are."

His palms were rubbing along her thighs, and he took her knees, spreading her wide, so that when he leaned down, his shoulders were between her legs, and his face was buried in her pussy.

She cried out then, not in fear but in sheer ecstasy. Keir had a tongue that could make her eyes roll back in her head. Damn it, his rhythm was slow and lazy as he made a path of slow licks and delicate circles. He was in no hurry to make her come, she realized.

"I can't wait," she panted as she pulled his hair.

"You have to."

"Keir, please."

"No," he whispered as he went back to licking her. Only this time, he slid his fingers deep inside her. She felt the flood of fluid seep out of her, which was followed by Keir's murmur of pleasure.

She didn't know whether to be embarrassed or pleased by his reaction.

"God, you're perfect," he murmured. "Made just for me."

She was crying now from the pleasure of a building orgasm constantly out of her reach. She wanted to scream for him to take her, but he was in control now.

"Put your arms over your head."

She clung to him, and he stopped, making her cry out. Fear flooded her. He smelled it.

"Give yourself to me," he murmured. "I'll keep you safe. Now, arms over your head."

She looked down at him between her thighs. She had never seen anything sexier than Keir with messy hair and lips wet from her pussy. She wanted this; this orgasm with him. She didn't want to feel fear anymore. She wanted to be alive for however long she had left.

"I'll stop," he teased as his tongue came out to lick. Only he didn't touch her, but just let her see what she could have if she did what he asked. "You want that, don't you, my tongue on you?" Then he smiled and lifted his body away from hers. "What if I let you tie me up, instead?" Rowan felt her eyes grow round. "You be in control," he murmured, "taking what you want, when you want."

The fear ebbed, allowing her to think. She didn't want this to end. But she couldn't be vulnerable to him—not yet. And the thought of having Keir all tied up and at her mercy was very arousing.

He produced two white strips of material; from where, she had no idea. But he held them out to her and moved so that his back was to the headboard and his arms were spread out at his sides.

The satin slipped through her fingers, and she bit her lip, wondering if she could really do this.

"You can," he said, detecting her hesitation and encouraging her. "And if you don't tie me up, I'll use magick to do it."

With a shy grin, Rowan straddled his thighs and went to work on his right arm. It was damned difficult tying him up, because his lips were on her cheek, near her ear, and then lower as he brushed his mouth against the curve of her breast. His murmur of appreciation as her breasts bobbed with her efforts made her blush.

"Let me touch you as you tie up the other arm."

She laughed and moved to his left. "Touch me with what?"

"My tongue."

Rowan gasped as he leaned to the side and flicked her nipple with the tip of his tongue. Floundering with the satin tie, she barely got it knotted before he sucked the nipple deeply into his mouth, pulling on her.

She moaned, arching farther into his mouth, and he smiled, his gaze locking with hers.

"That's what I wanted," he said appreciatively. "Now, cup them for me."

Rowan did as he asked, and he watched her, the way she kneaded her breasts and pulled at her nipples. He lowered his mouth to her once more, drawing her in and suckling her fiercely.

She was impatient against him, writhing on top of his muscular thighs. She needed more, the ache growing hot and hard inside her.

"Stand," he gasped, ordering her up.

She couldn't. But one look at his glittering eyes told her of the immense pleasure she could experience if she would only obey him.

Standing with one foot on either side of his hips, Rowan blushed as she looked down to find her sex level with his mouth.

He was staring at her, and she felt horribly exposed. But then he kissed her, and moaned, and she grasped the headboard tightly in her hands, trying to keep herself up as her legs threatened to go down.

"Closer," he demanded, and she pressed in until she felt his tongue parting her folds with one long stroke.

"More," he growled as he strained against the ties she had bound him with. His voice was dark, and needy, rushing up her spine in a delicious tremor. The sound, the sensation, peaked her nipples. "More. Onto my face, until you are all I can smell and breathe and taste."

"Keir," she cried as he moved his thigh behind her knees, bumping her forward so that she was shoved against him, her sex pressing against his seeking mouth and tongue.

His words had aroused her and had let her inhibitions break free. She was holding him to her pussy, her hands grasping his hair. She held his mouth to her and felt his tongue probing and parting, licking and circling; she cried out as she rocked against him, building her orgasm as she listened to their sounds—her breathless pants, his deep guttural sounds as he pleasured her.

And then she came, shaking and shivering until she collapsed against him. He kissed the top of her head, brushed his cheek against her temple, and allowed her to sink into him, taking his heat and strength.

His body was hot and hard beneath hers, and she felt him stir against her. She touched him, her fingers skimming along his jaw and throat, then down to his shoulder. He moaned, and Rowan lifted her head in time to see him close his eyes and tilt his head back.

Mesmerized by him, she let her fingers trail down his

shoulders and arms, tracing the intricate designs on his body. His lips parted, and she pressed forward, kissing him. He kissed her back but did not go any deeper. Frowning, she kissed him again. Again, he kissed her back—waited. And then she clutched him, kissed him hard, slipped her tongue past his lips, and kissed him as she had dreamed about.

It was long and drugging, intimate, and wanting. Her nails were biting his shoulders, but he only moaned, captured her mouth when she would end the kiss, and deepened it— claiming her.

When she broke it off, she was trembling, her nipples beaded and aching. She wanted to feel him, to memorize him— how he smelled, the texture of his skin, and the smoothness of his chest.

Bending over him, she inhaled the spicy scent of his skin and licked him, tasting the fine sheen of sweat that made his skin glisten. Closing her eyes, she absorbed every nuance of him—his size, the taste of his skin, the heat radiating out to her.

"Yes," he groaned as she licked her way down his neck, letting the tip of her tongue flick the hollow of his shoulder. He moaned as she went lower, her tongue tracing the swirling lines of his tattoos, which had turned a vibrant blue. Something was happening to him, and she was doing it to him. A sense of power infused her, and Rowan circled his erect nipple with the tip of her tongue. The tattoo around it glowed, and his breath came in short, harsh pants.

"No, don't!" Suddenly he was straining against the ties. "You're taking me away from you."

"How?" she murmured, and continued licking and sucking each nipple in turn.

"A divination. By touching them, you're starting one. And I want to be here with you. I don't want my spirit separated from my body. I want to be here with you—all of me—alone with you."

When she opened her eyes, he was looking at her desperately. "Don't take me away from you."

She smiled. "Then say I can touch you here."

She reached for his cock and let her fingers glide over the glistening head. His moan was her answer. She touched him again, this time squeezing the wet tip, then running her fingers up and down the thick shaft.

"Yes," he growled, his hands fisting and his arms straining against the bonds. "Touch me."

She did, with two hands, working her way up and down and watching as he thickened even more. How would she ever accept him into her body?

"Rowan," he said, his voice dark, beautiful in its huskiness. "Taste me."

She glanced down, wondering. "I don't know how. I've never done it."

"Just explore. Take what you want. Do what you want. Just let me feel your mouth around me."

Lowering her head, she licked his tip. He strained, and she heard the tearing of the satin. She lapped, nipping at him, and he growled, his whole body tense—dominant.

"My whole cock. Suck it."

His hands broke free of the bindings, and he gripped his cock, holding it out to her. With his other hand, he cupped the back of her head and moved her forward so that he was brushing his cock against her lips.

"Claim me as yours."

Something in his voice, his words, broke through her fears, and she sucked him in deep, roving her tongue along him as he thrust up into her mouth. His hand fisted in her hair, and his other hand claimed her breast, which swayed as she rocked over him.

He was breathing hard, his hips thrusting; then he stopped and pulled out. "I'm sorry. I shouldn't have done that."

"Why?"

"Too rough," he growled.

"No, it wasn't, and I wasn't afraid."

"Gentle and tender. That is how I need to be with you."

"No!"

She slapped at his shoulder, and he froze. "No? You no longer want me?"

"No. I want you. The real you. Not someone you think you have to be."

His eyes became hooded. "You wouldn't like it."

"I want *you.*"

His eyes flashed silver, and then he lifted her up and lowered her to the bed until he was above her, his hands twining with hers, the white tails of the satin strips winding between their clasped hands, holding—binding—them together.

She was breathing hard, her breasts rising and falling as they brushed against his. Her sex was pulsing, wanting more. She felt his cock nudging between her thighs, searching for her heat, pressing between her swollen, slick folds.

"Look at me, *beannaithe leannan*," he whispered.

She did, and when their gazes locked, he clutched her fingers and brought his mouth down next to hers. "*Beannaithe leannan* means sacred lover." He pulled away, catching her expression of wonder at the beautiful endearment. "Because you are. That is what you mean to me."

Slowly he entered her. She stiffened, and she felt the calming pressure of his fingers against hers, the brush of satin against her wrists.

"It's me loving you," he whispered. "My body in yours."

She nodded while she focused on his eyes and the feel of him moving lazily inside her. He was big, and he engulfed her.

"Can you feel me?"

He pushed against her, filling her, and she squeezed his hand. "Yes," she said, sighing, "and it's good." Oh, so good.

Keir kissed her cheek, letting his lips brush her skin as he kissed her ear. "Let me make love to you."

"Yes."

Moving so that he was directly on top of her, Keir blocked out the candlelight with his shoulders. He was all she could see now. He was above her, surrounding her. And he felt large and commanding as he thrust once, then twice deeply inside her.

Rowan let her body relax. She absorbed him, the feel of him. Her hips rose with his, and soon her hand was in his hair and she was whispering his name.

"Keir," she whispered as she rose one final time.

"I'm here," he answered. "I love you, Rowan. I'll always love you. *Mo bandia, mo aingeal, mo beannaithe leannan.*"

The world stopped, and all she heard were his words and the sound of his body loving hers. *My goddess, my angel, my sacred lover* . . . Rowan closed her eyes on the sensation of his love. She could feel it surrounding her, pushing into her, just as his body was pushing inside hers. And she opened to him, letting him in in a way that no other man had ever been allowed.

He kissed her, touched her, whispered into her ear as he filled her full. And when she was begging and pleading, he forced himself deeper, harder, faster. When she was crying out his name and gripping his hips with her thighs, he lifted her legs over her shoulders and drove into her, filling her so full until he brought her to orgasm, watched her beneath him as she came around him, then poured himself into her, stroking inside her until he was spent.

"You are going to need a lot of loving, *beannaithe leannan*. And I will give it to you. As much as you want," he said as he pulled out of her body.

Rowan turned in time to see Keir wipe his fingers along his cock. Bringing them to the black satin, he wiped the remnants of their mutual pleasure. He murmured something, then reached for the paper, which he ignited in the flame of the candle. Then his eyes met hers as he blew out the flames.

"What was that you said?"

Gathering her up in his arms, he kissed her.

"It was an urnai," he whispered into her ear. "A prayer for you. A prayer for us that we might be able to stay together—forever."

Rowan met his silver gaze. "It wasn't a prayer, was it? It was a spell."

"In my world, beautiful, magick is a prayer."

"It's magic what you're doing to me now."

He smiled. "Then let me do it some more."

Rowan felt his cock growing hard once more against her belly. Then he reached for her leg and placed it over his hip. They were face-to-face when he slipped slowly inside her. He closed his eyes as he penetrated her fully, the walls of her sex clamping around him. Rowan watched as his lips parted in ecstasy, allowing a low moan from deep in his chest. She was mesmerized by how beautiful he was, by the beauty of their bodies together, brushing and rubbing. He pleasured her, his rhythm slow and unhurried, as if they had decades of loving ahead of them. And when they were done, Keir repeated the spell, but this time, he folded the black satin and slipped it into a box before gathering her up into his arms.

"Wear the quartz," he reminded her. "It's how I'll always be able to find you."

CHAPTER FIFTEEN

Stirring beside Bronwnn, Rhys smoothed a hand over his face and glanced at the window. The big silver moon of Annwyn hung high in the sky, telling him he hadn't slept long. It was still night, and he had hours yet to spend with her.

"*Mo bandia*," he murmured. She stirred, mumbled something, then snuggled deeper against him, making his cock grow once more. With a groan, he moved away from her and caught a handful of her pale hair in his hand, allowing it to slip through his fingers. He liked the way it shimmered in the glow of the candles, and in the moonlight that shone through the window.

"Bronwnn. Take me to the reflecting pool."

This time she heard him. "No, it isn't safe. Cailleach," she mumbled.

"I want to see you beneath the moonlight. Walk with you, hand in hand in Annwyn. I want to see what my ancestors did. I want to feel, to understand my heritage."

There must have been something in his voice, because she

sat up and brushed her hair from her face. "Now? You want to connect with your Sidhe side now? It's the middle of the night."

He grinned and jumped out of the bed, tugging on the leather pants Drostan had summoned up for him. "Can you think of a better time? C'mon. Take me on a tour."

Tossing her his T-shirt, he motioned for her to get dressed. "And don't even think of putting on that gown Cailleach dressed you in."

She smiled and held the white tee to her breasts. "You're a wild one, Rhys MacDonald," she laughed. "You know the Supreme Goddess is just waiting for you to defy her so that she can kill you, and here you are pleading with me to take you out into her world."

"Highlanders," he said with a grin as he clasped the Celtic bracelets around his wrist and reached for the torc that sat upon the nightstand. "They're a brawny, brave breed of mortal."

Slipping the shirt over her head, she pulled her hair back and knotted it up. Loose tendrils fell around her cheeks, making her look messy and well loved. It was a look he particularly took pride in, since he had been the one who had made her messy. When she was finished, she held out her hand and clutched his fingers.

"Bring the adder. He'll follow and guide you to the pool."

"And where will you be?"

"Ahead. In wolf form. I can scent better that way. Make sure the *oidhche* isn't following us."

Rhys grinned and impetuously parted her lips with his finger. "You wouldn't have bitten Cailleach, would you?"

She snapped at him and laughed. "Careful, or I'll bite you."

He pulled her close and hugged her. "Biting, no. But a little nip here and there I'm game for."

"Come," she whispered as she traced the wolf head on his torc. "I'm eager to see if the big brawny highlander can keep up with the wolf."

"The big brawny highlander has a few moves he hasn't shown you yet."

The moon was still high in the sky as Rhys made his way through the castle and out into the night. The Sidhe king's court edged the forest, and Bronwnn, already in wolf form, darted into the trees. She scented the forest floor, then lifted her head into the night, sniffing the air.

Annwyn was calm and quiet. Nothing surrounded them but the smell of the trees and the passion they had shared.

Behind her, she heard the slight rustle of leaves, mixed with the dry pine needles that had fallen to the ground. The sound was too light, too elegant, and too rhythmic for it to be Rhys. It was the adder.

Blood rushed to her extremities, and a jolt of adrenaline infused her. Lunging deeper into the forest, she ran, padding softly along the floor, jumping over logs and twigs as silently as a doe. And all the while behind her, the adder slithered, leading Rhys to the sacred waters—and to her.

The thrill of the hunt warmed her, and soon she felt her blood burning hot, her lungs heavy in her chest, until she found the clearing, and the moon that reflected on the water.

She was about to break out of the foliage, triumph singing

in her veins, when she was tackled to the ground and held in a pair of strong arms.

"Got you, my bonny lass."

Bronwnn swiftly changed into her woman's form and tangled her arms and legs with Rhys'. She was breathing heavily, and he was barely winded.

"How did you beat me? The adder was behind me the whole time."

"Highlander," he said with a leer. "We can sniff out a trysting place from miles away."

She smiled and ran her hand through his dark hair. His violet Sidhe eyes seemed to glow amethyst in the night. Perhaps it was only her romantic imagining, or a trick of the moon, but she swore she could feel some sort of magick in him, if in nothing but his beautiful eyes and the way they looked at her.

"You're a cunning warrior, Rhys MacDonald. Any woman would be pleased to have you fight for her."

He pulled away and helped her up. Reaching for her hand, he strolled to the reflecting pool and sat down on the grassy bank. He was about to put his feet in the water, when she stopped him.

"Don't. You'll disturb the nymphs."

"Nymphs?"

She didn't like the way he cocked his eyebrow as if he were intrigued by the notion of naked sea women who lusted for men. The last thing she wanted was for Rhys to be accosted by a pack of nymphs. They were sexually promiscuous beings, bent on seducing any male. Their numbers had been dwindling for centuries, their men dying of a mysterious water illness, leaving the women unable to procreate. The nymphs were desperate for sex—and children. Rhys would make a delightful specimen for their amusement.

"Are they beautiful?" he asked, teasing her.

"Not as beautiful as a goddess," she said haughtily as she sat down beside him in the grass. She noticed the adder was curled around his bicep.

"As sex obsessed as the fairy tales claim they are?"

She narrowed her gaze. "Are you testing me?"

He laughed, caught her face in his hands, and kissed her. "Never, my love."

She huffed and glanced away. "Very well. Nymphs are stunning creatures and sexually bold. They come into . . . heat"—she blushed, not knowing what other word to use—"at every full moon. They're insatiable."

"Then I shouldn't put my feet in the water, should I? Because I already have an insatiable goddess, and I'm a poor mortal caught under her spell."

She slapped him, and he laughed before cuddling her closer. "It is gorgeous here. I love the water. The house that the Cave of Cruachan lies beneath was built by Daegan. He built it on the edge of a lake. It's beautiful. I like to lie awake at night and hear the sound of the waves crashing against the rocks."

She sensed the peace that stole over him as he spoke. "I would like to lie there with you."

He glanced at her, touching the ends of her hair before letting them slip back against her neck. "Then you will. As soon as it is safe to go back through the cave."

"Why didn't you tell me who you were?"

"You mean a mortal?" He shrugged. "I thought you knew. You know . . . from our dreams."

"No, I mean, why didn't you tell me you were kin to the king, and to Daegan?"

"I guess I didn't think of it. Our . . . common ancestry is not something Bran takes pleasure in. He made a sacrifice for Daegan to be with Isobel, and he was cursed because of it. I think he sees Daegan's weakness whenever he looks at me."

"I see only strength and courage. And those Sidhe eyes that see much more than anyone thinks."

He flushed and looked down, then pulled a few blades of grass free from the earth. "You're one of two people who think I have something in me that might prove helpful in this prophecy."

"You speak of the wraith." He nodded, and Bronwnn felt his emotions, so strong and powerful, all tied with the Shadow Wraith. "You care deeply for him."

"I do. Ours isn't the normal wraith-mortal relationship. In my family, it has always been a female to offer protection. But Keir came to me, and it . . . Well, it works for us."

Bronwnn knew little of wraiths, other than that they existed by absorbing emotions and feelings. In shadow form, they could take without knowing. She found herself wondering what the wraith took from Rhys.

"You should know that Keir and I are inseparable. We . . . share everything. Including women."

She should have been alarmed by such an admission, but instead her heart leaped. Suddenly all she could think about was how her *adbertos* might not keep her from Rhys after all. She had promised the goddess she would mate with the wraith, but if the wraith would share her with Rhys . . .

"It doesn't come as a shock to you?"

She shook her head, daring to imagine how she might still find pleasure in Rhys; how they might stay together. "The ways of Annwyn are not foreign to me. I can accept what mortal women might not be able to."

"I don't think I can share you," he said quietly. "As much as I love him, as much as I care, I *can't*. What I feel for you is more"—he swallowed hard—"more than what I feel for Keir."

She stopped him by placing a hand on his chest. "No, not more, but different. Our feelings are different than your bond with the wraith. But our bond is no more special than yours with Keir. You must not think that way, Rhys."

He held her hand and gazed deeply into her eyes. "I don't want to talk about Keir. I want to know about you."

"There is nothing more to know. I am a goddess."

"You mentioned something about women liking me to fight for them. What did you mean?"

"In my order, when we come to our sexual maturity, warriors are assembled before us. They fight one another for the honor of mating with us. It is a great pleasure for a goddess to have a male fight for the right to claim her."

"And now Cailleach has robbed you of it, by arranging your future with Keir."

There was no censure in his voice; only concern. "I will do as I am told."

"But you're sad. I see it in your eyes."

"Not about the fighting. But the Shrouding. I wanted that—to be shrouded with my true mate."

"Is the Shrouding like the Sidhe fating ceremony, where the wrists and hands are tied?"

"A bit. But it is more sacred and beautiful. A goddess lives for the night when her mate will lift the golden shroud from her body and claim her. It is a union of the body and soul."

"You'll have that, I swear it," he said in a hard voice that brooked no objection.

"No, I won't." She gazed at him, showing him everything she felt. "You're my true mate. I wouldn't want a Shrouding with anyone other than you. Besides, the shroud can only be given by the Supreme Goddess. She will not bestow it on me, because she does not hold me in esteem. She never has. And now, now she is livid that I gave myself to you."

"Just a lowly mortal, right?"

She shook her head, but he caught her cheek in his palm. "Bronwnn—"

"No, Rhys. Let us talk no more about it. The Shrouding ceremony is not to be mine."

"I'll get you the damned shroud, and it'll be me pulling it off you."

She smiled and pressed forward, kissing him. "I would like that. Your body climbing over mine, your scent covering me."

He made a little growl in his throat and kissed her, slipping his tongue between her lips. The hoot of an owl in the distance made them break apart.

"We must go," she hissed, jumping up from the grass.

"Wait a minute," he said, tugging her back down till she was sitting on his lap. "I will fight for you, Bronwnn. I will. I'll prove I'm your true mate, and we will be shrouded. Believe that."

She wanted to. How badly she wanted that. But it wasn't to be. She had offered an *adbertos*, and once offered, it could never be taken back.

"Come," she said, pulling him up. "Back through the forest to the castle. The *oidhche* will be there soon."

He pulled her up short, her body colliding with his hard chest. "We will be mates. And I will see you in the morning."

And then he kissed her, filled his hands with her bottom, and lifted her up against him, kissing her fiercely. She returned the kiss, fearing it might very well be the last time they were alone.

But the owl hooted again, and the adder on Rhys' arm began to hiss. They parted, and Bronwnn changed into her wolf form, silently following him back to the castle. When she was certain he was safely inside, she turned and made her way to the temple, where the goddess would be awaiting her.

"I need to talk to you."

Rhys sat up in bed and scrubbed his hands over his face. "What time is it?"

"Dawn."

Peeking through his lashes, he saw Keir standing in the room. Beside him, the bed was empty. How long had he slept, and where was Bronwnn?

"She's speaking with Cailleach."

"Now?" Rhys snarled. Jumping from the bed, he snatched his pants from the floor and pulled them up over his hips.

Keir shut the door behind him and prowled into the room. Rhys watched him, sensing his discomfort. Something was wrong.

"The Supreme Goddess has also spoken with me."

Rhys wondered when his turn would come, although he had no desire to meet with that coldhearted bitch. "When did you see her?"

"Just now."

Damn. He'd slept through a lot. And, of course, he'd been left out of everything—again.

Keir's gaze dropped to Rhys' chest. "I haven't apologized for leaving you. I am ashamed I left you unguarded."

"It's not a big deal. The way I see it, it's fate. If you hadn't, I wouldn't have found my mate."

Keir actually winced. "About that," he murmured.

Something about Keir's tone put Rhys on the alert. "What is it?"

"You really need to talk to Bronwnn."

"About what?"

"Damn it, Rhys," Keir snapped. "Just do it." He raked his fingers through his hair. "Sorry. I'm not myself."

"I can see that. What's the problem?"

Keir glanced at him. "There's more than one."

"Rowan?"

"She's one of them."

"How is she?"

Keir shrugged. "Weak. The weakest I've ever seen her. And this morning"—he swallowed hard—"I couldn't wake her. She was exhausted."

"You okay?"

Keir turned away from him and looked out the bedroom window. "I have to find a way to save her."

Rhys finally understood the consuming need that ran through Keir. He loved Bronwnn. He'd do anything, sacrifice anything, in order to keep her safe, just as Keir would for Rowan.

"I can feel her slipping away," Keir murmured. "I can see the light fading in her eyes." Glancing over his shoulder, Keir pinned him with his silver eyes. "Be thankful for your mortality."

Rhys didn't know what to say to that. He'd always believed he'd gotten the short end of the stick. But now he realized that immortality had its drawbacks—especially now. Keir was immortal. He'd live forever without the woman he loved.

"You need to feed?"

"No."

"To talk?" he prodded. Damn it, Keir needed something. He could sense it; he just couldn't understand what it was, or if he could even provide it.

"I came only to tell you that Cailleach wishes to see you."

"Why? To fry my ass?"

Keir barely cracked a grin. "She would have done that already if she was going to."

"Have you told him yet?"

Rhys whirled around to find Bronwnn standing in the doorway. He smiled and gathered her up in his arms. "Morning," he murmured in her ear. "You look good enough to eat."

She melted into his arms, and he held her close, savoring her. He felt like shit, considering that Keir was standing there worrying about Rowan, but Rhys couldn't help himself. Bronwnn was his, and he had only so much time with her. He was already thirty. The MacDonald men lived long, healthy lives, but they couldn't match immortality. One day, he would be parted from her, so he wanted to make every moment count.

"I missed you when I woke up." She smiled up at him and traced her fingertips over his lips. "You should have woken me when you were summoned by Cailleach."

"It was something I had to do alone."

The edge in her voice made him suspicious.

"Rhys, shake your ass."

It was Bran. He was standing in the hall with his arms braced over his chest.

"I guess the goddess can't be kept waiting, huh?"

Bronwnn stood up on her tiptoes and kissed his chin. "I will be here when you return."

"Good. And be waiting in that bed," he whispered, "because you aren't getting out of it for the rest of the day."

Leaving the room, Rhys closed the door, but not before he saw the shared glance between Keir and Bronwnn.

CHAPTER SIXTEEN

The wind was up, and the temperature had dropped. Rhys could see his breath—gray smoke, wafting up to the slate-colored sky. It wasn't a spring sky, but a winter sky with heavy gunmetal gray clouds that hung low on the horizon. As the darkness permeated more deeply into Annwyn, the trees had begun to drop their leaves, and as a consequence, the wind howled through the branches. It was a low, melancholy sound that wailed through the Otherworld. Even from up here, high atop Bran's castle, the sound swirled around him.

Rhys should have been cold, standing in the ramparts hundreds of feet up where the wind blew wild through the stone turrets. He wore only a short-sleeved shirt and jeans. The cotton was thin and well worn, and his arms were bare, except for the bronze cuffs, and the tattoo on his arm. Yes, he should have been shivering. But he wasn't. He felt nothing. He was numb.

A firebird circled overhead, and Rhys watched its graceful rises and falls, the dips and turns as it circled. He knew the Supreme Goddess had sent the phoenix Melor to watch him.

He was a prisoner here. But he'd have it no other way. This was where Bronwnn was, tucked inside her chamber. There was nowhere he wanted to be except close to her.

As always, his thoughts were of Bronwnn. Last night had been incredible—the best ever. The way she whispered in his ear drove him wild. Her voice was sultry, sexy, then soft and lulling, like that of an angel.

He would never forget the sight of her beneath him, or the way she felt, slick and hot against his fingers, or the taste of her on his tongue. That had been the biggest mistake, tasting her. Those memories made him hard and achy all over. Damn, it had been good—too good. But it was about so much more than sex with Bronwnn. It was dreams of forever; of nights spent holding her and mornings of looking at her across the breakfast table. It was images of a morning kiss and spooning together at night. It was all that normal shit he craved—a companion, a friend, a confidante, a lover. He'd actually dreamed last night of their Shrouding ceremony—what she would wear, and how she would look. He imagined seeing her round with his child.

"Rhys, descendant of Daegan."

Rhys whirled around, dagger pulled and drawn, ready to fight in an instant.

"You do not need that blade."

Hastily Rhys slid the dagger back into the sheath at his belt. The Supreme Goddess was standing before him, glaring.

"I shall have to have a word with the raven. He did not divest you of your weapon."

He didn't know why he felt the need to defend Bran, but he said, "It was well concealed."

The goddess stepped closer, her steady gaze scouring every

inch of him. She was dressed in a long silver cloak edged in white fur. Her voice was soft, womanly, yet commanding.

"You look like him." She stopped before him and gazed up into his face. "He was my favorite consort, you know."

No, he hadn't known. Daegan had never spoken of her, other than to remind Rhys of the curse she had cast.

"It killed a part of me to banish him from our world. It hasn't been the same without him."

"You could have taken him back."

She smiled, but there was no joy in her expression. "You've much to learn of our ways, Rhys MacDonald. Your great-great-grandfather offered an *adbertos*. Do you know what that is?"

"A sacrifice."

"Yes." She walked around him, her pale green eyes watching him. "A sacrifice cannot be undone. It is to be endured. That is the meaning of the word."

Rhys stiffened as she stroked her hand down his back. "The resemblance is uncanny," she murmured. "I can feel his power in you."

"Were you lovers?" he asked as he watched her circle him.

"No. I would have gladly given myself to him. And Annwyn would have been better for it if he had taken me. But he wanted the mortal."

"Hell hath no fury like a woman scorned," he snapped.

She tipped her head and studied him. "My curse was not born of scorn, but of necessity."

Rhys held his snort of indignation. He didn't want to do anything that might interfere with her loose tongue. He wanted to know more; to understand who he was and what he came from. He needed to learn about Annwyn, and what his role would be while he was here.

"You have no magick," she continued, "but there is something most powerful about you. Your destiny is in Annwyn."

"I guess my destiny trumps your curse."

Her eyes narrowed. "You would do well to hold your tongue, mortal."

Biting back a reply, Rhys struggled to tether his temper. Instead of lashing out at her, he watched as a slender, pale hand emerged from the sleeve of her cloak, only to trail along the cold stone battlements.

"Your presence here is a sign. It is part of the prophecy." She whirled on him. "Do you believe that the prophecy is changeable? That perhaps not even your God knows how it will all turn out or how it will evolve?"

"God is omniscient. All seeing. He knows what is going to happen."

"You forget there is another side in this war. There is magick in Annwyn. Your mortal rules do not apply here. And there is a Dark Soul—the Destroyer—to be fought over. There are many variables, and not even He can foresee what this Dark Mage will do. Just as I cannot see what will happen in your world. This is the beginning of a great battle. There is much at stake," she murmured, "and not enough time to prepare. The birth of the Destroyer is upon us. Bronwnn has sensed it."

Rhys stiffened. "It's treacherous to use her to find the Dark Mage. You put her very life in danger."

"We all have a role to play in this prophecy. It has been slowly evolving for the past thousand years. We must accept our part."

"And the Destroyer, does Bronwnn know who it will be?"

"No. But I believe the mage already knows the identity of this Dark Soul, even though we do not."

"This soul, it is already born, then? It's already turning?"

"Yes. But it does not yet belong to the Dark Arts. We can still prevent it."

"And why are you telling me this? I'm cursed, aren't I? What good am I to you?"

"Destinies change, mortal. And yours has."

The smallest flare of hope flickered inside him. "Bronwnn?"

"Has offered an *adbertos*. In exchange for your life, she will wed the Shadow Wraith."

"No," he growled. Heedless of the consequences, he reached for Cailleach and wrapped his hands around her elbows. She gave a little cry as he began to shake her. "Damn you, she's mine!"

"The sacrifice has been offered and accepted. You will live. You will aid Bran and his warriors in the hunt for Carden, and you will defeat the mage."

"No. I'll offer another *adbertos*. My life. I'll forfeit it before I do anything for you or Annwyn."

"You have Daegan's temper, his drive. Put it to better use than hating me."

Releasing her, he bit back an oath. He didn't want to be in Annwyn without Bronwnn, and he didn't want to do fuck-all to help Cailleach.

"Bronwnn has seen you," Cailleach murmured. "You are one of the nine. She sees the future, and your future is here, among us."

"But separate," he finished. "A mortal to be tolerated until the prophecy is fulfilled. And then what?"

"I am not a seer. I cannot tell you what your future holds."

He could—an empty life spent watching the woman he loved mated with the wraith born to protect him.

Fuck that, he thought as he moved away from Cailleach. He would make his own destiny.

"Your anger is a useful weapon," Cailleach called out to him. "Pit it against our enemies; not against things that cannot be undone."

"Go to hell," he murmured. There was no way he was living without his mate.

Clouds shadowed the room, darkening it. Beyond the window, the gray sky swirled, echoing what she felt in her soul—a tempest of swirling anger.

Bronwnn watched as the wraith stepped closer to the bed. Dressed all in black and with his black hair, he was nearly indiscernible from the shadows. His hand came up from his side, as if he were going to wave. In a slow arc he moved it. Instantly, the soft glow of the lamp on the nightstand flickered to life, displacing the shadows in the bedroom.

"What did you tell him?"

"Nothing—yet. I'll leave it up to you."

She sighed. "It doesn't matter. He speaks with Cailleach. He'll know what I've done."

Still, she clung to the hope that something might change. It was the only thing that gave her comfort.

"How is the mortal named Rowan?" she asked, thinking to change the topic that simmered between them.

"Dying."

Bronwnn swallowed hard. She felt the wraith's pain; she tasted his sorrow. "I'm sorry."

"You are sisters."

Brushing her hair from her face, Bronwnn slowly nodded. "I knew immediately when I saw her."

"I *knew* she wasn't fully human."

Gazing up at him, she swallowed hard. He was a dark and difficult man; nothing like Rhys.

"What do you know about her?" he demanded.

"Nothing more. We are sisters. How she appeared in the mortal realm, I don't know. I was told my mother died in childbirth with me. I do not know my father."

His gaze narrowed, clearly sensing her deceit. She knew her father was the Dark Mage. "It would be a betrayal to Rowan to discover that we are to be wed," Keir stated bluntly. "I will not allow anything to hurt her."

"I understand. I promise not to speak to her of what will happen between us."

"After . . . she dies," he said with a catch in his voice, "I will fulfill my part of your *adbertos*."

"Forgive me. When I offered my sacrifice, I was thinking only of Rhys and of protecting him. I didn't stop to consider your wishes."

"My wishes are the same as yours. The safety of Rhys. But . . . you must understand my love for Rowan. I will not betray her in life."

Clearly he didn't want to be with her, and Bronwnn shrank back, not knowing what to say or do. He sighed and put his big hands into his pockets.

"It is not that I don't want to be with you, but I think you know that in my heart, Rowan is my mate, just as Rhys is yours."

She gasped. "You read my mind."

He shrugged. "Our duty is to unite our races, and our powers. Together our divination magick will benefit our world, and perhaps the mortal realm. It is for the greater good, and the less selfish path. I can read thoughts, but once we are shrouded, I will give you as much privacy as I can. I'm usually successful at tuning people out. I'll try my best with you."

Bronwnn felt her heart skip a beat, then plummet to the pit of her empty stomach. This was not what she wanted. She wanted Rhys. Somehow she had mistakenly believed she could bring herself to accept a union with Keir. Now she knew deep in her heart she couldn't.

Keir was mysterious and sexy. He was tall, handsome, with a sexual intensity that any female would desire in a man. But Keir wasn't the one she wanted.

"I'll be kind to you. I'll treat you with respect, and I'll ..." He swallowed, then nearly choked out his next words. "I'll show you pleasure."

Bronwnn was speechless as she looked up at him. He was so virile and gorgeous, standing before her with his damp black hair and mesmerizing eyes. Yet, while she found him devastating to look at, she couldn't help but think it wasn't Keir she wanted pleasuring her.

"We have no choice. Our personal preferences have no bearing on this. Cailleach designed this, and your offer of a sacrifice has ensured our union. If it pleases you, and Rhys, we could all pleasure one another. You needn't give him up."

He had just voiced her secret hope, but the firm coldness

in his voice made Bronwnn look up. Keir stood towering above her, his eyes frigid and devoid of any feeling. He studied her as if he were some sort of machine, programmed to perform a highly specialized function. It would never work. She knew that now.

"This is a mistake," she began. "I can see it. Hear it. There's no inflection in your voice, no emotion. It's empty; there's no fire. No desire. Just duty, and duty is not what I want." She wanted only the pleasure Rhys gave her. She wanted his warmth. His fire.

Keir frowned at her words. "You're very pretty."

"Keir—"

"You have a beautiful figure. It's . . . voluptuous. I like it."

She thought of Rowan's figure, and she knew Keir was silently envisioning Rowan as he gazed down upon her. She didn't want to be a substitute for his lover. And she didn't want him being a substitute for hers. There must be another way to appease Cailleach.

"Keir, I'm certain there is a way around this. You don't really want me."

"We can have . . . passion," he said awkwardly. "There would be pleasure between us. I can guarantee that pleasure. Rhys will join us in bed, and all will be well."

"But what about love?"

His eye twitched, and he looked away, toward the stained glass window behind her shoulder.

"There will be pleasure."

She wanted more. She wanted Rhys. Oh, God, what had she done, offering such an arrangement to Cailleach?

Keir reached out and drew his fingers through her hair and

down her cheek till they rested against the notch in her throat. With a few fluttery sweeps, he brushed her bounding pulse. "You worry for Rhys."

"I do. We've ... shared intimacies. But I assume you already know that."

"I know you dream of him. That he dreams of you."

"I'm sorry." She shuddered as his fingers skated over to her collarbone.

"Rhys can be part of this."

"He won't accept that," she whispered.

"We have shared before. We will share again. I won't need your love, Bronwnn. I know it's for Rhys, and I won't ask for any of it."

"Do you touch him when you share your women?" She had no idea what prompted her to ask him such a thing, but she had been too afraid to ask Rhys. She couldn't understand it, but there was jealousy there on her part. She didn't want the wraith taking him from her.

"We have. But I won't, if you do not wish it."

"To survive, do you need to? Touch him, that is."

"No, not to survive. In the past, it has always been a mutual need, one that I can see no longer exists for Rhys. He has you now to fill that need—the empty place where one's mate should reside."

She was relieved. She understood that need, that empty hole that was left open and wanting as one waited to find one's mate. Keir and Rhys had taken care of each other, pleasured each other because it filled a void while they waited for their *Anam Cara* to take up the place where the emptiness beckoned.

Suddenly she felt for Keir, for his pain, for the loneliness and despair. If they shared each other, he would be the third wheel, the odd man out. He would be the one to watch but never feel; to yearn, only to be left hungry—and empty. "I'm sorry I am not the one who can fill the need in you."

"Don't be. I've always known your feelings. But some things can't be changed. For the sake of Rhys' life, and for Annwyn, we will do this. And we will make it work."

Bronwnn watched him walk away, but before he closed the door, he turned to her. "You will spare Rowan the knowledge of this?"

"You have my word."

He nodded and tilted his head to study her. "It will work."

Bronwnn watched as he closed the door. She didn't want to do this, but it was the only way to save Rhys. She would do anything for him. Endure anything.

Rhys pounded down the stone steps of the castle toward the opposite wing where Bronwnn was being kept from him. Ahead of him, the adder weaved over the gray stones, leading the way. His blood boiled; his anger, volatile and threatening, was erupting inside him.

How dare she give herself to Keir? How could she after what they had shared? After he had vowed to fight for her, to give her a Shrouding ceremony? She had looked into his eyes and made him believe that he was her true mate; that all the dreams they had shared were about them, and not Keir.

Damn it! He wanted answers.

Stopping at a door, the adder curled up, signaling that this was where he would find her—his goddess; his mate. And God help her once he did.

Taking a deep breath, he reached for the latch and forced himself to exhale slowly. He didn't want to hurt her, but he did want to know what the fuck she was thinking. She was not mating with Keir.

Inching open the door, Rhys watched as Bronwnn rose from the tub, the water sluicing over her curves. Her back was to him, and he watched the graceful movement of her spine as she reached for a towel and covered her body. He was seething mad; more angry than he had ever been in his life. He could feel the anger flooding his blood, but desire and longing swiftly replaced his anger.

Why was she doing this? Did she think him weak? Unable to protect himself because he was a mortal?

Christ, just looking at her made him want to lunge at her and take her, claim her as his. She wasn't going to Keir—no fucking way.

Coming up to her, he grabbed her around the waist and pulled her against him. Pulling the towel from her body, he threw it onto the floor and pressed her naked body to his. Having removed his shirt, he was now clothed only in jeans, and the feel of her silky skin against his chest made him rock hard. She moaned, whispering his name, and he whispered ruthlessly in her ear, "Yes—Rhys. Your mate."

With lightning speed, he turned her around so she was facing the wall. Reaching for her wrists, he held them above her, and Bronwnn gasped as he nudged the front of his jeans against her gorgeous ass.

He pressed his hard body against her back. She gasped

again when her breasts grazed the cold wall, but he didn't ease his hold.

"I love that sound," he murmured as he licked her neck. "It makes me hot and hard. Makes me want to sink my cock deep inside you, fucking you hard so that you never forget who you belong to."

He thrust against her once more as he nipped the tender flesh beneath her ear. "Who do you belong to, *mo bandia?*"

Bronwnn had never seen Rhys like this, so masterful and dangerous. She was aware of the barely controlled emotion simmering within him.

He clutched her fingers in his hand, his other hand, warm and soft, stroking the length of her back to her hips. Bronwnn held her breath, sensing the struggle waging deep inside him. He was hurting and no doubt feeling betrayed. She wanted to reach out to him; yet she instinctively knew he was beyond listening. He was all male now. Hurting and aching. And so was she. She wanted this—his desire; his power.

"How I love you like this. Bare-assed and willing," he drawled, sliding his hand down her bottom and cupping her. "I'll bet I could make you beg for it. God, I want that," he groaned, thrusting his erection against her. "I want to hear you beg me for it."

Between her thighs, she was wet and aching. His words unleashed an intense desire within her. She was completely at his mercy. "If that is what you want, I will beg you."

Rhys put his knee on the window bench and lifted her leg so that her foot was on top of his thigh. Coolness caressed her flesh, and she felt his fingers stroke her throbbing sex.

"Wet and throbbing," he drawled, trailing his tongue up the length of her spine. "I want to fuck you, just like this."

She tried to turn around, to release his hold, but Rhys only squeezed her hands and pressed them harder against the wall.

"Leave them up," he commanded. Then he turned her around, so that she was looking into his eyes, eyes that were burning with an intensity she had never seen before. Was it passion, or was it just anger glistening back at her?

Her hands were still raised above her head, and the position pushed her breasts forward, making her back arch so that she appeared to be flagrantly offering herself to him. His gaze skimmed her length, and she closed her eyes when she felt his fingers encase her throat, then slowly slide down her neck.

She was breathing hard, excited and aroused beyond belief. This dangerous part of him called to a buried yearning deep inside her.

"Rhys," she moaned when he circled her erect nipple. His finger stilled, and his gaze flickered up to meet hers. "Rhys, please. I burn; I ache."

"Then why did you offer yourself up to Keir?" he groaned, cupping her breasts and stroking her nipples. He tugged at them, and her womb contracted in response.

"Because I love you," she cried.

"Then why spend your life with Keir and not me?" he asked, raising her leg so that the ball of her foot rested against the cushion of the window seat. "Why not have this, this passion, this desire that flows between us?"

She tried to talk, but her teeth were chattering, and she was starting to tremble with desire. Her body literally throbbed for him. She needed his touch. *Needed him.* She needed to be filled with his cock; to be taken by him.

Rhys went to his knees, his hands stroking the undersides

of her breasts before trailing down her belly. His fingers raked through her curls, and she felt his hot breath against moist skin.

He licked her swollen folds, long and slow, and she felt her leg weaken, but he reached for her knee and steadied her, spreading her sex with his thumbs and exposing her to his gaze.

"No, Rhys," she whimpered, wishing she could run her hands through his hair. "Let me be with you. Let me touch you. Oh yes, Rhys, yes," she moaned, thrusting her hips out and rocking back and forth as his tongue greedily licked her. "Oh yes, I'll do anything for this, Rhys."

"Anything?" he asked, looking up at her as a slow grin parted his lips.

She reached for him, but he grasped her wrist and held her still. Freeing the buttons from his jeans, he slid them over his hips and kicked them aside. Then he reached for her and released her hands before bringing her to his chest, and she sucked in her breath, feeling the hot singe of his skin against hers.

He reached for his cock and stroked it slowly. Her gaze slid to his erection, watching the way he expertly stroked himself, but he tipped her chin up and forced her gaze to his face. "Make me come with your mouth."

Rhys pressed her down to her knees, his touch not ungentle. She looked up at him and saw that he watched her with his haunting eyes. Still stroking his cock slowly and sensually, he traced her lips with his free hand, his eyes searching her face.

Bronwnn trailed her fingers down his taut belly.

"Show me your mouth on my cock," he gritted between his teeth, and she looked down to see that he was eagerly pumping his erection. She sucked him and he groaned, but he did not loosen his hold; instead, he continued to pleasure himself and watch her as she sucked, then licked. "So good. Never have I felt something so damned good." She sucked him harder, faster, matching his rhythm and watching as the muscles of his stomach tensed and bunched. "Swallow me."

He came in her mouth, and she sucked him down as he held her to him, thrusting deep, his cry deep and primal, stirring the animal in her. When he was done, he was neither sated nor spent.

He slid from her mouth and picked her up, carrying her to the bed and laying her on her back. Tugging on her ankles, he brought her to the edge of the bed, kneeled down, and lowered his mouth to her, licking her with such intensity that she felt her orgasm upon her. His tongue was flicking madly along her sex, and she felt his finger dip into her wetness and slide along her bottom to the cleft of her cheeks where he circled her slowly, allowing her to accustom herself to the strange sensation. And then one finger entered her slit; another finger, the opening hidden between her cleft. She gasped, shocked at the intrusion, but then he groaned deeply and looked up at her, catching her gaze. "There is now no place where a part of me hasn't been, Bronwnn. I've marked you, and you're mine."

She trembled at his words, and at her approaching climax. He must have known, because his fingers continued to thrust in and out of both openings while his tongue flicked and laved. She arched her back, the ecstasy rising at a frightening pace. Her fingers clutched the coverlet, and her whole body tensed. "That's it," he said darkly. "Let me taste your cream."

He drank in her arousal, and when she had barely finished arching and squirming, he deprived her of his mouth and moved away from her.

"On your hands and knees," he ordered, and he stood back and watched as she did as he ordered. She thrust her bottom out at him, and he pinched her, just enough to heighten her arousal. "Gorgeous," he whispered, trailing his fingers along her bottom.

Slipping his fingers inside her, he pleasured her until she moaned and began to move her hips. Next, he slid his finger up her cleft and began to circle her; then he sank one finger within her. She moaned and pushed her bottom out against his hand. "Feel good?" he asked. She nodded her head and looked back at him over her shoulder. Her gaze dropped down to her bottom, and she watched as he again slowly sank his finger inside her.

His lids hooded his eyes, and she saw his sexy grin through the shadows. "Put your hand to your pussy," he commanded.

Her hand slid down her body, and with her fingers she circled the sensitive nub of flesh at the crest of her curls. She watched his gaze drop from her bottom to the shadow between her legs. She thrust her hips back and quickened her strokes, her lips parting on harsh pants.

"Do you want it? My cock in you?"

She nodded, and he moved his hand so that his index finger was plunging between her cheeks, and another finger parted her folds before sinking into her sheath.

Rhys parted Bronwnn's swollen folds and entered her in one thrust. She gasped, but she continued to finger herself. The sight was damned hot, and he stroked her hard, bringing her hips back to him as he stood before the bed. Her breasts swayed back and forth, and he reached around and fondled them, more roughly than he ever had before. He captured her breasts between his hands and pressed them together, thinking how he would like to put his cock between them. He swelled even more inside her, then released her breasts, only to watch and feel them sway against his hand. Their gazes met, and he could not resist purposely pinching her nipples and flicking them with his fingers till she was biting her lower lip in pleasure.

"Take me, Rhys." Her lips parted on a moan as he very slowly circled her nipple, then flicked it. "I want you, all of you, deep inside me."

He was taking her hard, but she just kept begging for more, making him more reckless, more hungry to possess her.

He was close, and the way he felt her clamping around his cock, he knew she was close as well. He felt his balls tighten, and he pressed against her. "I would do anything for you," he groaned, coming in long, hot spurts. "I would be anything for you, even immortal if I could. But I can't. So you'll just have to accept me as I am."

Rhys fell on top of her, still deeply inside her. Their fingers linked, and she kissed his knuckles.

"You're not leaving me," he whispered. "I don't give a damn about sacrifices or what you think you need to do to protect me. I look after what's mine, Bronwnn. I might be mortal, but I'll give every last drop of my blood for you."

CHAPTER SEVENTEEN

The scent of flesh permeated the tomb. Not human flesh; it was animal. He sniffed the air again, then grew still as the scent swirled around him. The faint flutter of wings whispered near him.

"Who is there?"

Only the echo of his voice answered him.

The clanging of metal, the loosening of his bonds made him not care who was there. His only thought was that he was free.

The wings fluttered again, and despite his blindness, he reached out into the blackness to clutch at the sound. *There!* He trapped it in his hands. The bird's hoot of protest made him smile.

It was a gift from the goddess.

The owl fluttered frantically in his hand, and he brought the bird to his face, inhaling the soft, downy feathers. Beyond the avian scent were those of the goddess and the heady, intoxicating aromas of moonlight and seduction. It was like the dew on the grass, the humidity in the air on a sultry summer eve. It was Cailleach.

Unraveling his fingers, he let the owl free, then stood, unsteadily—free at last. He could hardly understand it. He could not fathom why, after a millennium, the Supreme Goddess would come to his aid.

It didn't matter now. He needed to escape. In the distance, he heard the owl's flapping wings, and he took a step, and then another. Seeking to follow the bird to Annwyn.

Feeling along the wall with one hand, he made his way to the door. When he found it, he tore the thick oak door off its hinges, tossing it aside as if it were cardboard. Despite his blindness, he had found his way out of the pit in which Uriel had kept him and into the cavern where Uriel performed his butchering.

Circling around, Camael sniffed the air, which was heavy with the remnants of the candle smoke and the sweet scent of burned wax and ceremonial incense.

With a roar of outrage, he moved his arm to the side, trying to connect with something that might give him an idea of where he was. Metal clinked against metal. He'd cleared the altar of its magical items with one fell swoop of his thick arm.

"Uriel!" he roared, but there was no answer. There was only the sound of his voice echoing off the stone walls. "Where have you hidden them?" he cried.

Damn it. He wanted out of here—out of this pit; out of this black abyss. A hissing sound at his feet stopped his mental tirade.

It was Uriel's little viper. "Come to kill me, have you?"

The snake hissed again, only this time, Camael was certain he heard a voice whispering, "Follow me."

That would be the damned day, he thought with disgust. He'd followed Uriel down here from heaven, and look what it had gotten him. There was no way he was going to follow a snake, of all creatures.

"Trust . . ."

There it was again, that voice. It was a female voice, soft and beckoning. Camael stilled his mind and listened again. It had been so long since he had heard that voice.

"Follow me . . ."

And he did. Taking a step forward, he paused and listened, only to be rewarded with the sound of a hiss. Slowly, he followed the hiss, the sound of scales sliding against stone. He had no option but to trust that this snake would lead him to freedom. But there was every possibility that it would lead him straight to Uriel and his death.

"You would not be alive if he did not need you."

True. In his misery, he had always believed Uriel enjoyed torturing him, but even torture got old after a thousand years. No, Uriel needed something from him, and he was keeping him alive till he got it.

Giving himself up to the freedom he could taste, Camael followed the snake until he felt a shimmering shroud cover his face.

Annwyn.

He knew the feel of that magical veil; the scent of the woods. He could almost hear the trickling water of the reflection pool.

My God, he thought. He was back. After a thousand years, he was back in Annwyn.

"It has been a long time, Angel of War."

Every nerve he possessed jumped. Slowly he turned in the direction of the voice.

Despite his blindness, he saw red. How dare she? How dare this cold, heartless bitch come to him now? He'd kill her, just as soon as he could wrap his hands around her throat.

"You do not want to kill me," she said, her voice soft and gentle. The sound only fueled his anger more until it coated everything he sensed with rage.

"The hell I don't want to kill you," he muttered. "I'd love nothing more than to snuff the life out of you with my bare hands."

A twig snapped, the sound followed by the soft pad of her feet on the forest floor. In his mind, he saw her—blond and ethereal; cold and untouchable. She had destroyed him. She had taken everything he'd ever wanted from him.

"I can feel your anger, Camael. There is a darkness in you that will soon rule everything you are."

"And do I not have a right to my anger? Have I not suffered enough, Cailleach? Look into my eyes! What do you see?"

She gasped as he stepped closer. He could only assume that he had been shrouded in shadow, and now, whatever light bathed him revealed what he truly was.

"What do you think, Goddess? Do I not deserve my wrath?"

"You deserve vengeance," came the quiet voice. "I have wronged you, as well as my most treasured friend. I humble myself before you."

The swishing of her gown reached his ears, and he raised his hands, searching for her, but his fingers met only air.

"You took her from me."

"It has taken me a thousand years to come to terms with what I did. I was wrong. But I was young, then. No more than a child who was impetuous and proud. I am a woman now, with a woman's regret. And a heart that has been heavy for a thousand years."

"And what do you want from me?" he growled. "Surely you do not bow before me to ask only my forgiveness."

"I ask you to join us. To seek your vengeance against your rightful enemy."

"Did you not make an enemy of me, Cailleach, when you banished Covetina from your world? You turned her away, allowing Uriel to seduce her."

Suddenly there was a cool hand pressed to his cheek. He shook it off, but it returned, and with that touch, so did his sight. His vision was blurry, but clear enough for him to see Cailleach.

"Listen to me, Camael. I speak the truth. I made a mistake. I sent her away because I was envious of her. I . . . desired you."

Camael watched the way her body moved, the way her hips rolled beneath the material that hugged her curves. His body slowly came alive, and the feel of that awakening sickened him. He had only ever had one lover; he had only ever wanted the one. Their union had been beautiful, powerful. And to feel his body harden for this—this creature who had taken everything he'd ever loved, made his blood fill with rage and hatred.

"I followed my heart, not my head. I will atone for that sin. Just tell me how."

His hand shot out, capturing her around her white throat. "I need what you and my brothers took from me."

There was no fear in her eyes as he tightened his hold, and it angered him. He *wanted* her afraid; he wanted her to hurt just as he was hurting. She had freed a beast—an animal—not the angel she thought she knew.

"What you seek has long since died."

"Liar!" He lifted her up, her weight a pittance when compared to his immense strength. Her chin came up, and her hand clamped down over his, but she did not struggle, and he fought the urge to shake her, to kill her right then and there.

"They are dead, Camael. Covetina by Uriel's deceit, and his own hand."

"And my daughter?"

"I—I do not know her fate." He felt her hesitation, and he knew she lied.

"You lie! I would know it if she no longer lived. I would have felt her leave me. I know you lie," he sneered, shaking her.

"The pain you feel so deep inside? That is the loss. They are gone."

He refused to believe that his lover was gone. He couldn't— wouldn't—believe that his daughter was dead also. When Covetina had been taken from his bed, he'd made provisions for his child. She'd been hidden from Cailleach's wrath.

In her physical form she was easy to hold. Taking advantage of that, he pressed her back against a tree, pinning her with his chest and heavy thighs. "I want my daughter back. I gave her to Suriel so he could watch over her."

Beneath him, she stilled. "He spoke the truth," she whispered in surprise. He felt her warm skin beneath his palm. She locked her gaze on his, her eyes a mirror to her soul. She drew him in, and he felt his mouth lowering—lowering until he swore he could feel her breath caress his lips. For a second, he forgot where he was, who she was, and remembered another time when a woman's mouth had beckoned him with temptation, with forbidden pleasure.

But that had been another time; another woman; a woman he had loved. And this creature was the object of his hate; the cause of his despair.

Her palm came up to rest against his cheek. "The child you seek is called Rowan. My *oidhche* will lead you to her. I ask only that you join our fight against the mage."

She started to evaporate, and so, too, did his vision, but he clutched on to what he could, and she reappeared, her form solid and womanly against him.

"Why have the bird lead me, Cailleach, when you'll do so much more nicely?"

Resting on the bed, Rhys turned Bronwnn over and gathered her to his chest. "I'm sorry. I shouldn't have done that."

"What?" she whispered as she raised her head from his chest. "Claim your mate?"

"Come to you when I was feeling so out of control."

"I understand the rage that ruled you."

"I was rough."

"Primal."

"Angry."

She smiled. "Yes. And it's all right. I have never felt more womanly and . . . fought over in my existence."

"All the same, I'm sorry if I hurt you. I just wanted to . . ."

"Claim me. I understand. The claiming of a mate is a powerful thing. To find a mate, then be denied him is even more powerful."

"You are my mate."

"I know, but Cailleach—"

"Let's not talk about Cailleach."

Her fingers stroked his chest, and he closed his eyes, luxuriating in the feel of Bronwnn nestled beside him. They hadn't spoken of the future, but he knew damned well he wasn't letting the wraith touch her. Despite his love and caring for the wraith, Bronwnn was all his.

"My leg," she murmured as she moved his fingers away from her thigh.

He looked down between their bodies and saw the blue ink on her thigh. It was glowing. "Why does it do that?" he asked, pointing to the script that seemed to be getting brighter.

"He's close by."

Rhys sat up and looked down into her face. "What is it? How does this connect you to the mage?"

She swallowed hard and held his gaze. "He's my father."

Rhys sat up and pulled her against him. "What the hell do you mean?"

"I was conceived in a union between a goddess and an angel named Uriel. This is my link to him. When I touch it, it brings me to him."

"Jesus Christ!"

She rolled away from him and reached for her gray gown. "I should have told you earlier. At least I should have told you by the pool, when we were talking, and you believed I was worthy to be fought for. I will leave."

"The hell you will!" he shot back, tearing the gown from her hands. Putting his hands on her shoulders, he forced her back down. "Who else knows this?"

"No one. I'm ashamed of it. He is evil, and his black blood flows in my veins."

"There is nothing of him in you. Do you understand? No evil. No darkness."

"He is my father."

"I don't give a damn." The way she looked at him melted his insides. "We have to tell Bran, at least."

"Does it disgust you to know that I was spawned by such evil?"

His grin was slow, and he reached for her shoulders. "No. Does it disgust you that I'm just a mere mortal?"

"Of course not."

"Then why would it bother me to know who your father is? You're not like him. You've proven that."

"I didn't know until that night in the cottage, when I had the vision. It was then, when he and I were face-to-face, that he told me."

Rhys hugged her to him. "I won't let him hurt you."

She nodded and held on. "What will the others think?"

"They'll keep their thoughts to themselves, if they know what's good for them. And Bran . . . Well, I know for a fact he'll find a way to exploit your connection with the mage for his benefit."

"I will freely offer my knowledge."

"Not if it risks your life."

"Rhys, be sensible. I hold the greatest key to beating him. I can find him whenever I want. I have only to touch that mark."

"And the same goes for him. The minute you search him out, he can find you. No, I won't put you at risk."

"MacDonald," called the gruff voice from the other side of the door, "are you in there?"

Shit, how had Bran found him?

"I'm prepared to overlook you're someplace you shouldn't be, if you get your ass moving. We're preparing to leave."

"For where?" he and Bronwnn called at the same time.

"Rowan believes she knows where Carden is."

"I'll be there. Just give me a minute."

"Hurry it up. Cailleach will no doubt be coming over to retrieve her handmaiden."

"I'm going with you," she whispered to him, clutching him tight. "I might be able to help."

"No."

"Rhys, be sensible."

"I've never been more sensible than I'm being right now."

"No, you're not. You're being bossy, irrational."

Rhys looked down at her. "We're staying together, so you'd better get used to being bossed around by a temperamental mortal."

"How can you help?" she asked. She didn't need to add, *When you're a mortal?* He saw that reminder in her eyes.

"Thanks for the confidence. But I told you I have a few tricks up my sleeve."

She smiled and watched as he reached beneath the bed. Drawing out a bow and some arrows, Rhys flung them on the mattress. "I might not be magically inclined, but I can hit a bull's-eye every time."

"You made these?" she asked.

"Yeah. Keir brought them for me from the club." Whistling softly, he signaled his new pet. The adder emerged from the darkened corner and slithered across the floor, then up his arm.

It opened its mouth, and its fangs dripped venom, which Rhys poured onto the arrow tips.

"Not magical," he said to her as she watched him, "but we mortals can be resourceful."

In his study, Bran trained his gaze upon Bronwnn as she came out of her trance. "Did you see anything?"

"No, Your Highness. It is the same as always. A darkened cave with water, with symbols on the walls. Crosses, like Rhys' necklace."

"Christian." Bran clasped his hands behind his back. "I know little of the mortal religion. Rhys, what of you?"

"I know some, but I wasn't a regular churchgoer."

"Wraith, where is Rowan?" Bran asked impatiently. "She might know and understand these symbols."

"Give her a minute," Keir growled. "She has a headache and has been feeling tired. She said she'd be right down."

Bran rubbed his fingers over his forehead. "Forgive me. I didn't mean to sound inconsiderate."

"I will go to her."

Rhys didn't need to enter Keir's thoughts to know the wraith was coming unglued. There was more than tension in his big shoulders. There was fear. Something was wrong with Keir, a worry that showed in his face.

Watching the wraith leave the room, Rhys wrapped his arm around Bronwnn's shoulders.

"Something is wrong," she whispered. "I can feel it."

"With Keir?" he asked, frowning.

"No, with Rowan."

"Bran!" The cry rent through the air, followed by the pounding of feet on the stone staircase.

"She's gone!" Mairi gasped as she burst into the room. "Rowan's been taken. There're signs of a struggle."

The terror coursing through Keir nearly brought Rhys to his knees. When the wraith appeared behind Mairi, he looked murderous—far darker than Rhys had ever seen him.

"What do you mean, she's gone?" Bran demanded.

Keir held a crumpled piece of paper, which Bran grabbed from him. On it was a diagram, spread out like a Celtic cross. In its center was Rowan's name. Beside it was Camael's angelic symbol, and, on the other side, was the image of the gargoyle.

"I know where to look," Bronwnn said quietly beside him.

"How do you know?" Keir demanded.

"Rowan told us. The riddle."

"Mairi," the king called to his wife, "read us the riddle."

"'A house of mourning, a garden of pain, a path of tears. This is where you will find the first key.'"

"A key to what?" Bran demanded. "Carden? Rowan?"

"A key to the prophecy," Bronwnn replied. "The flame and the amulet are the keys needed to forge a weapon that the mage wants for his magick. When he speaks of keys, he means either the flame or the amulet."

Mairi cleared her throat, capturing everyone's gaze. "You know, this drawing has given me a thought."

Bran turned to her and reached for her hand. "What is it, my love?"

"It could just be a wild-goose chase, but Our Lady of Mercy orphanage was across the street from the church. Beside the church was a cemetery, and carved on each of the black iron gates was a cross that looked very much like the one in the diagram."

"It's a place to start," Bran agreed. "Let's—"

But Keir was already on the move, his shadow looming large and menacing as he swept across the floor and out the door.

Rowan was groggy as she felt her body being lifted. Her vision was blurry, and her head hurt like a bitch. She tried to see who was carrying her, but every time she opened her eyes, she felt like puking.

"Where am I?"

There was no answer. Her head lolled to the side, and she caught a glimpse of a brand of some sort. Narrowing her eyes to make her vision clear, she saw that what she was looking at was an angelic mark.

"You're an angel."

Again, there was no answer. She had no idea what was going on; she knew only that she was weak. Maybe she'd already died and this was the angel sent to take her up to heaven. If so, she felt cheated. She'd planned on saying good-bye to everyone, and now she couldn't.

It was dark. She expected the pathway to the hereafter to

be white and gilded, with fluffy clouds and radiant sunbeams. This, she thought, looked more like hell.

"Did I die?"

"Soon."

She knew that voice, but she couldn't recall from where, or to whom it belonged. And then the darkness became brighter, just a bit. It was nighttime, and above her, the moon shone brilliantly in the black sky.

As she looked around, she saw the familiar shape of an old Victorian building. Our Lady of Mercy was forever etched in her mind. She would know its Gothic outline anywhere.

Before she could formulate any more questions, she was placed on a cold slab of stone. The angel who had carried her moved before her and lowered the hood of his cloak, revealing his face.

Rowan screamed until blackness engulfed her.

CHAPTER EIGHTEEN

"We'll save her." Rhys clasped Keir's shoulder and gave him a gentle shake. "Did you hear me?"

Keir was in a deep trance, his eyes unblinking. There was no reaching him. But then he murmured, "It is too late. She's gone."

Rhys looked questioningly at Bronwnn, who shook her head. "I do not know. My connection with her is not strong."

"Bronwnn cannot feel her any longer because she is not alive."

Keir's voice was flat; indifferent. It was in direct contrast to everything that Rhys saw in the wraith's eyes. "You don't know that," Rhys murmured, trying to give Keir a bit of hope.

"I feel it. It is too late."

With his torch held high, Bran lit the stone corridor, illuminating the walls. "Christian symbols," he murmured. "We've left Annwyn."

"I've seen this place," Bronwnn announced. "When we were in the hall at the temple, when I touched your hand and told you where to find Carden," she said to Bran, "I saw this cavern."

Bran nodded. "Then we are on the right track." Lifting the torch higher, Bran surveyed the etchings. "Where the hell is Suriel? He's far more familiar with the mortal underworld than I am."

"The angel is not what he appears."

Everyone stopped walking and gazed back at Bronwnn. Her eyes were distant, and Rhys reached for her, holding her hand.

"He is in trouble. I can sense that much. His anger and rage paint the air. Can you not smell him?"

Drostan, the griffin, sniffed the air. "I do not smell him. But I could try to summon him."

"No." Bronwnn halted him with a hand on his arm. "That is not the intended path. He has chosen his path, and now he must follow it."

"You saw something," Keir snapped.

"I—I saw us finding Carden; that is all."

Keir halted her. "You also saw something else."

"A fleeting vision. Black wings. But I felt the anger. The pain. And it was not that of the mage, but of the newly born Destroyer."

"Who is it?" Keir demanded, gripping her arm. "It's Suriel, isn't it?"

"I could not see his face. There was only blackness."

"Now is not the time to worry over this," Bran grumbled. "The light from this torch wanes, and if we are now in the mortal realm, which I suspect we are, my magick will soon grow weaker."

"Rhys should lead the way," Bronwnn suggested. "He is mortal, but a warrior. He will lead us safely through the cavern."

"How do you know?" Drostan growled.

"Because he is my mate and I know his strength. He has shown me his exceptional tracking abilities."

"He's a mortal," Drostan snorted. "He has no abilities."

"My mortal," she said with a smile. "And a capable warrior."

The raven shared a look with Bronwnn, then immediately reached for Mairi's hand and fell back, allowing Rhys to step forward. Pulling an arrow from his bag, Rhys notched it into his bow. The adder wrapped around his arm hissed quietly, letting Rhys know the snake would guide him through the darkness.

"This way," he ordered.

Rhys was conscious of the others behind him, but most importantly, he felt Bronwnn. She stayed close to him, and he was glad of it. It allowed him to focus all his attention on leading the warriors through the winding cavern.

"What is this place?" Drostan asked.

"Shh," Rhys hissed. "Your voice will echo, and if the mage is here, he will hear you and be alerted to our presence."

The griffin glared at him, but Rhys didn't particularly care if he was affronted by a mere mortal. Rhys had spent enough time in the cave with the mage. He knew how the sound carried. Shit, he could still hear the screams of the woman as they ricocheted off the walls.

Something scurried across the floor in front of them, making Rhys pause. "It's just a rat."

"The *radan* is not favored in our world. As a shaman, you should know that," Drostan snapped.

"I'm a mortal," Rhys growled to the griffin. "I have no magical abilities, remember?"

"Anyone who can tame an adder is a shaman."

Ignoring Drostan, Rhys pointed his bow up and searched through the gloomy depths. It was safe to move forward.

As they walked the winding path, Rhys began to wonder if there was any merit to the griffin's claim. Perhaps Daegan had seen that in him. Maybe that was why he had spent so much time regaling Rhys with the stories of animal allies.

"There."

Rhys glanced over his shoulder to see Bronwnn pointing at a flickering silver light.

"Are you certain?"

She nodded and pressed forward, making to pass him. He held her back with his arm. "I don't think so." Their gazes met, hers unflinching; his just as unmovable.

"I'll be all right."

Rhys brushed the backs of his fingers along her cheek. "But I won't if something happens to you."

"Nothing will happen."

Keir pushed past them and climbed the steps. At the top of the staircase was a huge oak door, which the wraith easily pushed open. Candlelight brightened the dark cave, and Rhys took the steps two at a time. Moonlight flooded through stained glass windows, and he followed the silver moonbeams until they came to rest upon an altar.

"This is the chapel at Our Lady of Mercy," Mairi whispered.

"Are you certain?"

Mairi glanced irritably at Bran. "I've done penance here, many times. Trust me."

"What is that?" Rhys demanded, pointing to the altar draped in a white sheet. Moving quickly to it, Keir pulled the sheet, letting it fall away. On the altar was Rowan.

Keir and Mairi both cried out, and Rhys pulled Bronwnn into his side. "Stay with me."

"He's here," she whispered, trying to get free of him. "I can feel it. There is evil that surrounds this room."

"Rowan," Keir groaned as he pulled her limp body from the altar and hugged her close to his chest. "She's alive. But barely."

"Let me go, Rhys," Bronwnn commanded as Mairi ran to her friend. "I can find him."

"Not so fast," came a deep voice from the darkness. From the corner of the chapel, a tall man stepped out of the shadows. Before him, Cailleach was being held with the tip of her own athame pointed to her neck. His head tilted up, and, as he sniffed the air, his hold faltered, but he regained it quickly.

The man, who was obviously blind, clutched Cailleach closer to him. "Damn you, put your hands on me."

Reaching behind her, Cailleach placed her palm on her captor's cheek. The black eyeless holes filled with a pale white and blue flicker of light.

"Where is she?" he asked hoarsely.

The goddess pointed to Rowan, draped in Keir's arms. The man turned his gaze from Bronwnn to Rowan, exposing his neck. He was an angel, Rhys realized when he saw the marking. His arrow was notched in his bow, but the venom on the tip would not be enough to stop this angel. That much venom could only wound, not kill, and if this angel had the power to hold Cailleach hostage, then wounding would not be enough. They needed him dead.

Dislodging the arrow from the bow, Rhys stepped back into the shadows. The angel was utterly absorbed in studying

Rowan, but his absorption had not made him loosen his hold on Cailleach. Even now, drops of her blood splashed down her neck, landing on the pure white gown. Rhys didn't know if the angel even realized it.

Cailleach was struggling to stay upright, and each time she faltered, more blood spilled onto her gown. She was bound to Annwyn, he remembered. It was her sustenance, and now, deprived of it, she was powerless—and dying.

And Keir . . . God help him, Keir was frozen; immobile. He could think of nothing but Rowan. He was of no help to them now. And the others? He looked around their party, all unmoving, looking upon the angel with Cailleach—a helpless, dying Cailleach. Not even Bran gave direction. It was as if they were in a state of shock. And maybe they were, for in their world, nothing was more powerful than the Supreme Goddess.

Rhys looked to the angel once more. Was this the Dark Mage they sought? In the glow of the candlelight, he could make out only the marking, not the design. Rhys didn't want to kill him before they knew anything about him, but Cailleach was dying! Someone needed to do something.

Picking up the bow, he cocked an arrow, then focused on the angelic mark. Closing one eye, he aimed, then let the arrow fly. It landed in the angel's neck, just above the mark.

Instantly, he released Cailleach.

With a roar of outrage, the angel fought until the venom began to paralyze him. With a thud, he fell to the floor, his sightless eyesholes peering up at the ceiling.

Rhys ran to him. "Are you the Dark Mage?" he demanded as he started to search the angel's ragged clothes.

"Camael," he whispered, his mouth beginning to froth.

"What are you doing here?"

"My child."

Rhys followed Cailleach's gaze to Rowan. "Rowan is your child?"

"Yes."

"Where is the mage?"

"Hiding. Waiting for her death. He covets what is inside her."

"What is inside her?" Keir demanded.

"A symbol of great power," spoke a disembodied voice. It was followed by the sweep of a black shadow, a flash of light, and then Suriel was revealed. "Covetina's amulet. It is one of the keys he needs."

Suriel walked around the prone body of Camael and gazed down. "What has he done to you?"

Camael ignored Suriel, and, instead, opened his palm to Cailleach. He motioned to her. With great effort he spoke. "Uriel . . . is the mage. He searches . . . for his flame. The witch Morgan stole it from him and hid it within the one she cursed." He took a pained breath. "I was there when she did it. I heard the spell, but I do not know who it was. He is vulnerable . . . He grows more fearful as time passes without it."

"Carden," Bran said. "He was cursed by her."

Cailleach bent to him and reached for his hand. "You will be taken back to Annwyn, where my healers will rid you of the poison. And then you will join us," Cailleach said, her gaze pointed on Bran; then it focused on Drostan. "Griffin, summon Camael to the temple."

The griffin stepped forward and held out his palms. The

golden light of summon magick swirled in his palms, and then Camael was gone.

"Suriel!" Keir demanded. "Rowan is dying. Do something!"

Suriel bent to Rowan and brushed his hand along her hair. "This is the moment, wraith, when you will request something of me, and I must refuse you."

"Damn it, don't you play games with me, you son of a bitch."

"I cannot save her. Her path lies elsewhere, not with us. But I can facilitate her death. It will be painless."

"What can I do? What can I offer in return for her life?"

"Nothing. She might have been fathered by an angel, but now she is a mortal with a mortal's soul. She belongs to Him, and He wants her back."

Keir cursed at the sky, calling Him every foul name he knew.

"Please," Keir begged, and Rhys felt the agony that filled him. "I will do anything."

"There is nothing to be done."

"There has to be a way."

"Keir," Rhys murmured, taking a step toward him, but he heard Keir's voice, hard, biting, warning him back, wanting him away. But Rhys ignored it and placed his hand on Keir's shoulder. He looked down at Rowan, whose eyes were open, her face contorted in pain. Rhys could not bear to look at her. Whatever the mage had done to her, she was dying in pain and terror. "She suffers under his spell. Let her go."

"No!" Keir snarled, hugging Rowan to him. "No, she doesn't."

"The mortals believe in the afterworld, and you believe in transmigration," Suriel reminded him. "Is it not one and the same? The life essence or soul of a living thing passes immediately from the old body into a new life after physical death."

Keir shook his head, not wanting to hear anything other than that Rowan would live. But she would not live—not for much longer. Pressing his face to her, Keir kissed her, his large body protectively covering her as he held her in his arms.

"If you love her," Rhys murmured, "then let her last moments be peaceful."

Rhys felt Keir's inner struggle. His love was strong, but his grief was stronger.

"This is not the end for her, Shadow Wraith," Suriel said. "You will meet again."

"In how many mortal lifetimes? How many centuries will I have to wait for our paths to cross again?"

"I do not know your destinies."

Keir clutched Rowan to his chest. He wanted to be alone with her. Rhys heard his thoughts and honored them.

Motioning to the chapel door, Rhys nodded in the direction of the moonlight. Everyone filed out, including Suriel, to give Keir some privacy with Rowan.

With a sigh, Rhys clutched Bronwnn to his chest, holding her tight. He couldn't lose her—ever. He wasn't strong enough to endure what Keir was going through.

"Rhys, descendant of Daegan."

Rhys lifted his gaze to find the goddess leaning against Bran and Sayer. She was weak and frail, her powers swiftly draining.

"You saved me. Even though I would have killed you had Bronwnn not offered an *adbertos*, you saved my life."

He shrugged. "We mortals are like that. We forgive."

"Then I have much to learn," she whispered, "for I have never forgiven. I would offer you something in return—I would offer you Bronwnn."

Bronwnn turned around and gazed up at the goddess. "You would give me my mate?"

"I would. For he is worthy of you," Cailleach murmured. "And the wraith deserves to mourn his woman. The mortal is yours with my blessing. I must leave now. My soul is tied to Annwyn, and I cannot exist outside my realm. But it is my hope that you will both be able to find peace in Annwyn."

Rhys grabbed Bronwnn and kissed her hard, pouring all his love into that one kiss. While his heart was soaring that Bronwnn was to be his, he felt the pain of Keir watching his love slip away.

"Rowan," Keir murmured as he pressed his lips to her cheek, "don't leave me. Not yet."

She was growing cold in his arms, and he hugged her closer, rocking her. For the first time in his existence, he felt his eyes well up, and then a tear fell, only to land on her pale cheek.

"I would do anything, give anything, if only I could have you back."

She did not answer. She only looked at him with those blank eyes. And he knew it was too late to save her in this lifetime. But there was a way. He had seen it in his vision.

"One night is not enough," he said, his voice catching, then breaking. "It has only made me love you more."

He continued to rock her, to kiss her cheeks. His tears tumbled onto her, and he clutched her closer. "If love could save you, you would live forever," he whispered. But there was no reply, and he closed his eyes against the reality of what was happening.

"You have made me the thief of your heart," he murmured. "I am forced to take it, to steal it, and hide it away until you come back."

He knew what he must do, and he reached for the athame lying on the floor next to him. Then he pulled one of the satin ties from his pocket. It was one of the ones she had used to tie him up, and it still bore her scent. He closed his eyes, inhaling it, bringing her into his lungs, and filling his soul with memories of her. Then he placed the satin over her chest and picked up the athame.

"Your blood is precious. I will keep it with me, and, though you are unable to speak, I know you would have it so." Keir glanced at the quartz still around her throat. It was truth enough. He could find her anywhere as long as she wore it. And then he took the tip of the athame and pricked her finger, allowing three perfect circles of crimson blood to drop onto the white satin.

"I will find you anywhere you are," he whispered as he kissed her cold lips. "I have the power. Come to me when you are reborn."

Keir watched as Rowan took her last breath.

He had talked to her, whispered to her, told her they would find each other again, and he believed she had heard him. He had told her to come find him when her soul settled into its new vessel, and he believed she would. She had to, because he could not exist without her.

Butterflies circled, gathering around her. One landed on his shoulder, and he watched its white wings, edged in blue, flutter elegantly. On the windowsill, his wren sang a melancholy song that matched what was in his soul.

"We will meet again," he whispered to the woman he loved.

In his arms, her body turned hot, then slowly crumbled to ash, just as he had seen in a divination. Wind from somewhere came and spread her ashes, leaving nothing but dust in his hands—even the quartz pendant was gone—and on the floor, by his knee, a metal ring. Picking it up, he saw the triscale—the gems. With a start, he realized what it was. It was the first key to the prophecy, the amulet.

As he pocketed it, Cliodna sang out a warning, which he quelled with a dark look. It was a part of Rowan, and he would surrender nothing.

"Raven," Suriel murmured, "come with me."

Bran motioned for them to follow Suriel up a long, darkened path that wound uphill. At the top, Suriel stopped and gazed down at the little chapel. "A house of mourning. A garden of pain." Suriel's hand encompassed the manicured gardens that shone in the moonlight before he motioned to the set of trees behind him. "A path of tears."

Bran gazed at the angel, and Rhys began to understand. "The cemetery is beyond those trees."

"And where there is a cemetery, there is statuary."

Everyone began running, all but Rhys and Bronwnn who stood on the hilltop and held each other. Silently they watched the chapel, waiting for Keir to emerge.

When Rhys saw the little white butterflies begin to circle around them, he knew something had happened. Beside him, Bronwnn gasped.

"*Dealan-De*," she whispered. "Butterflies. Souls of the dead, and the keepers of power. No harm will come to you where you see butterflies."

And Rhys knew it for the truth. Butterflies were the souls of the dead. Rowan was gone, and Keir's anguish tore through him, making him stagger.

In the distance, he heard Bran's cry of triumph. Carden had been found. But the joy was short-lived, for Rhys was suddenly consumed with the wraith's need for vengeance, with a rage that swamped him and forced him to his knees. Bronwnn cried out and embraced him. But Keir had no one to hold him; no one to comfort him as Rowan lay dead in his arms.

CHAPTER NINETEEN

Rhys stared out the window and into the moonlit garden. It had been two weeks since they had found Carden, still cursed and encased in stone. Two weeks had passed since Rowan's death, and Keir had locked himself into his room, refusing to see anyone.

"You must eat something," Bronwnn whispered as she came up behind him and wrapped her arms around him.

Holding her hands, he dropped a kiss onto her knuckles. "I will."

"You worry for the wraith."

"I hate to see him this way."

"You don't have to."

Cailleach had lifted his curse, which had severed the bond between him and Keir. But although their bond was fading, Rhys could still hear Keir's thoughts and feel his pain. He was alone in that room, refusing to see anyone—even him.

"Go to him," she murmured.

Closing his eyes, he tried to think of a way to ease Keir's pain.

"Go," she encouraged. "I will be here when you get back."

"I won't be long."

She kissed him and smoothed her hands through his hair. "Have patience with him. The loss of one's *Anam Cara* takes more than a fortnight to heal."

Nodding, he left their room in Bran's castle, and made his way down the hall. Once he got to Keir's room, Rhys' nostrils began to burn as the acrid stench of smoke wafted up through the door. Keir had been going heavy on the incense. He was performing divinations day and night, trying to connect with Rowan. Rhys had felt his frustration and anger at his lack of success.

Rhys rapped his knuckles against the wood.

"I'm crashed," spoke the deep voice from inside.

"It's me."

"Yeah, I know. And I'm still crashed. Save it for the morning."

Rhys ignored the biting sarcasm and turned the handle, opening the door to a cloud of smoke. Keir was sitting on the bed, naked, propped up against the headboard with one knee bent. Beside him, the sheet partially revealed a woman with a bright red mop of hair. Rhys knew that hair. It was Abby, the waitress from his club.

He glanced from the sleeping woman back to Keir, who was shoving the butt of his smoke into an ashtray.

"How did she get here?"

"Sayer enchanted her. She won't remember anything."

"She's a complication we don't need right now."

Keir wiped his hands along his face. "I needed a fix."

"You don't even like her."

Keir's gaze pierced him. "But she likes me, and we all need

that sometimes, you know, to be wanted? And she knows how to screw; I'll give her that."

"So, what are you going to do with her now that you've brought her here?"

Keir shrugged and looked away. Rhys had never before seen him so callous, and never to a woman. "I'll probably do her again, then send her back. She'll be up for it. She's always up for it and what I can give her."

This didn't even sound like Keir. Christ, he was getting freaked out, looking at the wraith—the wraith he'd been tied to since birth—the one he no longer even knew. "When was the last time you slept?"

"I don't know. Weeks, maybe."

"Have you found Rowan?"

Keir laughed and reached for another smoke. "Would I be fucking someone else if I could connect with her?"

"I don't know. Would you?"

The lighter flared, and Keir took a drag of his smoke. He puffed out a big cloud before he spoke. "Leave it, Rhys."

"Does she help?" Rhys asked, pointing to the woman beside him. "Does she give you the kind of comfort you need?"

Keir glared at him. "Fine. Nail me to the cross for taking this one to bed tonight, but I needed a reprieve. I needed a few hours of mindless fucking. Is that a problem for you?"

"No, but I think it is for you. You don't have to do this. It can be different."

"Really? Is your new wife willing to share you?"

"Leave Bronwnn out of this."

Keir's gaze darkened, but Rhys continued. "You're hurting and grieving. I hate seeing you like this. Come by our room—"

"Oh, won't that be cozy," he snorted.

Keir could argue for hours. He was a stubborn son of a bitch who would never budge once he dug his heels in, and shit, he was dug in deep. Rhys turned his back and reached for the door.

"You don't really want this—or her."

"Our bond is severed," Keir snapped. "You no longer know what I want."

There was a pain in his chest when Keir reminded him of their bond. "Yeah, it's severed, but that doesn't mean I don't feel you anymore."

"Go back to your wife," Keir snarled, "and leave me alone."

There was no reaching him yet—not tonight, and not tomorrow. He was raging and hurting. Once the anger let up, he could find Keir once again. Until then, he could only wait—and hope.

"I'm around when you need me."

"I won't."

Rhys turned back to his wraith; his best friend. "She'd hate to see you this way, you know."

Keir's gaze flickered; then he looked away. "Well, she's not here, is she? Go away, Rhys. Go back to your mate."

Reluctantly, Rhys shut the door behind him. Christ! That . . . That had been a complete stranger. It wasn't Keir any longer, but someone else.

"Rhys?"

Turning, he saw Bronwnn standing in the hall. She held out her hand, and he walked to her, grasping on to her like a lifeline.

"You look as if you've seen a ghost."

"I think I might have. It was Keir."

"Grief has hit him hard. He's hurting, and knowing you have your mate is making him feel the loss of his more acutely."

"He won't let me help."

She stood up on her tiptoes and kissed him. "It's too soon. Everything is too fresh. But he's there, even in shadow. He hasn't left you."

Bronwnn dragged him into their room, kissing him, loving him, and he tried to put aside his fear, but he knew Bronwnn was wrong. Keir *had* left. But where he had gone to, Rhys didn't know. And he was afraid to find out.

Kneeling before the Supreme Goddess, head bowed, Bronwnn accepted Cailleach's gift—the Shrouding.

"It was wrong for me to have parted Covetina and Camael," Cailleach said as she hooked her fingers beneath Bronwnn's chin and tilted her head up to meet her gaze. "But I won't apologize for stealing you. If I hadn't, you would have been in Uriel's hands, and the light I see in your eyes would not be there. Fate has a way of making things right."

"'Tis true," Bronwnn replied. "I would have been his servant, his apprentice. He would have used me to destroy Annwyn and all that I love."

"I never intended to hurt, but I had to keep you separate from the others, because I was never certain where he was, and I didn't want him to know of you, let alone find you."

"That is all in the past," she whispered. "I wish to forge a future. With Rhys."

"Then you will have it. Go now and make your future."

Rising from her knees, Bronwnn's red gown glowed in the candlelight. "Thank you for this gift."

Rhys rose from the tub and pulled a towel from the rack. Quickly he dried himself, then wrapped the towel around his hips. He was headed for the room he shared with Bronwnn, when he stopped, caught a glimpse of something at the window, and headed for it instead.

Outside, something glimmered, and his gaze tracked it as it shimmered in gold and silver hues. Instinctively, he knew what it was, and he watched as the glimmer rose up again. Hurrying into his room, he shrugged into a pair of jeans. He had no idea what a man wore to a Shrouding, but he knew whatever it was wouldn't be on him long.

Dressed, hair brushed back, he ran down the staircase that led to the door that would take him outside.

"MacDonald."

Rhys stopped and glanced over his shoulder. Bran was leaning against the wall, his arms folded over his chest. A strip of white cloth dangled from his fingers.

"Cailleach has granted your goddess the rite of a Shrouding."

"I know. I'm just going." Rhys couldn't hide his smile.

"When a Sidhe warrior takes a mate, there is a ritual that must be completed." Bran handed him the strip of cloth. "Your hand must be bound to hers."

"A Sidhe?" he asked, swallowing hard.

"Yes. A Sidhe. Even dilute ones."

Rhys smiled at Bran's grin. "Any special words that need to be said?"

Bran shook his head. "Only the ones in your heart."

With a nod, Rhys opened the door, the white cloth fisted tightly in his hand as he searched for his goddess.

She was easy to find. In the garden, beneath a gathering of oak trees, was a circle of white-robed women. At the head of them was Cailleach. When she saw him, she raised her hands, and the glimmering cloud that hovered around them lowered, fell, and disappeared.

"Rhys MacDonald, descendant of Daegan, you are to be given this night to the goddess Bronwnn."

He was nervous. Bronwnn wanted this ceremony so much. He didn't want to mess it up. He wanted it to be beautiful for her. In the same way every bride wanted the gown and the flowers and the devoted, handsome groom, every goddess, he supposed, wanted this.

"Thank you," he murmured, not knowing what else to say.

Cailleach's eyes flashed, this time not with anger, but amusement. "Is it your intention to take this goddess as your mate?"

"It is." He said it with deep conviction.

"Then your union is to be consecrated this night. Here, beneath the ancient oak of the Sidhe and the golden veil, which represents the power of the goddess."

Then Cailleach and the others departed, moving outward from the circle and revealing a woman covered in a glistening silver shroud that hugged the outline of her body. She was on a low bed of sorts, which was draped in silver and white satin and littered with pillows.

Rhys took a step, and then another, letting instinct guide him. He walked all around the bed, studying her still form. Up close, he saw how transparent and gossamer the cloth was, clearly showing her nakedness beneath. Reaching out, Rhys stroked one full breast with his hand. The nipple rose and pressed against the gossamer cloth.

His own body responded to the sight. She was gorgeous, like a pagan princess from a fairy tale, just waiting there for him to take her.

Unable to stop touching her, he slipped his palm lower, down her belly, where it lingered over her navel. He thought of her pregnant, rounded, and he wondered if it was too soon for her to be carrying his child.

Soon, he told himself. Perhaps it would happen tonight.

His palm left her belly and descended slowly to her thighs, then to the junction of her sex. She had been shaved, her sex now smooth and white. Kneading her with the heel of his palm, he listened for her intake of air, but she lay perfectly still, serene beneath the cloak.

He guessed he was supposed to pull it off, but he wanted to savor this moment; to do it his way.

Stepping to the bottom of the bed, he lifted the shroud, just enough so that he could come to her from beneath it. That was when he saw the markings on her body. On her shaved mons was a crescent moon, the symbol of the goddess. Around her navel was an infinity knot, and between her breasts was a painted triscale. In her hand was an athame, with a large moonstone gem on its hilt.

"*Mo bandia*," he whispered as he kissed his way up her thigh and over to her slick sex. "I have come to claim what is mine."

She stirred, spreading her thighs. Her hand left the athame, only to join her other hand as it skimmed down the curves of her pale body. "I am yours, Rhys MacDonald."

With a swipe of his tongue, he parted her folds, tasted her, teased her. Then he eased his way up her body, the gossamer veil covering them both. When he was fully on top of her, his arms on either side of her shoulders and his gaze locked with hers, he lowered his head and kissed her, his tongue slipping effortlessly into her mouth.

Bronwnn allowed her hands to rove over his shoulders, which felt as unyielding as rock and as contoured as a sculpture. Sliding her hands down, she ran her palms over his chest. Then she fingered his nipples and felt them grow taut and erect.

Tilting her head back, she looked up into his face and saw that he watched her with unblinking eyes, his body rising up for hers, his back covered in the silver shroud that cocooned them. He was the most beautiful man in the world to her.

"Tell me what to do. I want to make this perfect for you."

"It already is, Rhys."

He smiled into her eyes, then lowered his face to her neck, nuzzling the sensitive patch of skin beneath her ear. "No, not yet. Not until I hear you cry out and come so hard around me."

Her body shuddered. She knew he felt it, because his cock was pressing into the smooth, hairless skin of her sex.

The torches that had been lit around them filtered softly beneath the transparent blanket, making it intimate and erotic beneath the shroud. Normally, the covering was to be removed, revealing her body for his inspection and pleasure. But Rhys had made the ancient ritual his, and she felt it was perfect for them.

"I want you so much, Bronwnn. I want to savor you, to kiss and lick every inch of you."

Her womb clenched, and the muscles of her core tightened in yearning. Bronwnn felt his wide palm slide up her calf, then her thigh, nearly engulfing her flesh in his hand. He caressed her to her hip, running his hand appreciatively up and down the rounded contour.

He reached up, above her head, and she saw the white cloth of the Sidhe fating. He wrapped their hands loosely together and gripped her fingers with his.

"Bound now, you are to me."

"Yes, my love."

Sliding his unbound hand beneath her neck, he raised himself slightly above her. He was so beautiful—so strong—looming over her.

Reaching for his hand, she placed it on top of her breast. But before he could take her nipple between his thumb and finger, she reached for his head, bringing him to her so that she could offer her breast to his mouth. "Suck me," she whispered into his hair.

She arched like one of Rhys' taut bows when he curled his tongue around her peaked nipple. Her fingers gripped his hair, and her head was thrown back by the time his hand was kneading her and his mouth was tugging at her nipple.

She moaned, the sound erotic in the silvery light. Rhys responded by freeing her breast and claiming the other one. This time he bit down gently on the nipple. Her hand flew to her belly, her body tightening. His palm followed hers, down below her rib cage, to the crescent moon that had been placed on her mons.

"I want to give you my baby," he whispered. "I want to feel this skin stretched with life."

"Yes," she moaned. She wanted that. The instinctive need to conceive welled up inside her, and she knew that this night, she would take Rhys' seed inside her and create their child.

She gasped as he nuzzled his mouth against her nipple, making it harder and making it strain against his lips before he kissed his way from her breast to the soft, scented valley between, only to capture her other waiting nipple between his lips.

On a hiss she arched into his mouth, and he covered her hand more forcefully. She imagined him taking her when she was full and heavy with their child. She knew he shared her thought when his movements became more intense, more aggressive, and possessive.

Rhys slid down her length, his tongue burning a path down her midriff to her belly, and she rubbed her thighs together, feeling the slickness pooling between them.

His beautiful hand gripped her bottom; then he lowered his mouth and lapped at her. The way his tongue slowly slid up the length of her made her ache to hold him there.

But soon she was restless. He was going too slow, and she was rubbing against him, struggling to find the right rhythm, the right pressure that would make her shatter.

And then, just when he moved his tongue against the spot that ached, she moaned and felt two of his fingers sink deep inside her, drawing out her arousal and then sinking inside again. She groaned, emitting a deep sound of need and release; then he set his tongue to her clitoris and pressed against it, feeling it throb. She needed to touch him, to feel her hand stroking up and down the long, thick length. As she grasped his cock, he moved his tongue in a furiously fast rhythm that had her nearly convulsing and crying out his name.

"Faster," he moaned.

Rhys could barely breathe as he watched her work his cock with her hand. A drop of pearl-colored fluid leaked out the slit of his sex and onto her fingertip.

He knew he wouldn't last. He knew he'd ruin this ritual if he came in her palm.

Slowing things down, he moved to the side. Their hands were still bound, but he still had one free hand to play with her. But she was intent on something else—the athame that lay at her side.

Picking it up, she gave it to him. "I am to shed blood for you tonight."

"*What?*"

She smiled and kissed away his frown. "Normally, it is my virgin's blood, but you have already claimed that."

"Yes, I did," he said with a possessive growl.

"But our blood must mix tonight."

Taking the athame, she poked the tip into her thumb, drawing out a drop of blood. Then she poked his finger, allowing his blood to drop onto the blade and mix with hers.

"Hold the handle with me."

Wrapping his free hand around hers, as well as the hilt of the athame, he watched their blood mix and run together down the blade.

"Now we must plunge the blade into the earth, consecrating our union."

Together, they leaned a bit to the left. The bed was not high off the ground, and the tip of the blade easily pierced the earth. Bronwnn's fingers clutched his, both on the athame and beneath the white binding that clasped their hands together. He could feel her pulse, a steady thump against his wrist. Above them, the shroud glimmered more brightly, casting little shadows on her body that reminded Rhys of starlight.

Bronwnn's eyes lit with wonder as she looked up at the veil that draped over them. "Our union has been accepted."

"I love you," he blurted out. It wasn't very mystical, or original, but it was all he could say.

"My mate," she whispered as she wrapped her thighs around his hips, guiding his cock into her slick, hot core. "My mortal. Come. Claim your goddess."

Never allowing their gazes to break, Rhys lowered himself on top of her so that her breasts scraped his chest and their eyes were locked together; then he sank himself deeply inside her, reverently, slowly.

"Take me. All of me."

He knew she could. He was so deep inside her, he felt her pulsating around him. And when he began to enter and withdraw, he heard each gasp she made with his measured strokes.

Bronwnn placed her free hand, palm up, against Rhys', and they stayed like that, palm to palm, bound hand to bound hand, for long seconds before he entwined his fingers through hers and brought their joined hands back behind her head as he thrust deeply into her, claiming her fully.

Bronwnn had never known this euphoria before—this oneness of mind, body, and spirit. As they looked into each other's eyes, as his hand gripped hers tightly and his body slid along hers, Bronwnn knew she would never, ever feel this connection with anyone else.

"Don't close your eyes. I want you looking into mine as you come," he rasped.

And then he stabbed her deeply, and she fought to keep her eyes open as she trembled beneath him. She was shaking and shattering in his arms, and he thrust up into her once more, his fingers pressing against her.

"Take me," he said, thrusting up hard against her. "Claim me."

She did. Lifting her hips to meet his, she thrust back, joining with him. With her teeth, she nipped at his throat, and he groaned, pouring his seed deep inside her.

"*Mo bandia*," he breathed against her. The binding had come loose around their hands and slipped to the ground, allowing Rhys to pull her into his arms. They were still covered by the shroud, and Bronwnn thought it the most intimate, beautiful moment she would ever experience.

"My mortal," she whispered back. She felt him, so deep inside her, swimming in her blood.

"I can feel you," he said, his heart beating heavy against her